THE
SPARE

T0182216

By Ava Rani

THE
SPARE

A BIOTECH BILLIONAIRES NOVEL

AVA RANI

AVON

An Imprint of HarperCollinsPublishers

THE SPARE. Copyright © 2023 by Avi Rani. Bonus epilogue copyright © 2024 by Ava Rani. All rights reserved. Printed in the United States of America. No part of this book may be used or reproduced in any manner whatsoever without written permission except in the case of brief quotations embodied in critical articles and reviews. For information, address HarperCollins Publishers, 195 Broadway, New York, NY 10007.

HarperCollins books may be purchased for educational, business, or sales promotional use. For information, please email the Special Markets Department at SPsales@harpercollins.com.

FIRST AVON TRADE EDITION PUBLISHED 2024.

Originally published as *The Spare* in the USA in 2023 by Ava Rani.

Interior text design by Diahann Sturge-Campbell

Mandala illustration © Anlomaja/Stock.Abobe.com

Library of Congress Cataloging-in-Publication Data has been applied for.

ISBN 978-0-06-341360-3

24 25 26 27 28 LBC 5 4 3 2 1

*To all the girls that saw the expectations set for them
and said "screw that"*

CONTENT NOTES

This story contains topics that maybe sensitive for some readers.
This includes parental death (off page).
For a full list of content triggers, please visit: authoravarani.com

Chapter 1

SLOAN

I had to stop getting into prank wars with Xander. It was fun back in college and grad school, but now it was a little juvenile. Okay, it was still fun.

But it was starting to get out of hand. And I was getting a little tired of losing.

All I did was lock him on the roof of The Soho house overnight. It was the middle of summer, and he was fine. I wouldn't have done it if he hadn't baby-proofed my entire townhouse. It took me three days to figure out how to open my cabinets.

We had three rules: No bodily harm, no ruined reputations, and no foreign interference. I abided by all three.

His response was a disproportionate escalation. Calling the University of Pennsylvania Alumni committee and volunteering me to chair this year's annual alumni gala was cruel and unusual.

I smiled maliciously when I felt a buzz from my phone. I hoped he enjoyed walking, because the team I hired to wrap his Aston Martin in a hundred pounds of plastic wrap had just arrived at the garage at the Ritz, where his car was parked.

The annual UPenn Charitable Foundation Alumni Gala usually pulled an impressive guest list—from captains of industry to politicians and socialites, the list went on. Scanning this year's list of attendees, I searched for one name in particular and smiled when I saw that he would attend. A delightful shiver danced up my spine at the memory of those piercing gray eyes.

The prestigious university counted some of the most powerful in the world among its graduates. Its sprawling campus was one of the first places I had ever visited in Philadelphia. My grandfather, and every Amari after him, attended the university. My grandfather went on to start one of the most successful pharmaceutical companies in the world. My older brother, Henry, was being prepared to take over whenever the time came.

Walking through the stone corridors with the autumn leaves crunching beneath my feet filled my mind with memories of college.

I stood in front of the historic library where the gala would be held and ran through the obsessively organized checklist I had made. I may have had to spend my Saturday morning overseeing the setup, but I was now done, and the day was mine.

Well, mine and Xander's.

"Sloan?" a heartbreakingly familiar voice called from behind me. Recognizing it instantly, I paused. I handed a few items to the caterers and the final guest list to the event coordination team. I peered down the path to see him jogging toward me.

It couldn't be. Fate could not be that cruel. My heart started to race as I confirmed what I had feared.

Broad shoulders. Icy gray eyes. Dark brown hair.

Marcus Sutton.

My long black hair was rolled up in a bun, I was wearing glasses instead of contacts, and I hadn't applied a stitch of makeup. Not how I wanted him to see me after so long. I wanted to look devastating.

Instead, I looked like a librarian.

Clearly coming from a run, Marcus slowed down on the cobblestone path in front of the library.

"What are you doing here so early?" Marcus closed the distance between us, catching his breath between words. The body of a Roman statue pushed against the Dri-fit running shirt he wore.

I was about to go in for a hug when I realized he was sweaty from his run. He chuckled in amusement at my awkward shifting.

Giving up any attempt at grace, I released a resigned sigh and fidgeted with a folder full of papers in my hand. "I was roped into heading the committee this year."

"Ouch." He feigned a grimace and looked around, likely for his brother, who was almost always by my side. "Is Xander with you?"

"It's a little early." My eyes tried to find an appropriate place to land. "I'm going to lunch with him later. Want to tag along?"

Because, apparently, I am a glutton for punishment.

His smile made my legs wobble. It was subtle, a small tug at the corner of his mouth. He always looked at me like I amused him. "Of course you are. I wish I could, but I have to get some work done. I got here pretty late last night from Manhattan."

I nodded and wished I could think of something, anything to say.

"I'll see you at the gala tonight?" he asked.

I nodded again, and he was off, leaving me with a smile I would replay for hours.

But first, I texted Xander. He would have feelings of his own about his brother's return.

* * *

WE SAT TUCKED away in the corner of a brunch spot we'd visited for years. Xander and I had driven in from Manhattan last night. We opted to stay in Philadelphia for the weekend to reminisce about our college days.

He took a sip of his coffee. His green eyes were distracted and unable to meet mine. "You saw Marcus? Where?" he asked.

"At the library." I shuffled a bit on the chair.

"He texted me this morning before you did," Xander said as he swiped his dirty blond hair from his eyes. "Does this mean he's back for good?"

"I didn't ask." Mainly because any intelligent thought jumped ship when he gave me *that* smile. "He did say he came straight from Manhattan, so maybe?"

He nodded, and his brows scrunched in confusion. We all lived in Manhattan, but Marcus had been all over the globe for the last two years working.

Xander Sutton and I met almost fifteen years ago. Our older brothers were assigned as roommates during their freshman year in college, and since then, the Sutton boys had been a permanent fixture in my life. Xander started at Penn two years later, and I followed two years after that. He became my ticket to being the coolest college freshman—knowing all the cute upperclassmen was important currency for young college girls. The fact that Xander was a college heartthrob-slash-soccer-star didn't hurt either. Our friendship had grown and changed over the years, but it was one of the few things I could always count on: unwavering and unconditional support. I could rely on him for anything.

"Maybe." Xander's voice lowered from shock to disappointment. His older brother was the definition of living to work. And that kicked into overdrive a couple of years ago when he began traveling and prioritizing it over everything else.

Over the last two years, it had become clear that for Marcus, his company came first. It hurt Xander more than he cared to admit.

A tense couple of minutes passed; meanwhile, he gently swirled his coffee cup as if it were filled with wine.

"Thanks for being my date to this thing," he finally spoke up, forgetting he had done me a favor by escorting me. There was no better way to keep the inevitable set-ups at bay than having Xander run defense. "I don't think I could scrounge up one for this."

That was categorically false. He certainly could get a date for the gala, but he was usually powerless to deny me a favor. The Sutton brothers were unreasonably attractive in different ways. Between his gorgeous green eyes, sculpted body, and charming smile, Xander had no trouble with women.

Our conversation shifted to work, particularly my hesitance to tell my family about my latest accomplishment.

I was the dutiful Indo-English daughter of an Indian-American pharmaceutical heir and his high-society English wife. The expectations set for me were offensively low. While Henry, my older brother, was poised to become CEO one day, the only thing expected of me was to sit still and look pretty. The fact that I was one of the youngest junior partners at my firm was an adorable hobby to them.

I was the spare, after all. The heir had expectations. I had charity galas.

But a six-month assignment in the London office to help strengthen my firm's mergers and acquisition group was a game changer.

It was an important task and wasn't usually given to new junior partners. The UK was essential in large-scale merges because it was almost completely regulation free. Any firm that wanted its hands in global deals needed a strong team there.

Ensuring a stable and effective group would provide dividends for decades to come for the firm and a senior partnership for me.

"You still haven't told them?" Xander asked, with a disappointed sigh.

"I'm going to tell them at Thanksgiving." I leaned my head on my hand and pushed the eggs around my plate.

"Nervous?"

I shrugged. My mother wouldn't be happy; her parents lived in London. To say they didn't get along was a massive understatement. There was enough family drama to fill a Tolstoy novel. We only visited on rare occasions, staying in a townhouse my father had purchased to avoid being around them for long periods. Henry and I hadn't even met our cousins on that side.

We all liked to ignore the reason for their disdain, but it loomed over me like an omnipresent cloud. Henry could ignore it better than I could. He *looked* the part, while I was unequivocally the picture of "mixed."

The last thing I remember about my grandparents was seeing them for a few minutes at the townhouse. It was the last time I was in the property—the one I planned to stay in while working on the London project.

"You know, you could work from London for a few months." I offered.

It was an idea I had rolled around in my head more than a few times. Xander managed investment portfolios at one of the largest hedge fund firms in the country and lived the exact lifestyle one would expect from a drop-dead gorgeous banker. Given London's appeal to bankers, I was sure it would be an easy sell.

"You need to learn to live without me." He winked.

He wasn't wrong, but that wasn't my concern. The last couple of years had been hard on him with Marcus being gone so often. I didn't want to make it worse. Marcus was his only remaining family member after their parents passed a decade ago. The brothers recovered in their own ways, but it was a wound that Marcus's absence may have reopened.

After their parents' death, Xander spent his time avoiding commitments, and Marcus spent his time avoiding any feeling at all.

Over time, they both seemed to get back to some degree of normal, but the last two years had flipped that stability on its head.

"Besides," he continued, "my brother has a private jet; you can't rid yourself of me by being in London for a few months."

"I wouldn't dream of it."

"Oh." He perked up. "The team you hired has successfully wrapped an Aston Martin in plastic wrap."

Why was he so happy that I won? His smile indicated that I'd been bested. "Henry's," he finished.

Dammit. I forgot my brother was planning to drive down today as well. If I weren't planning this gala, I would have been there to oversee my retaliatory fire.

"Checkmate, Amari." He was practically giggling. "Better luck next time?"

"Fine." I hated losing. "You win this round."

He bared his teeth in a smug grin. "You're losing your touch."

Chapter 2

MARCUS

I sat at the kitchen island in my Philadelphia penthouse. I bought it years ago and never stayed in it. The only time it ever got any use was when Henry or Xander visited Philly. Everyone lived and worked in Manhattan now, so there wasn't much use for it outside of being a decent investment. I held on to it for that reason.

The bright white marble reflected the sun's rays throughout the room. I spent an hour trying to get some work done. Instead, my mind replayed seeing Sloan this morning. The run was meant to clear my head.

I could have ignored her; it would have been easy enough. She hadn't seen me. But she was Xander's best friend, and Henry's sister.

Neither of those reasons was why I stopped. I stopped because I couldn't seem to break the magnetic pull she had on me.

She was always effortlessly elegant. A navy-colored wool coat wrapped tightly against her body, and her hair had been pulled into a neat bun, a few rebellious strands framing her face. Her black tights pulled my attention to her alluring long legs as she adorably fidgeted with her folders.

By that point, I was staring. So, I gave in to temptation and stopped. It was oddly gratifying to say her name out loud.

Our interaction was short, but enough to defeat the purpose of the run.

I shook off the memory. My coffee grew cold as my laptop went into sleep mode again. Instead of the work I intended to do, I turned my phone around in my hand. I had texted my brother earlier, but he still hadn't responded.

Refilling the coffee cup and regaining some focus, I reviewed the strategy for our next acquisition—Gant Pharmaceuticals. The goal was to finish this deal as soon as possible. Acquire, destroy, and move on.

Another email confirmed that my company's bid to acquire Ellory Incorporated failed. It was acquired by Amari Global, the Amari family's company, just as I had planned.

Sutton Industries, my company, was largely born of luck. One very lucrative sale meant I had the chance to recreate the success Rishi Amari, Henry and Sloan's grandfather, had decades before.

I took it.

That was probably the first time I felt deserving of the praise Rishi lavished on me. I was always very cognizant that Henry, my oldest friend and Rishi's heir, was never graced with such approval. It was compounded further by his captious father and the great expectations of being the Amari heir.

My success had never driven a wedge between us, nor did the competition we engaged in between our two companies. Our friendship had always trumped everything else—we were lucky in that respect—but I had a sinking feeling that luck was going to run out soon.

* * *

ANOTHER COUPLE OF hours passed, and still no response from my brother.

The sound of keys at the door pulled me from my thoughts. A

smile stretched across my face when I saw my little brother walking into the entryway.

"Xander." Something about seeing him after so long reminded me of when we were kids. When our parents were still alive, before we'd ever met the Amaris.

It felt like a lifetime ago.

"I left lunch early to come here and yell at you," he snapped with no malice. I'd seen him briefly several times over the past two years, but not long enough to make any real impact. "Sloan sees you before I do? Imagine a world where Sloan Amari is better informed than I am."

"I can; it's the one we live in." I sat down at my computer, hit send on one last email, and closed it.

An annoying tingling sensation found permanent residence in my chest at the sound of her name. I ignored the mounting desire to ask about her. I knew the headlines, but the details eluded me. She'd broken up with Julian Waldorf while I was away. They'd started dating right around the time I left. That was all I knew about her personal life.

Xander rounded the kitchen counter and hopped up to sit on it. He grabbed a bottle of water and made himself at home. "You're coming to the gala tonight? Are you going back to London after?"

"Yes, and I go back in January."

Xander's face fell, only for a second, but I saw the disappointment in his eyes. Sutton Industries had a few international offices, and I'd spent most of the previous year working out of the London office.

"I'll be back permanently after that, though," I added. It was a decision I hadn't made yet, but seeing that look on his face made me sure I would figure it out. All the reasons I had to be away didn't make much sense anymore. All but one.

"Yes! The gang's back together."

We'd become something of a family, the four of us, especially after my parents died a decade ago. I was just out of business school, and Xander was a senior in college. Even before then, Xander and I spent most of our time with them. Me and Henry, Xander and Sloan.

It wasn't long until Henry walked in unannounced. Sloan likely told him I was back.

"You didn't want to tell your best friend you were back on this side of the world?" he called.

We turned to see him walk in from the entryway. His dark brown eyes fell on me with some disappointment before dissolving into an excited smile. He pulled me into a hug. We hadn't seen each other for two years, apart from a couple brief visits. We were practically inseparable before I left. I shook off the prickle of guilt.

Henry and I were randomly assigned as roommates in our freshman year of college. We were teammates in rugby and tennis and, as fate would have it, the same major. We went to the same business school and competed with each other in everything. He was my greatest friend and competitor.

"He didn't tell his brother either," Xander added. "Guess who he went to see first?"

Seeing Sloan was purely coincidental.

"Your sister. I saw her on my run," I corrected.

"You saw Sloan?" Henry's brows furrowed, and he turned to Xander. "She's been avoiding me; any idea why?"

"Nothing I haven't told you before." Xander shook his head with some disappointment. "But think about it. I'm sure you'll figure it out."

Henry sat down, and we picked up like no time had passed.

Chapter 3

SLOAN

Xander and I arrived a bit early to the gala, giving me time to ensure everything was in place. Luckily for me, the budget for this event was always astronomical, so once I checked in with the coordinators, I was free to mingle.

"You okay?" Xander asked. We stood at the entryway as guests began to file in. I turned to him and nervously adjusted his tie. He immediately recognized the nervous energy being funneled into keeping my hands busy. "Why are you so nervous?"

"Your tie is messed up," I answered without looking up at him, knowing he could spot my lie from a mile away. I had no idea why my heart was racing, but it was. Almost imperceptibly, Xander motioned to a waiter, and handed me a glass of wine.

"Relax. Everything looks fine. Besides, if you mess it up, they'll never ask you to chair it again."

"But what if some asshole volunteers me again?"

"Handsome asshole," Xander corrected.

"Sloan! Xander!" A small, excited voice drew our attention from my nerves to a petite blonde with flowing hair entering the library. Charlotte Cummings, or CeCe as we often called her, was a friend of mine and Henry's since we were kids. She was in my graduating class at Penn. We remained close over the years.

We all walked further into the library. The books and shelving had been cleared to make space for the event.

"You look stunning; give us a twirl," she demanded. CeCe was always the life of the party. Xander laughed as he held his arm above me for me to spin under. My dress, red with a high neckline and fitted mostly but flared a bit at the bottom, gave a less dramatic swirl than I'd hoped.

As I brought my arm down, completing a turn, I looked to the entrance for a split second, where a pair of familiar eyes found mine.

Xander followed my gaze and called his brother over. "Marcus."

At that moment, I realized the reason for my nerves. They had nothing to do with the party. It was the same reason I checked the RSVP list a hundred times for a name. Same reason I bought this particular dress.

The Sutton brothers were tall, which became more obvious as they stood next to each other. Marcus was slightly taller than his brother, who was probably around six-three, and there was some family resemblance. Xander had the all-American boy look down with the mesmerizing green eyes, inviting smile, and dirty blonde hair that often fell in his face. Marcus was more a smoldering and brooding handsome. He was serious and buttoned up, his gray eyes always deep in thought while a war raged inside. They couldn't be any more different. Xander was gregarious and charming. Marcus often seemed guarded and cold to the unknowing observer.

I was one of the few people who got to see his face soften and the endearing features come through; being the little sister of his best friend gave me that privilege. He smiled as I went to hug him.

"Marcus." I tried to keep any hint of whatever was happening inside me out of my voice. Having held on to a crush for so long was getting a little embarrassing, even if I was the only one who knew about it.

"Sloan," he said softly as I breathed him in. His cologne smelled of musk and spice. It was so familiar. I hadn't realized until that moment how much I had missed it. After taking an extra second to relish the feeling of his arms wrapped tightly around me, I pulled away.

"You're back."

Obviously. Say something smarter.

I unconsciously stepped back next to Xander. "At least for now," Henry said as he joined us, arriving a few steps behind Marcus.

I was half tempted to talk to Henry, but decided against it. Lately, anytime we spoke to each other, it ended in sniping. He was getting more pressure to take the reins at the company, and his stress often spilled over to the people around him. Admittedly, I wasn't very sympathetic. I didn't want to be. I had spent my entire life performing at the same level but was never once considered good enough to take on the responsibility he was given.

The same cycle would repeat itself. He'd say something he thought was harmless, I'd give him a scathing retort, and down the rabbit hole we'd go. I was just as culpable as he was for the recent thorniness in our relationship. Sometimes it felt like we were speaking different languages.

The four of us didn't have much time to catch up. We got pulled in different directions. But things felt like they used to for the first time in a while.

* * *

THE GALA WENT on without a hitch; if the heiress and lawyer thing didn't work out, it would seem I had a promising career in party planning. The historic library was enormous, and the party often spilled outdoors onto the large lawn. The twinkling lights and lanterns were set up beside heat lamps all along the green, so stunning at night that you might forget that fraternity row was only a few blocks down.

I spent most of the night glued to Xander's side, afraid of where I might wander if he wasn't right next to me. He came alive at these types of events. He had a personality that drew you in, and an effortless grace with strangers. For as long as I'd known him, he was the type of person everyone wanted to be around. It was one of the many benefits of being his best friend; I was never bored.

Xander had gone to get us drinks, leaving me alone to take in the event, but I could only think about one thing. I could feel Marcus close by but refused to look around for him. He had been talking to Henry for a while before Henry had to leave early. Now, he was talking to someone else, but I was firmly focused on not letting him distract me.

"Don't get mad." Xander returned with a drink and handed it to me. An endearing smile adorned his face. It was the best way to deliver bad news. "I have to leave."

I stepped back as if slapped.

Absolutely not. Being abandoned at this thing was mortifying. "They'll write that on your headstone," I warned.

"Sloan. I'm sorry, it's work." He gave a deep apologetic sigh and raked his hand through his hair, as though the tricks he used to get out of trouble with other women would work on me. "You know I wouldn't go if it weren't important."

"Work? I want the real reason." Xander wouldn't leave a dentist appointment in favor of working, let alone a party.

"That is the real reason."

"Xander."

"Barcelona," he blurted. It was all he had to say. I owed him, and he was settling up. There was no way I could deny his request.

My jaw dropped. "I can't believe you would call that in now."

"I wouldn't if it wasn't important," he repeated and looked around the room and smiled when he caught sight of his brother and waved him over. "I have to go, but I am not leaving you alone, because Marcus will be my stand-in."

"What the hell are you talking about?" Marcus stood beside me; his tone wasn't amused.

"I have to go. Take care of my girl for me?" Xander patted his brother on the shoulder.

"Do I get a say in this?" I interrupted, noticing the pinched expression on Marcus's face.

"Barcelona," Xander reminded me as he turned away with a wink. Annoying as hell sometimes, but damn if he wasn't charming.

"I'm going to kill your brother." I glared at Xander as he walked quickly out of the library. "Sorry," I added, turning to Marcus, who probably wasn't pleased with the idea of spending the night with me. I did remind myself that he didn't bring a date. It provided me with more satisfaction than it should have.

"You need better friends." His tone was lighter this time, probably out of pity.

Marcus and I were friends, kind of. We were mostly pushed together by proximity, but we had always been comfortable around each other. That was, until the last few times I saw him, the time leading up to when he left.

The air always seemed heavy.

I couldn't quite pinpoint when it happened, but something was different. It felt like I annoyed him.

"If I'm going to be any good as a stand-in for my brother, I should probably ask you to dance." He offered me his hand.

I smiled and accepted. A shiver rolled up my spine when he placed his other hand on my waist.

We danced in silence as I tried to think of something, anything, to say. "You're back." It came out as a statement, even though I meant it as a question.

Over the last decade and a half, I had come to expect his piercing eyes and finely chiseled body at get-togethers, nights out, and the holidays.

He and Henry attended business school together after undergrad. After that, they both started at Amari Global, my family's company. He was the closest thing our grandfather had to a protégé. Henry would never admit it, but he had always felt like Marcus was the heir Grandfather expected while Henry was the one he got. Marcus quickly rose in the ranks and ended up leaving for a startup that sold not too long after. He made a killing.

In today's world, success in the biotech industry was less about discovering the next great drug or device and more about acquiring its intellectual rights. Marcus's company, Sutton Industries, did that with surgical precision. Thus, the legend was born. He started his own company and quickly became my brother's only real business rival.

"In the flesh," he answered after a few seconds, pulling me from my thoughts. "I have some work to do here until after the new year."

When Marcus left to travel constantly for work, the four of us became three. Henry became increasingly solitary, which only left Xander and me. None of us had mourned what was lost, but we all felt it.

"Are you going to stay?" My voice cracked, sounding far more emotional than I meant it to. "Xander misses you." I melted a bit when I saw his features soften at the sentiment. "We all do."

Anyone who knew Marcus, really knew him, wasn't surprised by Sutton Industries' meteoric rise. Marcus put his work ahead of almost everything. The only time I'd ever seen anyone come ahead of his career was when Xander needed him.

He didn't answer. His eyes moved around the room, anywhere but on me. He looked almost pained with the question, so I tried to think of something to lighten the mood.

Marcus beat me to it. "Barcelona?" he asked. I looked up to see a small smile tugging at the side of his face. An eyebrow rose, and his eyes finally met mine. "I don't remember any calls from the Spanish police."

My heart fluttered at the lightness in his tone.

"You heard that? We took care of it." I lifted my chin to look confidently at him. "I'm not some Fabergé egg that could break at any moment. I can handle myself."

His smile grew wider. He peered down at me with intrigue in his eyes. "So much so that Xander is blackmailing you with it?"

"He has his cards, I have mine. I'm not going to waste them on a gala."

His hand slowly moved from my waist to the small of my bare back. It splayed, almost possessively. Liquid fire trickled down my spine, warming and rolling chills through me at the same time.

"What would you waste them on?" he drawled. His eyes remained locked on mine; the heavy weight of his full attention bore down on me. Except now, it didn't make me nervous. What it did to me was a different feeling entirely.

After a long pause, I realized I hadn't answered. "Bribing government officials." My expression was flat, my tone serious.

He laughed.

Xander's senior year of college was the year their parents passed tragically in a car accident. Every year around that time, Xander and I would take a trip somewhere to get his mind off it. The annual trip grew into a ritual.

We often got into some mischief on those trips. And whenever one of us needed to be bailed out, so to speak, we had a fun little game of lording it over the other. The stories were top secret between the two of us. The Barcelona I-owe-you was a particularly salacious story that made me glad Henry was the Amari who got hounded by tabloids, not me.

"Sloan Saanvi Amari, you are full of surprises." His smile felt like sunrays after a snowstorm, a warmth that cut through the chill.

"They aren't very surprising if you know me." I scrunched my nose playfully.

His eyes stared into mine again. "I've known you for years."

"You've known Henry for years," I corrected. "You hardly know me."

Beneath the soft fabric of the tux, I could feel his muscles tighten; he looked offended. It snapped me back to reality.

It was true. In the last two years, the only people he'd kept in contact with were Xander and Henry. That contact was minimal. All I got was a birthday text both years and an offensively generic gift.

He didn't *want* to see me. I knew there wasn't malice there, but after knowing him so long, I hoped he'd have at least missed me.

"I mean . . ." I sputtered, feeling instantly aware I must have upset him. "I mean . . . uhh. Nothing."

Way to stick the landing, Sloan.

He grinned, seemingly enjoying watching me stumble incoherently over my words. "I hope you're better at making an argument in court," he mused.

"I don't litigate."

The tempo of the music began to pick up. He pulled me closer, his pace hastening to match the new timing.

I inhaled sharply. "My work is . . ." I swallowed hard and eagerly anticipated the brief brushes against his marbled body. A fire settled and roared low in my belly. "It's more cloak and dagger."

I blinked to try to shake off whatever that was. I'd never danced *this close* with him. Actually, I don't think we had ever danced together. Usually, Xander or whoever I was seeing took me to these types of events.

Surprise and *something else* washed over me.

"Mergers and acquisitions, right?" His eyes scanned the room. His palm pressed harder against me for a short second as he pulled me through a sweeping turn.

I nodded.

"Huh, interesting," he said. The music slowed, and a drawn-out decrescendo followed. The song was over. I pulled away from him and got my bearings.

He motioned his head in the direction of the bar.

"Why is it interesting?"

I found myself appreciating just how chiseled he looked in his tux. The way the fabric pulled in when he moved and outlined the muscular body beneath was enticing. The black fabric contrasted deviously with his alabaster skin.

"You left your family fortune behind to do the same thing as Henry?" He grabbed his drink and handed me mine. He took a sip, placed the whiskey glass on the bar, and turned it in his hand.

"Fortune is still mine." I scrunched my nose. I became a lawyer to strike out on my own. I was more than an heiress. "The family bullshit isn't."

"I always knew you were the smart one."

Chapter 4

MARCUS

I sat in front of my laptop on the island in my penthouse's kitchen. If I was not going to be able to sleep, I should get some work done. But, again, I couldn't focus. The sun was barely up; nobody would be bothering me for hours.

Getting distracted from work was a new phenomenon; time away meant fewer distractions. But my mind kept drifting back to last night. I couldn't think of a time when I'd spent an entire night with a woman fully clothed, let alone just talking. But then again, Sloan wasn't just anyone.

I had almost forgotten how incredible she was. Smart and independent. Not to mention sexy as all hell. Her lithe body fit perfectly into that backless red dress. Her hair was scooped into an elegant updo, with a few locks left loose, begging to be tucked back. The diamonds she wore glistened against her olive skin.

Annoyance and maybe guilt radiated through me when I thought about how many boundaries I was crossing. I was thinking about things I shouldn't entertain, wanting something I couldn't have.

It didn't matter. I didn't *actually* want her, she was simply . . . stuck in my head. I'd find a way to get her out of there eventually. Besides, she was off-limits, for too many good reasons.

My best friend's little sister.

My little brother's best friend.

My mentor's granddaughter.

That same loop of thoughts continued for a couple of hours until I heard footsteps coming down the hallway. It would pass, that much I knew.

"What time do you wake up?" Henry asked.

I'd heard Xander wander in at some point last night, and Henry had ended up here in a drunken stupor at some point as well.

"Early." I scrambled to close an email. Now that I was back, I had to be more careful.

"Is that why you're always two steps ahead?" Henry laughed and poured himself some coffee. Henry had become my family over the years. Our drunken college adventures evolved into a friendly rivalry in our professional lives.

"That and talent." I glanced up from my laptop to offer a smug smirk, then returned to my work—not that I had managed to do anything productive since dawn.

What he was about to say was interrupted by a knock at the door, followed by an agitated "Xander Philippe Sutton!"

It was Sloan.

Henry walked over and opened the door.

"Is he not up yet?" Sloan asked. She glided right past him into the kitchen, brows furrowed. Her jet-black hair swept down to midback, a slight curl at the ends. The yellow dress she wore shone against her skin. It was inappropriately short for the weather.

"I brought scones." She placed a box in front of me on the counter, and her tone was suddenly sunnier. "I figured they'd soak up whatever the three of you got into last night."

"What makes you think he's here?" Henry asked. "Weren't you guys staying at the Ritz?" He looked down at his phone and got distracted.

She shrugged. "He texted last night; said he was here."

"What's he done this time?" I asked mildly.

"Oh, nothing." Her brown eyes sparkled with mischief. "I figured he'd be hungover, and I can't miss the opportunity to torture him. Besides, we're going to brunch with CeCe."

"Can you and Xander just get married already?" Henry let out a frustrated sigh as he looked at his phone and pushed it back into his pocket.

I choked on the scone.

Take care of my girl for me kept ringing in my ears. *My girl.* I tried not to think about the idea of Sloan and Xander dating, even though I fully understood that it was a real possibility. At times, it seemed inevitable.

It shouldn't bother me.

It didn't bother me.

They both scoffed at the idea. For years, they've fended off questions about their relationship. They insisted anything more than friendship was ridiculous. But it couldn't be platonic. How could anyone not want more with Sloan?

She was beautiful, quick-witted, a relentless contrarian.

More facets than the Hope diamond. Equally flawless and equally rare.

You'd have to be insane not to fall for her.

Hypothetically.

She laughed loudly at the suggestion. "Get the family off my back for once," Henry groaned.

She slapped him on the back of his head. "Maybe if you stayed out of the papers, you wouldn't need me to clean up your PR nightmare."

Henry tended to relieve stress in unhealthy ways. Drinking and womanizing, mostly. It was problematic for anyone, but their family's very public image made it lethal.

He rolled his eyes. "Easy to say when they have no interest in bothering you."

"Heavy is the head that wears the crown." She didn't hide the resentment in her voice. Sloan grabbed a scone from the box and hopped onto the counter. Her dress rose slightly, revealing more of her thigh. My mind drifted to the idea of those long legs wrapped around my waist.

"What?" Henry asked, annoyed.

"It's *Henry IV*," I answered, and kept my attention squarely on the screen in front of me. A silence passed, and I looked up to see the same look of befuddlement scrawled across his face. "It's Shakespeare, man."

Henry rolled his eyes. "You didn't answer my question."

I shouldn't—it didn't bother me, but I didn't want to have to sit around and think about it.

Someone, please change the subject.

As if answering my silent request, Xander's voice echoed from the hallway. "It was a ridiculous question." He appeared with a bright smile as he swiped his hair out of his eyes.

"Already working?" he asked me. "It's Sunday morning. Take an hour off; nobody's gonna think you're any less perfect, I swear." He walked past me, squeezing my shoulder before stopping at the counter next to Sloan.

For a split second, she looked up and our eyes met. She broke away instantly, peering back down at my brother.

"Are you still mad I had to leave?" Xander asked, looking up at her innocently. My little brother could charm his way out of a murder conviction. "I heard you middle-naming me earlier."

"Get over yourself." Sloan rolled her eyes, placed the scone next to her, firmly planted her hands on the counter, and leaned forward. "I actually had a very nice time without you." She looked up, and her eyes pulled mine in again. She granted me a small smile.

"Uh-huh." Xander's mouth hung open slightly, and he looked at us skeptically.

"Do you guys realize this is the first time in over two years we are all together, just us?" Sloan asked, hopping off the counter. "I miss this. All of us."

Nobody bothered to answer her. It was something we were all thinking—she happened to be the only one brave enough to broach the subject. Her face fell at the silence. I hated seeing the pained look she tried to hide. I hated even more that I was a large part of why it was there.

"We better get going," she said after a long silence. Xander followed behind as she headed to the entryway. "Will you be at Thanksgiving?" She turned at the door, her body halfway through the threshold. Her voice picked up, and she looked directly at me. "You missed the last two."

If that was meant to make me feel worse, it did.

I nodded, and her face brightened. She flashed me a smile before the door closed behind her. The room felt empty with her absence, but maybe I could get some work done. I turned back to my computer.

Agreeing to spend Thanksgiving weekend with the Amaris was like signing up for camp. There would be games, activities, and sports of some kind. All of which were mandatory. The time I would use to catch up on work would instead be filled with an overly competitive game of Taboo.

Henry sat down next to me and turned his coffee cup around in his hands for a second before finally speaking. "Are you ever going to tell me what happened?"

I let out a heavy sigh and closed the laptop. "I was working."

"For two full years, nonstop? All over the world?"

"Henry, you of all people understand what a global company means," I scoffed. He was the heir to the world's largest pharmaceutical company. At one point, the same had to be done for his company.

"In between any of the cities you went to, there wasn't a single week you could've made it back?"

"What are you implying?"

"It wasn't just work. Obviously." He rolled his eyes.

"What else do you think it was?"

"I don't know." He stood and paced around the counter. His voice went up an octave. "You're a stranger to me now. I only know what's going on with you when I read an SEC filing about it. If it weren't for those, I wouldn't know if you were alive."

"I visited."

In my defense, I did have to go back to work after each visit. I could have stayed longer, but the global expansion was addictive. I faced a new challenge every day; it was thrilling. When I stopped, my mind would wander. It was best to keep moving.

"Three times." Henry was terrible at keeping his cool. The Amari temper was not something to be taken lightly.

"I'm sorry." We sat there a few seconds longer. Silence became more comfortable and tempting, but Henry deserved some explanation. "Look, Sutton Industries expanded faster than I could have expected. I shouldn't have shut you all out."

He nodded. "Then why are you back?"

Henry had the annoying talent of asking all the right questions. I was never supposed to be away as long as I was. The actual work of expanding Sutton Industries was done months ago. I was stalling. I wouldn't need to go back until the new year, and then it was to transition operations back to U.S. headquarters. It would be a few months at the most.

When the invitation for the alumni gala came across my desk, it was decided. I'd never made a snap decision like that before. The invitation should have kept me away, but it drew me in. Her name was on it.

"No real need to travel. Most of the international offices are up to speed." I hadn't even decided to stay until Xander's face made me feel like absolute shit yesterday. I could've stalled a while longer.

"I could have used a friend here," Henry said so quietly that I almost didn't hear it.

"Are you okay?" He seemed different, more agitated than usual. I noticed more gray among the rest of his jet-black hair. We were the same age, thirty-four, a little early to be graying. He was stressed. Something was going on beyond what I knew.

"I don't know." He sat back down. "Dad and Grandfather have been awful; their idea of grooming me to take over is probably banned by the Geneva Conventions."

"Is that why you've been such a colossal ass to your sister?" I asked. In the past twenty-four hours, I'd heard the two exchange jabs about the company's future more times than I could count.

"She's throwing a tantrum because she's not going to be CEO."

"Going to law school and becoming a partner instead of taking orders from you isn't a tantrum," I said mildly. Their competitive sibling dynamics weren't new, but the vitriol was. "If anything, it's a giant fuck you."

His eyebrows furrowed, almost as though the thought had never crossed his mind. As if all the memories of him treating her like a spoiled heiress and not the intelligent and capable woman she was came to him all at once. He let out a loaded sigh, guilt working its way into his expression as he raked his hand through his hair. "Right."

"This can't be news. She graduated law school three years ago."

He huffed another long breath. "Want to go play tennis or something?"

A quick stab of guilt hit me. It was our tradition. After graduating, we would use that time to work out some of our competitive aggression—a game of tennis, a round of boxing, or a chess match, anything to spend some time together. Our friendship spanned almost two decades, and the weekly tradition was hardly, if ever, missed. I didn't answer. Instead, I got up and headed for the door.

Work would have to wait.

Chapter 5

MARCUS

"Would it kill you to put up a picture?" Henry's voice asked from my doorway.

After the gala, I was back to working out of my old office in Manhattan for the first time since being away. I smiled at the intrusion. We used to interrupt each other's days all the time.

"It might."

"Well, I guess it's good that it looks like a coffin in here," he added, sauntering in and taking a seat.

My office wasn't adorned with photos or personal effects. I considered a family photo once, years ago. It brought up too many memories, and I didn't need a reminder of the past. It was easier that way.

"It's an office, not a TGI Fridays." I didn't look up from my computer screen, quickly closing anything he might see.

He paused. "What the hell is that?"

"Your 'trust-fund baby' is showing," I said. Henry and Sloan didn't have a regular upbringing on the Upper East Side. I was hardly a man-of-the-people these days, but I grew up like a regular kid. On the other hand, Henry took his family's private jet to boarding school in Switzerland.

He looked around wistfully. "I haven't been here in two years."

Guilt weighed on me. I hadn't meant to be away so long. I knew it affected Henry, but I told myself he was busy with his own company. As for Xander, he had Sloan. She was the only one who didn't seem upset with me, only upset that I hurt Xander in my absence. I never meant enough to her to hurt her.

A knot tightened in my chest. I ignored it.

I huffed a breath after a prolonged silence and decided to breeze past it. "You know, when you're in charge, you will have to work weekdays."

"This is work-related. I came to do some recon on the competition." He smirked and folded his hands together.

I chuckled. "It's cute you think it's a competition."

His expression changed to curiosity when he noticed something on my desk. He leaned forward, reached across the desk, and grabbed a dark brown leather-bound journal. He flipped through the mostly blank pages. "You still have this thing?" he laughed.

Henry always picked up on little details. The only blind spot he had was Sloan. When it came to his little sister, he often looked past the obvious and saw what he wanted to see.

I snatched it back in a flash with more ferocity than expected. There was almost nothing in it, and certainly nothing I needed to keep hidden. A few random notes I scribbled down over the years.

"Why carry it around if you never use it?" He put his hands up in innocence and sat back down.

An awkward silence passed for a minute.

"We just acquired Ellory," Henry said. Sutton Industries made a show of trying to acquire the company, but the plan was always to have Amari Global get the acquisition. It meant the Ellory owner got a seat on the Amari Global board, and that was far more important.

"You always remember your first," I mocked.

"You know anything about Marie Ellory?"

"No more than you." He knew very well that whatever I did know, I couldn't tell him. Being competitors meant that type of advice was largely inappropriate. Although those were rules we often bent. "Why?"

"They just got a board seat. A new one. It came with the acquisition." Henry sighed aloud. "I guess it's fine. It just seems weird."

Being away came with the benefit of not having to lie to him. Lies of omission were easier, especially when I was an ocean away. "It's not unheard of in acquisition deals. Rishi approved it?"

"Yeah, my grandfather was fine with it." He still seemed worried. I was a little impressed. He should've been wary. It was suspicious.

"What are you worried about?" I probed.

The board seat was technically Ellory's, but she was a proxy, something Henry was unaware but may have started figuring out on his own. Henry's instincts were impeccable. But a lifetime of second-guessing them was his weakness.

"Honestly, I don't know. My grandfather wouldn't approve a shareholder vote to add a seat unless he felt secure with it. I feel like I'm always missing something." He sounded practically defeated.

"I'm sure it's for the best," I reassured him after a few tense seconds. I glanced out the window to the gray, miserable day outside. "Lunch?"

"You gonna tell me why you left?"

He wasn't going to let that go. "You know the reason."

"You'll tell me at lunch." He grinned and pushed himself up.

Chapter 6

SLOAN

The week after the gala was hell. We needed to close several deals before the end of the year. With the holiday season starting, the pressure was mounting.

"Do you have the Hightower Energy file?" Penelope walked into my office, not bothering to look up from the file she was reading. Her smooth, British-Singaporean accent filled the room.

Penelope Astor was a junior partner at the firm. She and I met when we took the same position as associates during our first year out of law school. We'd grown to be something of a dynamic duo at work.

"One of the paralegals is checking the draft merger conditions." I stood at my desk, distracted, as I reviewed another merger. Two sizable private banks with numerous financial trade commission concerns were attempting to merge. It was a legal minefield. "The W. Burton merger is equal parts mess and possible money laundering."

"Van Der Baun is here and asking about it." She finally looked up from her file, making my concerns about possibly aiding and abetting mercenaries disappear. "Hightower Energy, I mean." She adjusted her sleek black hair and nervously ran her hands over her pencil skirt.

Lars Van Der Baun was the managing partner at the London office and led the entire mergers and acquisitions team. Our firm did the most M&A work globally, with our team responsible for making some of the biggest deals in the world.

Adrenaline poured into my veins. He was the partner who explicitly asked that I join the team to expand the M&A department in London. I was responsible for almost half of the largest deals struck in the past three years. I knew I could take it on. I just wanted to make sure it was worth my time.

I wanted to be a partner at the firm, and then I wanted to be managing partner.

It wasn't more than a couple of minutes after Penelope's warning that Reese Atkinson, managing partner at the U.S. office, and Lars Van Der Baun knocked on the doorframe of the office. "We hope we aren't interrupting." Reese looked at the two of us, and I nodded.

"Not at all." I gestured for them to enter. They didn't sit. Instead, they stood there menacingly. It was a scare tactic. They would continue to walk around the rest of the offices and probably make a few associates cry.

"You've met Amari and Astor, our best junior partners," Reese said with enormous pride. Getting him to respect me had been a herculean task, but now that he did, he quickly became a mentor.

"Yes, quite the duo." Lars's German accent was surprisingly endearing. His demeanor was the exact opposite. He was a tall, towering man and middle-aged, with short salt-and-pepper hair. He had whatever the male equivalent of resting bitch face was. "Ms. Astor has agreed to join the London project, but we wait with bated breath for Ms. Amari."

I couldn't tell if he was annoyed, rude, or trying to be charming. "Won't be much longer, I assure you."

"Good. Take care of the U.S. regulations for the Burton merger before you go. You'll handle the UK side once you're there," Reese reminded me, not that he had to. If I was successful, I would be the youngest senior partner in the firm's century-long history.

Not bad for the spare.

"Well, I look forward to seeing both of you in London." Lars gestured to Reese, and they made their way out of my office.

Penelope had a confused expression when the door clicked closed, and she looked over at me. "I thought you already accepted."

"I will." Managing partner was the goal, and this was the next logical step. "I was going to tell the family this weekend at Thanksgiving. It's always a perfect time for a fight, so why not pile on?"

"Ooh, an American Thanksgiving." Penelope often waxed poetic about American holidays, as if experiencing each one in a truly "American" way was on her bucket list. Born in Singapore to the wealthy Chen-Astor family, she spent most of her childhood there. Her high school and college years were spent in the United Kingdom. She had never experienced a proper American Thanksgiving.

Not that ours was ever proper.

My mother was English, so the entire holiday was foreign to her. My dad, born and raised in Manhattan, insisted on a traditional American Thanksgiving every year. But it often devolved into a screaming match.

"You're welcome to join ours." I offered.

"How fun. I cannot wait." She accepted gleefully.

"Wait for what?" Xander's voice pulled our attention to the door opening. He leaned casually at the doorframe of my office at noon on a Friday, his laptop tucked underneath his arm.

"I'll be joining the Amari family on Thanksgiving," Penelope said excitedly as she clocked the time. "How is it that you hardly work? Are all bankers so highly suspect?"

"Nothing suspicious about it." He casually strolled into my office, took a seat next to Penelope, and put his feet up on my desk. "I happen to be good at most things." He winked.

She laughed.

"Besides, that's big talk coming from a Chen-Astor," he continued.

The Chen-Astors were the Kennedys of Singapore, a well-known political family with a wealth that was hard to calculate. Although, like the Kennedys, there were many of them by this point, and their wealth was well distributed between them.

Watching Xander and Penelope spar over the years made me question whether they liked, hated, or wanted to have sex with each other. I was leaning toward "like" since Xander never took very long to close the deal.

She rolled her eyes. "I would love to continue the sparring, but I have work to do."

"Always a pleasure, Astor," he mocked.

"Is that how people see our interactions?" Grimacing at what I just witnessed, I turned to Xander.

"No"—he feigned a gag—"I'd never flirt with you."

I rolled my eyes and skated past the insult. "Do you want to tell me why you're here five hours earlier than expected?"

"Figured I'd make you leave work early."

I managed to get another hour of work done, and Xander worked a bit too. Then, we decided to leave early. I tucked my laptop in my bag, expecting to work on the weekend to make up for it. We were headed to get something to eat and probably watch a movie, unless any of our friends were planning to go out.

"I might be late for Thanksgiving. I'm going to try to finish the Hightower merger offer before I leave," I told him as we left my office.

"I'm driving to the house early, so I'll meet you there. I can take Astor," Xander offered. We all lived and worked in Manhattan, but

Thanksgiving was always at the Amari country house in upstate New York. "You should go with Marcus. He's driving up a little later too. Make sure he shows up this year."

"Oh, really?"

Xander nodded.

I had tried my best to keep my mind clear of him the past week, but the memories of the gala replayed in my mind. We had fun—at least I did. I couldn't remember a time when he and I had spent so much time together, just the two of us.

I had to remind myself that he danced with me and listened to me ramble on about work all night to be a good stand-in when Xander had to leave. Nothing more than that.

"I'll text him," I said.

Me: We're driving over to Thanksgiving together

Me: You've been deemed a flight risk

Marcus: A GPS ankle monitor would be easier, don't you think?

I spent way too much time thinking about how to respond. Then I remembered that I was madly in love with Marcus's car. His black McLaren Artura was the car I wish I had a reason to drive. Most of the time, people like Marcus and Henry traveled with drivers for ease and the ability to hold meetings while en route. Being able to drive was a rare treat. And if driving was a treat, then indulging in a fine piece of machinery was necessary.

Me: An ankle monitor isn't nearly as entertaining

> **Me:** Besides, I need to spend some time with the Artura

The feeling of the engine humming and sending a faint vibration through the car as it sliced through turns was heavenly. Watching a ten-part movie series centered around illegal street racing starting in my hormone-driven teenage years did something to me.

> **Marcus:** I'm driving

Chapter 7

SLOAN

Xander and I ended up going out.

We met some friends at an upscale lounge in Chelsea. Upon arrival, we beelined to where they'd congregated and were waiting with a table full of drinks, clearly having started without us.

"Sloan!" The guys were quick to get up and welcome me, making me feel like a goddess among men. We were a rambunctious bunch.

"You need to come out more," Tristan said, and wrapped me into a hug. He and Xander got their first jobs out of school together. If you could distill the essence of a golden retriever into a human, it would be Tristan Alders: cute, with his big hazel eyes and dirty blonde hair, lovable and fiercely loyal.

I scanned the group. It was the usual suspects—Tristan Alders, Jackson Prince, and Rohan Malhotra—until my eyes landed on Henry. "I would if you'd stop inviting my brother." I retorted.

"Trust me, I would, but your husband insisted." He motioned at Xander while his arm was still wrapped tight around my waist. We often engaged in harmless flirtation, primarily out of boredom. It would quickly stop when either of us found something more interesting. Or someone.

"Hi, Sloan." Henry rolled his eyes.

"Why is he here?" I turned to Xander, who got lost in conversation with Rohan. He was too preoccupied to answer me.

I turned back to Henry. On the rare occasions he'd joined Xander and me on a night out in the last couple of years, he always managed to ruin any fun for me. "Shouldn't you be out on some romantic dinner with Marcus now that he's finally back?" I asked Henry.

"He's not really my type," Marcus's voice said from behind me. My smile dropped, and I heard Xander stifle a laugh. I felt Tristan's arm retreat as he pulled away and walked over to the opposite end of our occupied tables. Whatever face Marcus gave him, it wasn't pleasant. I turned around to find Marcus beginning to laugh at my expense.

He answered the question that popped into my head. "Got here a second ago, right behind you two."

The group of us occupied a few high-tops toward the back of the bar and a couple of lounge sofas. It was secluded enough to talk, but not so much so that we couldn't dance.

Henry sighed with annoyance. "Can you go a single day without throwing a hissy fit about—"

"Hissy fit?" I snapped. He was the one being crushed under the pressure of taking control of the company, yet I was the one being reprimanded. "I don't know, Henry. Can you go a single day without making it on the cover of a tabloid?"

"You wouldn't be nearly as haughty if you had them following you around."

"Well, they don't, so find something else—"

"Because nobody *wants* to see you." He recoiled after he said it. Somedays, I went too far. Other days, he did. Like everything else about us, our tempers were equally matched.

Xander quickly crossed the short distance between tables and interjected. "I feel the need to remind both of you that we are, in fact, in public."

Hearing Xander's voice with that serious intonation was like being doused in ice water.

"Relax, Sloan. I'll leave you alone," Henry grumbled and allowed Xander to drag him away to the other end of the group, getting another round.

I turned back to Marcus, who looked stunned and then winced. "That bad, huh?"

"Yeah."

I shifted uncomfortably at the high-top next to the couches. That little tableau happened a lot these days and was not something I was proud of. After a drawn-out pause, he skeptically looked at my dress, lingering on my legs. "You look . . ."

Did he just check me out? I stifled an inner laugh at the idea.

"Devastating?" I twirled. After saying it, I realized how silly I felt.

"Cold." Half a smile crept up the side of his mouth. "You're wearing a cocktail napkin."

My dress was short, purposefully so. I had long legs, and there was no point in hiding them. The rose gold sequined fabric complimented my slightly tan complexion.

"A sparkly one." I put my drink down next to his. "I wasn't expecting to see you out."

"I gathered that much." He looked at me intensely, as though he was trying to solve a puzzle. It was unnerving. "I didn't mean to interrupt whatever was going on with Tristan."

He had known Rohan, Tristan, and Jackson for years and knew nothing was happening between us.

I scoffed. Why did he care? "We're friends," I reminded him.

"Doesn't look like it," he said plainly.

He'd been witness to enough nights out with all of us to know better. Usually, CeCe would have joined us. The six of us ran like a pack sometimes. We got into our share of antics, enough stories to fill books, but we kept things close to the vest. It was an agreement between us. We figured things out on our own.

"What does it look like?" I crossed my arms in annoyance.

"Like he wants to sleep with you." His tone was detached, almost chastising. It was a line I had never crossed with any of them. I was mildly insulted at the insinuation that it would happen.

We had an interesting dynamic. Of course I found them attractive; they were attractive. Over the years, they became as alluring as Xander, which was not at all. Most importantly, they'd always been good friends to Xander and me. The trio helped pull Xander through some of his darker days. A time we kept largely concealed from Marcus at Xander's request. The pedestal he put his older brother on was sky-high, and the thought of disappointing Marcus was too much for Xander to gamble on.

"So, what if he does? Does that mean he gets to?" I pushed. Tristan didn't want to sleep with me, that I knew. But I was annoyed at Marcus's insinuation. "Besides, if I wanted to sleep with someone, they'd be slept with."

"Oh?" he said mockingly.

One syllable blew the fuse. He didn't see it, but I was an attractive woman. "I know you've sworn loyalty to Henry's royal guard, but you're still a man." My voice dripped in defiance as I ran my eyes down my body and back up to meet his eyes. "And I'm wearing a cocktail napkin."

Surprise papered his usually unreadable face. Whatever else he was thinking, he hid it well. I had no idea what his motive with this conversation was, outside of pissing me off.

I wasn't entirely sure why I was trying to argue with him, but I didn't hate it.

After a few drawn out moments, *that* smile grew on his face. "A sparkly one," he added.

"Can we drop it?" I begged, but my tone lacked any seriousness. He nodded.

Talking to Marcus was like getting sucked into a different world. He was well-traveled, well-read, and knowledgeable about a wide array of topics. There wasn't much he couldn't keep you engaged in. And when in conversation, he spoke to me like an equal—high praise, given all he'd accomplished. I loved every second of it.

We were deeply entrenched in a conversation about the World Bank when I noticed the same blonde walk by us, again.

Although strut was probably more accurate.

She wore a tight pink dress and sky-high heels; her short blond hair was pencil-straight as it swept along her shoulders. She was cute. And transparent, having walked past a few times by now.

I couldn't help but laugh.

It was pretty brazen, given I was standing right next to him. I didn't know what irked me more—that everyone always assumed Xander and I were together, or the snap assumption that Marcus and I couldn't possibly be. He was older, sure, but not by that much.

Marcus raised an eyebrow.

"Eleven o'clock." I tilted my head in the direction of our spectator. "You have an admirer."

He turned, saw her, then looked right back at me. He shrugged.

"Please." I rolled my eyes. "You can't tell me you didn't notice that."

He remained quiet, flicking another passing glance in that direction before looking back to me. "What would you suggest, Counselor?" His mouth quirked.

My stomach fluttered.

He was messing with me. Provoking me, maybe? If there was one thing I knew for sure, it was that Marcus Sutton had no problem closing a deal, business or otherwise. I'd had a front-row seat, for a long time, to his and Henry's escapades.

"Counsel for Marcus Sutton? No thanks."

He scrunched his nose patronizingly. I hardly ever saw that side of him. Glimpses of it emerged at the gala and had me in a tizzy for days. "Yeah, I probably don't need the help."

"I'll leave you to it then. You have your admirer." I gently shrugged off the annoyance and glanced back at the table Tristan and the rest of our friends occupied. "I have mine."

He gently grabbed my elbow as I turned to rejoin the guys. "If you leave me here to politely decline conversation with her, I'm going to ruin your night."

"I'd like to see you try." I didn't know why I said that. He and Henry were always happy to ruin my chances of having any fun. Marcus was infuriatingly good at it.

"Is that a challenge?" He playfully threw his arm on my shoulders. The heaviness shot electricity through my chest. "Henry isn't the only one who can scare off anyone who wants to talk to you. If I remember correctly, I'm excellent at it."

"You're *that* put off by the prospect of talking to a beautiful woman?"

"I'm already talking to one." He took a sip of his drink. "And I know this one can hold a conversation."

Chapter 8

MARCUS

I could kill Xander.

Why the fuck didn't he stop her from going out in that dress?

Her long legs were on full display. The dress would lift when Rohan danced with her. Tight enough that it wouldn't lift entirely when he spun her, but there was still enough of her bare thighs to get the attention of almost every man in the bar.

It made me wish I had never agreed to come out tonight. Henry roped me into it, and a mixture of guilt and nostalgia convinced me to go.

She and I were left to talk for a while until a beat played that practically took control of her body.

After the dance, he told her something that made her laugh. It shouldn't have set my jaw on edge the way it did. They were friends. They were all friends. I kept reminding myself of that fact, hoping it would extinguish the white-hot anger every moment she wasn't next to me.

It never used to bother me this much. But now, my mind was consumed with monitoring every person that even looked at her. It was nearly impossible to listen to whatever Henry was saying.

She ignited a strange feeling in me, and it needed to stop.

She floated between sitting beside Henry and me and getting up to dance for a few minutes. Luckily, sitting between us meant nobody would be hitting on her. If only she could sit still.

Bopping along to the music, she sat beside me when Henry got up. "Are you going to scowl all night?"

"I'm not scowling, I'm thinking."

She laughed. "I have trouble believing anything Henry said required additional thought."

"Remind me not to upset you."

She rolled her eyes.

"Why not dance?" she asked and took another large sip of her drink. She was less inhibited and more flirtatious. It bothered me until she sat beside me. Then I found it endearing. "I know you can."

Henry was a few feet away. And just like Xander had witnessed all of Sloan's past, Henry witnessed mine. He knew my history and wouldn't let me near his sister if he knew even half of what was happening in my head. If I put my hands on her, we'd have a problem. Filling in for Xander at a black-tie event was one thing. Dancing with her in a bar was another.

"Why not sit still? I know *you* can."

Her gaze stuck to mine for a moment. "Dancing seems insane to anyone who can't hear music." She looked down and played with the straw in her drink.

My heart faltered. It was a slightly modified quote from Nietzsche.

Sloan did that on occasion. She read everything. Classics, fiction, biographies, fantasy, all of it. She had a bizarre fascination with revolution biographies. For years, she'd thrown obscure references into conversations. I didn't think anyone ever noticed she did it. A pretentious little game she played, but nobody else was playing.

I always caught them, even if I had to covertly look them up. I almost never said anything.

"German philosophers are a little heavy for a night out." I focused all my energy on slowing my racing pulse. She beamed. I won that round.

She took another large sip. I got distracted momentarily by what looked like something happening behind her. I saw Xander's brows furrow as he and Tristan talked. Seconds later, Xander walked toward us. Tristan turned to join the rest of the group.

"We're leaving." Xander's uncharacteristically serious voice was low, like it was restraining concern. Most of the time, my little brother was hard to take seriously. But the look on his face was one that I didn't see often.

Sloan turned, likely to question him, but she complied. One look at his face and hers turned in a flash. It was enough that she complied without question, no small feat when it came to Sloan.

"Okay." Her voice was soft. Almost scared. Not the unyielding woman I knew. "Let's go."

I was lost. Usually puzzles and ciphers were a breeze for me, but with this group, they were impossible. My side felt an emptiness when she moved away from me in favor of retreating beneath my brother's arm.

In seconds, Rohan, Tristan, and Jackson surrounded them. Xander turned for a second, his eyes meeting mine, and he motioned for me to follow.

They were stone-faced. A departure from their normal demeanors, their expressions were serious. I complied, wondering what caused my little brother's serious tone. I caught Sloan's eyes darting across the room as they left. The frantic search stopped when she saw something.

I got delayed when trying to find Henry to let him know we were leaving. By the time I made it outside, I caught only the end of their conversation.

"She's right," Rohan agreed to whatever Sloan just said. "If he wants to fuck around, he can find—"

"No." Xander wasn't convinced. He looked down at Sloan.

He? A bolt of protectiveness shot through me. It was Julian, her ex. I saw him from the corner of my eye but didn't register it until I was halfway out the door. Why did seeing him summon that type of reaction?

"I don't want to leave," she said. I couldn't hear the rest, but her lips read: "We did nothing wrong."

Xander's eyes were reluctant. He was worried. "Is it worth it?" I could barely hear it. With that, she caved.

There was so much I wished I knew.

"What was that?" I finally managed to find my voice.

They gathered on the sidewalk; Xander's jacket was draped over Sloan's shoulders. They exchanged looks. The group had struck a silent agreement, one I wasn't privy to.

"Nothing," they said almost in unison, with a casualness that felt rehearsed.

"Let's go to Xander's," she squeaked out a few moments later. "CeCe is going to meet us there."

"Not until someone tells me what just happened," Henry demanded, finally stepping outside. He trailed behind me when I finally got a hold of him.

"Nothing." Again, in robotic unison. Their little clique wouldn't let Henry or me in on the real reason. They were annoyingly loyal to each other. I should've been thankful. I knew enough to know they'd looked out for Xander.

"Come with us or don't, Henry." Sloan rolled her eyes in agitation. She was hiding something. Her fidgeting was her tell. "It couldn't matter any less."

"You're okay?" I looked directly at Sloan; the desire to protect her overrode everything else.

She nodded and smiled.

I called it a night.

Sloan had her knight in shining armor, who happened to double as Prince Charming whenever she needed, and an entire royal guard to match. She was in good hands.

If I told myself over and over that it didn't bother me, I was bound to believe it at some point.

Chapter 9

MARCUS

Sloan's Park Avenue townhouse oozed of old money. It was a beautiful stone structure with a grand entrance that you'd see on the pages of architecture magazines.

"Coming!" I heard in the distance after knocking on her door. A *clacking* sound neared. Unlike the rest of the family, Sloan refused to have staff. She was hell-bent on defying any expectation set for her.

At times, Sloan was a walking contradiction, a puzzle I couldn't figure out. But fuck, I wanted to spend all my time trying.

A wealthy heiress who pursued law rather than live as a socialite with a multibillion-dollar inheritance. Independent, almost to a fault, she nonetheless did everything to keep our little group together. Immovable one moment, incredibly accommodating the next.

Only after she began law school did I realize she was very serious about being her own person. I respected it. Not to mention, it was sexy as hell.

She opened the doors with a swing, the cool fall breeze pushing her hair back and lifting the edges of her dress. Her dark lashes lifted to meet my gaze, and she smiled. Her expression was soft and inviting. I silently reminded myself not to say something rude and push her away. Now that I was back, an actual friendship was the endgame.

"I'm going to grab a couple of things." She fiddled with a lock of hair while the rest flowed mid-back, sweeping along the long-sleeved merlot-colored dress she wore. It was form-fitting until her waist, then it flared and ended just above her knees, giving me a peek of her bare legs.

Those legs. They went on for days and consumed too many of my thoughts, especially after that night out.

"We're going to be late," I said mildly.

"We're already late." She turned quickly. Her dress lifted slightly again. A pair of knee-high boots were responsible for the clacking sound as she walked along the hardwood floors. "Come in. It should only be a few minutes."

I had been inside her townhouse dozens of times. It looked the same, but somehow it felt different this time. Was it that I couldn't peel my eyes off her body?

Maybe.

The thought of her bare legs wrapped around my waist while I fucked her on the large kitchen island was new.

"Aren't you going to be cold?" I said, still staring, in a judgmental tone.

"I have a change of clothes." She stopped at the marble island in her kitchen, placing a few items in a tote bag, ignoring my tone.

I leaned against the counter, waiting for her, when a copy of the *Odyssey* caught my eye. Sloan's love of reading was something we had in common. Absent-mindedly turning through the pages as I waited for her, I realized the book was written in Greek.

Henry spoke four languages, and, not to be outdone, Sloan spoke five. But I didn't think Greek was one. "You can read Greek?"

She looked over her shoulder, and a smile stretched across her face. She lit up. "No, I've been having a colleague at the firm help me translate it page by page." She put the bag she was packing on the counter and walked over to me, close enough to inhale the intoxicating scent of her perfume.

"It's the first publicly available translation from ancient to modern Greek by a female scholar." The excitement was evident in her voice. Her fingertips grazed against my skin to take the book, leaving sparks in their wake. She opened it to display the translations she'd done so far. Taking a step closer, she continued. "Turns out, some of the translations were a little off. It changes how you see Odysseus and so many of the adventures he found himself in."

Watching her talk about something she loved was captivating; I couldn't take my eyes off her.

"I thought of you when it came in," she said. "There's an English version available of her translation, but this is like solving a puzzle."

"Yeah?" My love of reading came from my mother. She had a particular interest in French literature. I had read all the greats by the time I was in middle school.

She laughed and nodded.

"Henry and Xander never cared much for stories that weren't presented in HD." Closing the book, she looked up at me. Her luminous brown eyes drew me in. I didn't say anything. My mind had a nasty habit of going blank when she was too close. I merely took in the light her gaze cast.

"We should go," she said softly, shook her head, and her eyes darted down to the floor. She looked over to the bag she'd packed. When she began to pull it from the counter, I stepped closer and held it for her.

I motioned toward the door silently, ignoring the buzz the short encounter sent ricocheting through my chest. She grabbed her coat, and we walked out of the townhouse.

On my way out, I noticed a few familiar book spines along the bookshelf in her living room and smiled.

We made our way to my car, where she stopped abruptly.

"Should I leave you two alone?" I asked as she drank in the beauty of the Artura. She had an interest in fast cars.

"I love this car." Her brown eyes remained transfixed as she walked to the passenger's seat. I dropped the items she'd packed in the front trunk. "But this car, on the Spa-Francorchamps, that's the dream."

Sloan didn't want the things most heiresses wanted. She wanted to be a lawyer and, apparently, race on an F1 track.

"I meant what I said earlier." I opened the passenger side door so she could take a seat. "I'm driving."

"I didn't ask." She settled into her seat and looked up at me innocently. She stretched her hands along the dashboard. "You better treat her right."

* * *

THE DRIVE UP was quiet. After leaving the city limits, there weren't many cars on the country roads. It was nice until I realized that the quiet meant my mind would drift to places that it shouldn't.

I tried to focus on the road. "Those locations you and Xander will randomly call out to shut the other one up," I began, and immediately regretted it.

Never ask questions you don't want the answers to.

"Hmm?" She perked up. I had pulled her from her thoughts. She smiled and looked over at me. "Oh, those. It's calling in an I-owe-you. We name them after where the incident in question happened," she explained casually, as though it hadn't been a burning question in my mind for years. "I owed Xander a favor after an undisclosed incident in Barcelona."

I heaved a quiet, relieved sigh. Henry and I used to guess what some of their shorthand meant. After so many years of friendship, they developed their own language. The location shorthand was particularly grating to me. I finally realized why.

"I'm surprised you never figured it out; you're always looking for a puzzle you can't solve." She took in my expression, and her eyes went wide. "What did you guys think it meant?"

I didn't answer. A wild smile grew on her face, and crimson spread along her cheekbones.

"Oh my god." A hand covered her mouth momentarily. "You guys thought that was something sexual? And we would scream it at each other in mixed company?" She giggled in delight at the thought.

I didn't find it funny.

I still didn't answer, unsure of how to. "What you and my brother do is none of my business." It came out more harshly than I intended. It was supposed to be light, but the tone helped serve as a reminder. One I needed.

My eyes drifted to her for a second. She looked taken aback. She opened her mouth to deliver what I was sure would have been a scathing retort. Instead, she closed it and leaned back into her seat.

Chapter 10

SLOAN

Pulling up to the family compound in the country was like driving up to the best parts of my childhood. The beautiful French Renaissance–style home was nestled on a couple of acres of rolling hills in upstate New York. It was our own personal Versailles.

My favorite time of year at the house was autumn, when my grandfather threw our annual Diwali parties here. It was when the house was the most beautiful. The trees around the property were adorned with colorful leaves that checkered the perfectly manicured lawn.

The crisp autumn air was a refreshing change from the strained air in the car. Part of me wished I'd driven up earlier that day with Xander and Penelope.

Marcus was hard to read. One minute he was delightful and endearing. The next, he was back to cold and closed off. I couldn't figure out what to make of him these days. A part of me wondered if the Marcus I used to know was fading away. It was like he was closing himself off again, as he had when his parents died.

He was never warm and gregarious like Xander. Marcus picked his moments to be wonderful, and the rest of the time, he was just a little . . . serious.

We walked in to find the whole family seated in the salon. Xander and Penelope had arrived from Manhattan earlier that day, an hour or so before Henry. Xander made himself quite comfortable, seated on the couch with his feet up on the coffee table. To this day, he was the only person allowed to do it. My mom had the biggest soft spot for him.

My mother was on the couch, and my father nowhere to be found—a common occurrence over the last couple of years. The pressure of taking over once our grandfather decided to step down was getting to my dad. It was beginning to strain his relationships.

By now, everyone assumed it would be Henry taking over entirely whenever our grandfather did step down.

Marcus sat next to Xander on the couch, leaving only one spot for me—right next to him. I leaned against the arm of the couch, putting as much space between my body and his as I could. He was wearing a coat earlier, so I hadn't noticed the navy crew neck sweater he was wearing.

I tried not to notice the way it fit his broad shoulders and muscular arms. It left me to imagine what hid beneath the less snug parts.

"I told your family I'd never been to a proper American Thanksgiving." Penelope pulled me from my now R-rated thoughts. She sat on a plush armchair, Henry on the floor next to her. "What's on the schedule?"

"Games, overeating, fighting." Henry counted on his hand. "The big three. Speaking of fighting, Taboo is on the banned list of games now."

"Why can't we play Taboo?"

Xander smiled widely, tilted his head, and turned from Penelope to me. "Sloan?"

I rolled my eyes. "Someone *may have* been injured last year."

Henry laughed. "Sloan threw the buzzer at Xander for missing *Casablanca*."

"It barely grazed him." In my defense, he was hardly trying and making a mockery of the competition.

"It flew past me and hit an eighteenth-century candy dish." Xander beamed in regaling the story. Penelope's eyes were wide. Never having seen a true American Thanksgiving, our family may not have been the best one to start with. They were always a departure from anything Norman Rockwell would have painted.

"As I said that day, I was under duress at the time," I defended. The duress was a terrible mood from an entire night with my family that I treated with a glass of wine. The glass turned into a bottle.

"I say we lean into it." Xander leaned forward, running his hands through his hair. "Let's do football on the lawn again. Sloan can get all her aggression out." He and Henry laughed, only to be joined by Marcus a few moments later.

"I will take the grief from them," I said, turning to look at Marcus, "but you are in the doghouse for missing the last two years."

He smiled. *That* smile. The stiff air between us from the car was forgotten. Instead, it was filled with comforting familiarity.

The conversation thankfully changed to reminiscing about previous Thanksgivings, and we gave Penelope a full history of the Amari family dysfunction. She seemed to find it endearing. Sitting in the salon, all of us together again, filled me with a calm I had forgotten existed.

* * *

DINNER WAS ALWAYS very formal. My mother, a proper English society woman, would have it no other way. She'd softened over time, but assigned seating and formal dress were required. It meant most of us had to change beforehand. When she and my father married, it was a bit of a scandal. He was new money, which was scandalous on its own. Throw in a first-generation Indian-American, and it probably made our Thanksgivings seem friendly.

But true love prevailed. I grew up listening to the stories of how they fell in love while in college together. It was an impossible bar to meet.

"Sloan, when are you going to London?" Xander asked when there was a lull in the conversation, knowing I hadn't told my family yet. He liked to keep me honest that way.

"London?" Henry looked up from his plate.

"I didn't know you accepted the project." Penelope perked up in her seat.

"London?" Henry repeated, and my mother joined him.

"Won't you miss home?" she cooed.

"Terribly, but absence makes the heart grow fonder." Xander grinned. I threw a roll and mouthed "*fuck* you" at him.

"Language, Sloan," my mother interjected. The entire conversation devolved into what it did every year. Everyone had something to say, and no one was listening.

"I think it's a wonderful idea." My grandfather interrupted the group momentarily. "Marcus can look in on you while you're there."

More discussion erupted. Right on schedule, dinner got unhinged.

I buried my face in my hands for what seemed like hours. In reality, it was probably only a minute. Everyone needed to weigh in on whether it was a good idea. The promise of six months away sounded sweeter with every minute that passed.

"I don't need a nanny," I finally snapped into the cacophony of arguing voices. "I'm going, it'll make me a partner, and I do not need supervision." My voice rose until I was screaming. I pushed myself back from the table. My hands shook in anger as I got up and left a table of shocked faces.

* * *

I FOUND MYSELF angrily pacing on the patio overlooking the back of the estate.

Xander would come looking for me out here soon enough. This wasn't the first time I ended up out here after a tense dinner. Most years, after whatever caused me to end up on the patio, he would come out and let me rant awhile. Eventually, he would change the subject, and we'd laugh, drink wine, and head back in.

My pacing halted when I heard the door click open and closed. I turned to see Marcus walk out onto the patio, a blanket in one hand and a glass of whiskey in the other.

"They're setting up for a rousing game night." His voice dripped with sarcasm as he handed the blanket to me. I was freezing; this dress was meant for indoor events, and the blanket was appreciated. It didn't help the argument that I didn't need someone looking out for me.

Marcus didn't acknowledge my taking the blanket, letting me hold on to a semblance of my pride.

"I figured I'd check on you and try to avoid aggression-related injuries this year." He walked past me to the railing. He leaned his arms against it and kept his gaze forward, not looking at me. I was grateful for it, still a bit embarrassed at my outburst. The autumnal evening sky was ablaze with bursts of red and orange, casting shadows along his sweater where his muscular arms and back made enticing dips.

"I'm okay."

He nodded. "London?"

"Yeah. I meant to tell everyone today anyway. I just hadn't planned on screaming it." I crossed my arms, keeping the blanket wrapped tightly around my torso. "I leave a week or so after the New Year."

"Sounds like a great opportunity." His tone was bland, bored. "To become a partner."

"Yeah. You've been in London this whole time?"

"I've been all over, but global offices are there, so that's where I stayed between trips."

He'd traveled for work before. Why didn't he visit more? He saw Henry and Xander maybe three or four times during that period. Never me. Didn't he miss us? *Me?*

"I didn't mean to imply that you would be a nuisance or anything. I won't know anyone there except Penelope, so a familiar face would be nice." I suddenly felt nervous and started pacing again. My fingers pulled at a loose thread on the blanket. "I'm just sick of being treated like a child."

He didn't say anything. He took a sip of the whiskey from his glass, looking directly ahead at the sunset.

After a few silent minutes, he stood, turned around to lean his waist against the railing, and looked at me. His gunmetal eyes were soft, making me feel all the worse for my outburst. "For what it's worth, everyone already knows you're incredibly capable."

He walked to the door.

"You don't need to prove anything to them," he said, gesturing to me to come back inside. "Except maybe that you can go one game night without any injuries."

I smiled, basking in the warmth of knowing I was privy to *this* Marcus. It was because of his love for Henry and Xander, but the result was the same. I walked past him through the threshold and took his glass from him.

"This will probably help." I took a sip and continued to the salon for a rousing game night.

Chapter 11

MARCUS

Thanksgiving weekend at the Amaris' almost always included a fight. Yesterday, it was Sloan. Today, it was Xander. The arguments hardly ever came to blows. But sometimes they did. Today was one of those days.

It all started as an innocent game of touch football. It was a tradition in the family for as long as we had been attending Thanksgiving weekends. Xander threw a pass to Henry, which an overly competitive Sloan fairly intercepted. She ran it back for a touchdown. She did an adorable touchdown dance and jumped to hug me after—we were teammates, after all.

Something about that play pissed Xander off. Whether there was an actual infraction, we won't ever know. What we did know, with absolute certainty, was what happened next.

Xander bolted over to me, and with one hard shove, it began. Once the fighting started, Sloan directed everyone else to go inside and have lunch. They left us to duke it out until we worked through whatever was wrong.

It was a tried-and-true procedure by that point. There were probably only a few years on record where nobody fought and nothing was broken.

Xander managed to land a few punches, something he had never done, and I tried my best not to hit him back. After a few minutes, his anger dissipated. We sat on the ground feeling foolish, mud and dirt smeared across our clothes.

"What was that about?" I finally asked after a few minutes of silence. I was pretty sure I knew.

"I felt like hitting you," he said flatly. He sat on the ground with his knees bent, elbows resting on them.

"Fair enough; anything else?"

"You leave for two years, we never talk, you're back, and the only person you choose not to spend any time with is me?" He didn't look at me and maintained a hard stare at the ground. I was still shell-shocked that he threw a punch. Xander was never the type to resort to physical violence. His approach to everything was far too amiable.

"It's not just the time you were gone," he continued in a huff. "Why is it that Henry and Sloan have seen you more in the last few weeks than I have?"

He was jealous *of* Sloan, not over her. That didn't seem to add up. Nevertheless, that's how he felt.

"I'm sorry." We always had a good relationship; the last few years fucked that up.

"That's all you have to say?"

We sat in silence for another few minutes.

"Xander," I said, then paused. I had spent my entire life looking out for him, and in the span of two years, I undid all the good. "I shouldn't have shut you out. I'm sorry. It won't happen again."

He took a deep breath and looked at me, and a nervous smile emerged. "I think I fucked up your eye." Xander stood up and dusted the dirt off his pants. He didn't accept my apology, but it was close enough.

"Yeah." He offered his hand to help me up. I couldn't open my right eye too well.

"Sorry, bro."

We came into the entryway just as Sloan left the dining room and stopped. Her eyes went wide when she saw us. She inhaled sharply and rushed over.

"Xander! What did you do?" She rushed to my side and smacked the back of his head.

"I didn't mean to."

She shooed him to the dining room, not wanting to hear his explanation or cause a stir, and warned him to behave. Sloan grabbed my hand and led me to the kitchen. She filled a bowl with water and got the first-aid kit.

"Don't move." She stood on her tiptoes and assessed the damage. "It's not too bad," she assured me as she opened the first-aid kit.

Sloan took the warm washcloth and wiped the dirt away from the abrasions around my eye. It wasn't lost on me that I could very easily tend to my own eye, but I didn't mind the attention. Her attention. I flinched at the sting of some antiseptic hitting my skin.

"Sorry." She winced. "You're going to have a headache. I sent Xander and Pen to get something for that."

"Thanks."

She smiled. "I guess you'll have to hit Henry or me next year. Fair is fair."

"Probably Henry. I don't know if I want to end up like the candy dish." I tried to concentrate on the pain and not that she steadied herself by leaning her hand against my chest.

That close, I could smell the citrus of her perfume and the lavender scent of her hair. Her breath scorched my neck. The soft warmth of her fingers buzzed through me like a live wire. That's when I realized I was running my fingers along the hem of her shirt. I resisted the urge to touch the soft skin beneath.

I could enjoy that while still being her friend. Look and not touch. How hard could it be?

It was temporary anyway, until the feelings passed. And they would eventually. Distance may not have blunted whatever it was, but time had to.

Aside from coming to blows with my little brother, the situation ended half decently. Sloan was solely focused on me. With everyone else in the dining room, we were left to the quiet solitude of the kitchen.

"Hopefully it'll look less harsh by Monday." She stepped back, snapping me out of the trance she had me under. "But concealer should cover it if you have anything important to do."

"You want me to wear makeup?" I laughed for a second before I ran the words back in my head. It hit me. Fury thrummed low in my ears. Why the hell did she know how to do that? "How do you know so much about covering bruises?"

Sloan stopped, looked down, and tamed a worried expression about half a second late. I caught it. And I wouldn't believe whatever lie she was about to tell me.

She stayed silent.

"Sloan." I lifted her chin to face me. For the first time in a long while, I was having trouble controlling an emotion. The anger began to fester. The bar. They saw her ex and immediately left. I needed to know what had happened. "Don't lie to me."

"Women know how to use makeup. If you don't like it, blame the patriarchy." Her demeanor was calm, voice steady. She wasn't half bad at lying.

"Sloan."

"Xander was there." Not an explanation, but she knew the mention of his name would blunt the worst of my concerns. My mistake for trying to pull information out of a lawyer. "It's been taken care of. I'm fine."

I tried to ignore the caustic jealousy bubbling in my gut. She didn't need someone who looked after her, but if she did, it would be Xander. Not me. "Who?"

"This is why we don't tell you two anything." She walked away from me, went to the cabinet, and grabbed a bottle of wine. She placed it on the table before walking back to get a couple of glasses. "You overreact."

You two. I hated that she saw Henry and me as the same. Older brother types. To her, the idea that I could care for her in any other way was unfathomable. "How is this an overreaction?"

"You know *literally* nothing, and you're getting bent out of shape." She stopped and put the glasses on the table. "For all you know, Xander and I could have been in a West Side Story–style dance fight."

I laughed. Dammit, I wanted to be angry. "I need a na—"

"No, you don't. It's been handled." Her tone lost its razor edge. A small laugh snuck through.

"Sloan."

"Saying my name over and over again isn't going to change the fact that it is a story I am not telling you." She looked at me and pointed to a chair. "Sit."

I took a seat and dropped it for now.

"Don't tell Henry." She poured the wine, giving me a look of warning, and awaited my compliance.

"Under the condition that you will tell me what happened at some point."

"Fine." She handed me a glass and took a sip out of hers. "That should help with the pain, at least till Xander and Pen get back."

Silence blanketed the room. I felt nauseated. It was getting harder to deny the feelings that bubbled up whenever I saw her, thought about her, or heard her name.

The anguish must have been apparent on my face.

"You know, therapy would be less painful," she said as she

pushed an ice pack across the table in my direction. Her mood was lighter. It pacified the gnawing in my chest.

"Yeah, but this is faster."

"Everything's sorted then?" she asked, with a soft sigh, and swirled her glass at the base. She watched the wine as it lazily lapped around the goblet.

I smiled. She was worried. "Yeah. Don't worry. He won't be throwing any more punches. Unless we beat him at touch football again."

She beamed. "So, you'll be around? Strictly for punching purposes, of course." The heaviness of our earlier conversation dissipated, and her laughter filled the kitchen.

"Punching purposes? I'm the reason we won." It was an easy hack, playing into her competitiveness. I wasn't ready to have her attention move away from me.

"The hell you are," she snapped playfully.

"You had one lucky catc—"

"Lucky?"

"Xander can't throw for shit." He played soccer his whole life. The entire premise was not using your hands.

"Based on your face, I'd say his aim is pretty good." She laughed loudly at her own insult. "I was the one to score. Did the blow to your head make you forget?"

"And all the other touchdowns?" I reminded. She was silent. "You need me, Counselor."

"Fine." Her smile became a smirk. "Let's run that back next year with different teams."

"You'll be begging to change teammates," I warned.

A spark lit in her eyes. "Top of my class. Best at the firm. Impeccable instincts," she listed off, as if I needed a reminder of all the reasons she set my blood on fire. She leaned in and crossed her arm. "Sloan Saanvi Amari begs no man."

Our eyes locked and the entire world stilled for a moment. The air between us crackled; my throat went dry. "A thousand apologizes," I drawled, ignoring the sudden heat that ran through every fiber in my body.

She laughed again, cutting through the thick haze. "Where's this guy been? I've missed him." She took another sip of her wine.

The idea that she missed me sucked the air out of my lungs. The door opened and closed.

"We're back." Penelope and Xander's voices filled the quiet house.

I didn't have her to myself anymore.

"In here," Sloan called. She didn't look away until they neared.

* * *

At the end of the long day, I found myself in Rishi Amari's office, sitting on the upholstered leather chair in front of his desk. A bookshelf that spanned the entire wall was behind it, filled with books in different languages.

Sitting there always felt like being sent to the principal's office. In our more rambunctious years, Henry and I would often get called in to get a talking to for whatever nonsense we got ourselves into. The patriarch of the Amari family, he was the reason for their massive success and wealth. He was also the reason for mine. Rishi was the one to recognize my talents and help find me opportunities to excel.

I owed my success to him.

"That's quite a shiner." He took a sip from his glass and his brow furrowed; the deep wrinkles against his brown skin were more pronounced these days. His dark brown eyes were rounder as he laughed jovially. "Xander must have been upset."

"I deserved it." I let out a lighthearted chuckle. I sat up a little straighter. "Sloan said it wasn't so bad."

"My granddaughter has a big heart and propensity for white lies." He laughed another deep, rolling laugh. "That's why she's a good lawyer."

I smiled at the mention of Sloan. Even though I was the one who mentioned her. I couldn't get her out of my head.

"How are things at work?" I knew what he meant. Work specifically for Sutton Industries was fine, but that wasn't what he was asking.

"No misfires yet." Our conversation was to be succinct. It was hard to gauge how much Henry knew about what was happening. For things to go smoothly, we decided to play everything close to the vest. "When do you think they'll call a shareholder meeting?"

"Next one isn't until the summer, as scheduled. The board can't call an emergency one, not while I am around as CEO anyway." He smiled.

I shifted in my seat and released a heavy exhale. "You're sure?"

"Yes," he assured me with a nod. "And thank you. I know this isn't a simple request, but you're the only one I trust with it. Henry and Sloan can't know."

I was well aware of how plausible deniability worked.

I shrugged. Lying to Henry was one thing, but this encompassed everyone. It felt like poison.

"Is that why you were gone?" he asked, the billion-dollar question. "I was surprised you were away so long."

I did get more work done from further away. Fewer distractions. It did feel like my life was paused for the time I was gone. But while my story wasn't moving, everyone else's ran right past me and left me behind.

I shrugged again. We shared a comfortable silence before he grilled me on other non-work-related things, the things you would expect from a mentor-turned-friend. To no one's surprise, my answers were largely unsatisfactory for him. No chance of settling down anytime in the near or distant future. Disappointment painted his expression.

"Oh, and Marcus." He stopped me as I prepared to leave. "Look after Sloan. You'll be in London around the same time. I'd feel better knowing she's got someone in her corner."

"I'm still working on the last favor you asked me," I reminded lightly.

"Last one, I swear."

Chapter 12

SLOAN

I spent the rest of the night with Xander. Marcus and Henry watched the football game, and Penelope went to bed early.

I spent the better part of an hour trying to figure out what exactly happened during the game earlier. As far as I could fathom, Xander was annoyed at Marcus for not spending time with him. The thought made my heart hurt for him.

He always used to put Marcus on a pedestal. He still did. Their parents passed away when he was a senior at Penn. After that, it was just the two of them. They had us, sure, but it was just the two of them in terms of an actual family.

"It's probably easier for him around us," I told Xander. "We aren't his little brother. We don't expect the same things from him." We also didn't remind him of all he'd lost.

"What do *you* expect from him?" He was annoyed. While there wasn't anything in the way of romance between Xander and me, he did get oddly territorial when I became close friends with other people. Hence the animosity toward Penelope.

"I think the better question is, what do you?"

Excellent dodging, Counselor.

The nickname Marcus gave me did things to me that I couldn't explain. Goose bumps, butterflies, all of it.

"I don't know . . ." he began. His mood had been deflated all day after the incident. "I want it to go back to how it was, when we all knew what was going on with each other because we were there."

My heart sank at the thought that he'd be away from us again soon. "Come to London, Xan." I knew that wouldn't solve the problem, but it would make the next few months easier for both of us. "Stay at the house with me. It'll be like college all over again."

"Your solution to my inability to move on from an idealized past is to pretend I don't have to?" He laughed. He'd already turned me down twice. A part of my request was selfish; if I had a live-in best friend, I would never be lonely. "You're a bad therapist."

"Yeah, that's usually why you don't go to lawyers with these problems," I countered as some levity rejoined the conversation. "Give him some time. Whether you're angry or not, he's still your brother, and he is trying."

"Maybe."

"Definitely," I corrected. "If he weren't, you'd have a black eye too."

* * *

SATURDAY MORNING AFTER Thanksgiving was when everyone prepared to return to their lives. The day was spent lazily getting things in order and packing. Everyone usually headed out later than planned because of a game, conversation, or argument.

"Sloan." My mother peeked her head out from the kitchen when I walked through the hallway; my weekender bag was packed and in hand. She didn't say anything else. She walked back into the kitchen and took a seat at the table.

I followed the unspoken command and took a seat next to her. The table sat in front of a large window overlooking the back of the property. Sunlight streamed through and filled the room in the morning.

"This London trip," she began. Her hands clutched her coffee mug tightly. "Are you sure it's necessary? You have such a wonderful position at the firm as it is."

Don't snap at her.

I had grown accustomed to the bewilderment my career aspirations caused among my family and some of our family-friends. But my mom's concerns didn't have anything to do with my career and everything to do with her estranged family.

The parents that disowned her and the family that disinherited her lived in London. My mother always seemed to worry that Henry or I would reach out to them at some point, only to be met with the same rejection she faced.

"I have no plans to see any of *them*," I assured her.

The part that burned the worst was that I tried so hard to be someone they could love. I insisted on going to finishing school, on being presented to society in an archaic debutante ball, all to maybe find a place in their world. That silly little girl learned long ago that she could act like them as much as she wanted, but they'd never really see her.

I only wished I'd come to that revelation sooner in life and loved myself then the way I did now. It would have saved me a lot of heartache.

She sighed. Her concern softened. "They don't deserve to know you."

She didn't say anything else. I stood up and hugged her. My parents had always maintained some distance from me and Henry growing up; it didn't really change until we were much older. I spent a lot of time being angry about that too, but the annoyance over their expectations thinned over time. Nowadays, it was easier to let go of it in deference to keeping the peace.

* * *

Marcus drove me back home. I intended to wait for Xander to leave and avoid another awkward drive, but when I left the kitchen, he already had my bag in his hand. He gestured to the car, gave me *that* smile, and I was convinced.

I loved the drive. The city blended into the mountains; before you knew it, you were in an entirely new place.

"You're so lucky to have grown up around here," I said aloud. The lush fall colors blended as we zipped past them. The words came out of my mouth before I remembered who I was sitting next to. I winced. Xander and I loved to reminisce about the trips our families would take together during fall breaks in college.

Since Henry and Marcus were best friends, our families often got together for school-related events like parents' weekend or homecoming. By the time Xander and I made it to Penn, it was a tradition. The summers always included a week at my parents' house in East Hampton, and the autumns always had hiking and pumpkin picking around the Sutton family home.

Marcus didn't say anything. He never brought them up.

"Sorry," I said after a drawn-out silence.

More silence passed before he finally put me out of my awkward misery. "No, it's okay, I don't talk about them enough."

Xander had an expected reaction to his parents' passing. He went off the rails. Marcus went from shocked to numb and stayed that way for a while. Over the years, it started to peel back.

"You were great, you know." Again, the words came out of my mouth without regard to how he'd feel about it.

Marcus and Henry were just starting out at Amari Global when it happened. Afterward, Marcus would drive back and forth between Manhattan and Philadelphia to keep an eye on Xander for months. Every weekend. Like clockwork.

He still owned the Philadelphia penthouse to this day, like a reminder to look after his little brother. "All that time, going back and forth. You were infallible to him. Still are," I added.

He didn't say anything as a heavy look scrawled across his face. He didn't believe me.

"I loved your house," I continued. A part of me screamed to shut up. But maybe he needed a push to talk about it.

Their house felt like an actual home. Their mom loved to garden. Every spring, the entire yard smelled of peonies, which wafted into the house. It felt like a fairy tale. I leaned back into my seat and listened to the gentle hum of the engine.

"Xander and I would call it the country house." I smiled at the memory.

A small, sad smile tugged at the side of his face. "We used to go up there a lot."

"I loved it. You and Henry always ended up getting Xander in trouble." I was always spared because their father adored me, and I was usually left out of their shenanigans.

"We got in so much trouble when we left you out of things." His voice lightened. The boys tended to be awful, especially when Xander was goaded into ditching me. "Mostly Xander, though."

"You were bullies."

A laugh almost made its way out of him. "You were fine."

Those visits were only fun for me when I got to hang out with Xander. "I was sixteen and dragged away from my friends. Xander was all I had, and you two tried to take him."

Something about that statement made him pause. His softness was lost, his features closed up again.

It was quiet for a few minutes after that.

"Yeah, but look at how tough you are now. You're welcome." His voice broke the mounting tension.

I smiled and spent the rest of the ride trying to convince Marcus to visit his old house with Xander one day. He was surprisingly receptive.

Chapter 13

MARCUS

After Thanksgiving, I realized how many problems had cropped up while I was busy getting assaulted by my little brother. And other holiday activities.

I needed to focus on work, but I had a quickly healing black eye reminding me that I had amends to make.

"The eye looks back to normal," Henry said as he took a seat beside me at a bar at the Augustus, a high society club in Manhattan that the Amaris belonged to for two generations. Xander and I gained access a few years ago.

The bartender delivered our drinks. "I invited Xander, but he declined," I told him. Xander said he was busy with work, but we all knew he wasn't. There wasn't much when it came to mental pursuits that he wasn't good at. His work didn't take up much of his time or hold his attention very long.

"He's still angry."

I took a sip of the whiskey and relished the smooth burn. "You're not?"

He shrugged. "I don't know, probably. I don't think I have the time to be angry with you."

"It's not going well?" I asked. His grandfather was always kinder to me than he was Henry. That had more to do with the impossibly high bar he set and expected Henry to surpass.

Henry shrugged and ran a hand along his jaw. "How the hell did you do it?"

It sounded half like an actual question and half like an accusation. Sutton Industries expanded exponentially over the last few years; it was a feat. Still, it was primarily due to constant work and the acceptance of all I'd probably lost because of it.

"Talent?" It was meant to be a joke, but he wasn't amused, and I wasn't sure how to answer his question. I had help. The same help he had, but sometimes his father and grandfather tortured him by withholding that aid. I think they thought it made him stronger. It just made him resent them. "And a comfort with bending the rules."

He shrugged. "I guess. You know, my grandfather will still like you even if you have the occasional misfire."

My smile faded. He'd hit a nerve, and he knew it. I never had the level of comfort with the Amaris that Xander did, constantly feeling as though I had to prove myself. Maybe it was always going head-to-head with Henry that started it, or maybe because I felt indebted for my first real opportunity. Either way, a part of me thought I had to be perfect to prove I was worth the investment.

I tried to shield Xander from it, made sure he knew his success was his own. I told myself that was why he fit so well with them while I always felt like a guest. I tried not to give the more painful reason any credence—that he was just someone people could love while I was someone who could achieve, and my place in their lives wouldn't outlive my usefulness.

Henry shifted in his seat uncomfortably in the long silence. "Sorry, I didn't mean anything by that."

"Don't worry about it. Did you come here solely to piss me off?"

I had hoped getting drinks would reset some of the animosity that came along with my absence. I shook off the annoyance and wondered how many of those shots I'd have to take before we were even.

"No, that was just a fringe benefit." He grinned. "Actually, I did want to ask you about this Sloan thing."

My mind raced for a moment. I reminded myself that, technically, there was no Sloan thing. There never was. "What?"

"I think she's up to something."

"What does that mean?" But I knew what it meant. He'd suffered bad press all summer and was taking out his current slippery position with the board on her. The idea that his little sister was doing something to undermine him was outrageous. If he believed it, he was doomed.

He gave me a stern look.

I pinched the bridge of my nose. "Do you want to consider who's at fault here? Sloan didn't push you into bed with every ballerina in the city."

"Not *every* ballerina," he scoffed. "You're keeping tabs on me?"

"You don't make much effort to keep it a secret."

"Are you the best person to lecture me on *that*?" Henry turned the glass in his hand. "If I recall correctly, and I do, you had a different girl every weekend. At least I know their names."

"I didn't live under a microscope," I reminded him.

The rules were different for me. I wasn't from one of the wealthiest families in the city. I didn't grow up in society. I was new money, and that came with benefits. Nobody cared about what I was doing until I started showing up in the *Financial Times*. Even then, hanging out with Henry meant he absorbed the glare of the press.

"I guess." He shifted uncomfortably again. "She seemed to enjoy the onslaught of bad press this summer."

"I doubt that," I snapped. "Look at all the evidence. She's leaving the continent to pursue a career away from her family. If she wanted your seat, she's doing a shitty job of getting it. And we both know she's too much of a perfectionist to have done a shitty job at anything."

"Then what's going on? Why does she hate me?" His voice was low, like he was talking to himself.

"You dismissed her and said she was throwing a tantrum and then a hissy fit. The second one was to her face, in front of her closest friends." I didn't even mention his comment that nobody cared about what Sloan did. Even I wanted to punch him after that crack.

Clearly frustrated, he ran a hand through his hair. "Shit. You're right."

"I usually am."

"Oh, and do me a favor, look out for her while she's in London, will you?" He looked genuinely worried. Before they started competing viciously to prove who was the better fit for CEO, they were close. And he was always protective. "She has fucking terrible taste in men; you would've hated the last guy she dated."

He was right about that. "He was that bad?"

Why do you care what Henry thought of her ex?

"Awful." Henry rolled his eyes. He finished his drink and motioned for another. "Then there's my fucking CFO, who thought it would be a good idea to ask me if she was seeing anyone after he saw her at some event."

"Preston Scott?" My molars smashed together. We worked together before I left Amari Global to strike out on my own. I never liked him. He was a high society clone of every other proper gentleman that Sloan seemed to attract.

He was also a couple years older than Henry and me. He worked for her brother. How the fuck was that appropriate?

"Yeah." Henry lifted his fresh glass and took a sip.

"Fire him."

Henry laughed. I didn't know why; I was entirely serious. Now I was stuck thinking about Preston hitting on her every time she went into the building.

"At least he had the decency to ask before hitting on her," Henry said.

"I guess."

I was initially a little annoyed that Sloan and I would be in London at the same time. Seeing her alone felt like a temptation I needed to avoid. But it provided me the opportunity to keep her away from guys like Preston for another few months.

Hopefully long enough for whatever it was that I felt for her to finally go away.

Chapter 14

SLOAN

The knock at my door on a late Saturday afternoon was odd. I wasn't expecting anyone.

I stood in the kitchen and ran down the list of people it could be. Usually, if my parents or grandfather wanted to see me, I was summoned. Xander had a key and never knocked.

"Sloan? It's Henry," I heard after another knock.

Henry? My heart raced. Something must be wrong. I dropped the wooden spoon in my hand, turned off the stove, and ran to the door.

Henry never visited these days. Not unless something happened.

"Is everything okay?" I almost screamed in anxiety as I swung the door open. My frantic eyes were met by my brother's. He was calm and collected and held a bottle of wine. His smile was one of a psychotic fool who yelled fire in a movie theater.

"Yeah, I wanted to come say hi." Brushing past me, he invited himself into my townhouse.

Shell-shocked, I stood on the threshold for a moment.

My mind raced, and I tried to make sense of his sudden intrusion. "Are you high?"

I closed the door and followed him into *my* house.

He laughed, walking from the foyer to the kitchen overlooking the living space. He put the wine down on the countertop and sat at the island. "Smells good. What are you cooking, Saan—"

"Nothing." I cut him off before he used my middle name. He only used it when he tried to be nostalgic.

"How are you?" He got up and busied himself by opening every cabinet in search of a corkscrew and wineglasses. "Are you seeing anyone?"

He found two glasses, and I got the corkscrew from the drawer. If we were going to do this, I needed wine.

"No. Are you?" The room fell quiet. I sat on the seat next to him, crossing my arms. He gave a resigned sigh and finally yielded.

He ran a hand through his short black hair. "I was talking to Marcus."

I sat up straighter at the sound of his name. I found myself wanting to see Marcus more. Henry had a chance to cultivate a better relationship with Xander in his absence. I wanted the same with Marcus.

Okay, I probably wanted more, but I knew better than to fill my head with silly fantasies about Marcus. The man had more commitment issues than Xander. And that was a high bar.

"I haven't been a good brother these last few years, have I?" Marcus got Henry to understand that? It was obvious, but months of Xander screaming it at him hadn't done anything.

"Not really." I poured two glasses and went to the stove to get the food I made. Dhal and rice; I was in the mood for comfort food. "I haven't been great either," I admitted.

In the last three years, Henry had changed from being a pretty decent guy to someone I hardly recognized. Utterly consumed by living up to our father's expectations, he began to alienate those closest to him. Marcus's absence probably made it all worse.

I didn't exactly help matters. I was angry for years that he was the presumed heir, even though there was never a discussion as to whether someone was better suited.

When I accepted it, I tried to move on and make my own way. I knew my last name helped open doors, but I was still proud of myself for everything I had accomplished. I never minded when it was met with apathy from some members of the family. When Henry discounted it, it filled me with a rage I often saved and summoned in the worst ways.

"Tell me about London." His expression was sincere. He was trying to make amends, and I had to undertake the enormous task of swallowing my anger and letting him.

I talked to Henry. For the first time in a long time, it was like talking to my big brother again, not the douchebag in a suit cosplaying a CEO. Seeing genuine pride in his eyes when I told him about my chance at partner gave me a feeling of acceptance I thought I would never have. His opinion of me mattered more than I liked to admit.

He confided his concerns about his eventual ascension and some of the trouble he was running into as he started taking on more responsibility at Amari Global. In the past, that was something he and Marcus would talk about. It made sense, given they had essentially the same position at different companies. While it never bothered Xander, who was decidedly uninterested in anything to do with the industry, I always felt a little cheated.

"I think he's going to pass it to me directly," Henry said after a few moments of silence, anxiety hanging on his words.

Our father was never meant for the CEO job, and the pressures were getting to him. It was evident in his noticeable absences and how my mother seemed utterly lost lately. The man she married was gone and replaced by someone who was never meant to lead a company.

"Grandfather isn't planning to retire for a while." He hadn't told us of any plans to retire soon; Henry had time to prepare.

"I could probably use some help whenever it does happen." He focused his gaze on the stem of his wineglass. He rarely asked me for help. In those moments, Henry reminded me of what he was like when we were kids. He was my confidante, my best friend before I had Xander. We were close for so long, until the reality of who would lead the company sank in.

I'd been given the pitch to join the leadership ranks before. I did consider it, but my career was taking off. It felt like a step down, even if it meant being the second in command.

I wanted to be first. And with the firm, I had a real shot at it.

"I think Marcus may be a better advisor than me." It wasn't an answer. And realistically, it wasn't an option. Sutton industries was a behemoth now. The conflicts of interest alone were enough to get regulatory attention.

The conversation drifted from work to our personal lives. Neither of us was interested in the details of the others' romantic ventures. The headlines were good enough. Henry went through women like Kleenex, so I tried not to ask any specific questions. Aside from a couple of wild streaks that Xander was sworn to secrecy on, my love life was not all that interesting. I worked a lot; there had been a few flings here and there.

Henry was worried last year when Julian and I split. Only having met him a couple of times and not being fond of him, I figured he wouldn't pay it much attention. He must have caught word from Xander at some point about it because he asked again.

"You're sure you're okay, after everything?"

Julian Waldorf was a mistake I would love to forget. When we met, he was easy to talk to and seemingly perfect—doting on me and taking time to impress Xander and curry his favor. The first six months were something out of a dream. I thought I'd met someone who actually saw me and cared for me as I was.

In reality, he was a terrified little boy who clung to his family's opinions as if they were the air he needed to breathe. I'd never forget the Waldorf family dinner I was forced to endure. I spent the entire evening getting thinly veiled insults about my "breeding" or how our family was "so new" to many of the charity boards they headed.

It didn't take a genius to decode their actual problem with me: skin too tan, money too new.

"It was almost a year ago. I'm fine." I nodded with a small sigh. I mostly felt embarrassed that I was so taken with him and just wanted to forget it happened.

He nodded, knowing I wasn't telling him the whole story. "You know the Feds froze his family's assets?" He laughed. "It was all anyone could talk about at the club a while back."

"Pity." I smiled. It was cute when Henry was protective, but hardly necessary; I could take care of myself. Julian knew that first-hand.

Chapter 15

MARCUS

S itting on the front porch steps of our childhood home for the first time in years was eerie. It felt like a lifetime ago that we lived here; a part of me had a hard time believing we ever did. The cold fall air smelled of rotting leaves and smoke.

I used to love this house. It was the only place that ever felt like home. After our parents died, I hired a caretaker and pretended it didn't exist.

"Marcus?" Xander called from behind me. "You don't want to come inside?"

I blinked away what welled in my eyes at the memory. Xander ran out from inside the house. When we arrived, he'd run into the house like a bat out of hell. I made it as far as the steps. The large brick façade that held my childhood felt intimidating.

I nodded and got to my feet.

The house seemed smaller when I walked through the front door for the first time in years. The larger pieces of furniture were still there, and photos still hung on the walls.

The memory of that night tended to replay without provocation. The night they died. Henry and I were at a business dinner. We left the restaurant and were deciding where to get drinks when he got the call from Sloan. The blood drained from Henry's face when he hung up and looked at me to tell me the news.

Sloan and Xander were just a few miles behind them and soon came upon their car. Sloan was the one to call EMS and shield Xander from seeing their mangled bodies.

"Finally." Xander rolled his eyes when he saw me walking around inside. "See, not so bad," he joked, and walked into another room.

I didn't know what Sloan and Xander did when they came here, but I guessed it was about the same. Xander's mood was hard to read. At times, he was excited and chattered about memories from the house. In other moments, he was quiet.

I found myself stuck at the bookshelf that spanned the entire study wall. It was our mother's favorite room. The spine of each book was worn from years of multiple reads. Her journals were interspersed between the books, each the same navy blue with a golden fleur-de-lys along the spine.

"Why don't you ever come back here?" After a long silence, Xander came down the steps. I found myself walking out of the study and aimlessly through the hallway.

A couple of years after their death and after we recovered, whatever that meant, Xander would ask me to come here with him on occasion. I always found a reason to avoid it. Eventually, he stopped asking, and Sloan came instead.

"Never really saw a point." That was the truth. We'd suffered enough. "It was easier to stay away."

Henry tried to get me to face it too. He brought them up yearly around the start of fall and at Christmastime. Every time we were remotely in the area, he suggested we come by.

His lips thinned, and he looked hurt. "Does that apply to me too?"

"I'm back for good after this next trip," I assured him. "And cut me some slack. I'm trying."

He fidgeted for a while and looked down at the floor. "Do you resent me for how I reacted?"

The fact that he needed to ask felt like a gut punch. He was my baby brother; I was there to protect him and tried my best at the time. After our parents died, it was my job to make sure he had what he needed to be happy. "No. Of course not, you were grieving."

"Yeah. I was." He didn't look up and shifted uncomfortably. "Because of that, you never got to."

I had tried to handle it stoically. I was twenty-five, and I learned as I went. I had to figure out how to settle an estate and execute last wishes.

An adult, but not a useful one. I had no idea how to do any of it, but someone had to step up. Xander lost all control for months. He went from despondent to unhinged at the drop of a hat. Someone needed to steer the ship and ensure their demise didn't spell ours. I tried to keep Xander from dealing with anything other than getting through it. He was never good with change.

Once the immediate needs were met and Xander was mostly steady, I buried myself in work. It was easier. It was something I could control.

"I'm fine." That was probably true.

The pain from their death was long buried. We'd all moved on, and things leveled out. That was until a couple of years ago. The unfamiliar feelings that bubbled up whenever I was around Sloan started to change things. It would stir up emotions I'd rather keep buried. I was figuring that part out.

Coming back here wasn't as bad as I thought it would be. It was actually kind of nice.

"Then why'd you just leave?"

I ran my hand down my jaw. "It didn't have to do with this."

"Then what?" Irritation crept into his voice. "And don't say work."

It *was* work. Mostly. What else would I have been doing for so long?

I didn't answer.

"Fine. But between me, Henry, and Sloan, someone will get it out of you." He gave me a shove and went to the backyard. Whether or not it was for the best, I was back for good.

* * *

WHEN I FINALLY returned to my place, I looked at my phone and smiled at the name that flashed on the screen.

> **Sloan:** I don't know how you did it, but thank you for fixing my brother

> **Sloan:** I owe you

Henry must have taken my advice. The fact that I helped make her happy pleased me more than I thought it would. I hadn't expected how the text would lift my somber mood either.

We could be friends. Keeping away from her wasn't a practical solution now that I was back. Besides, I enjoyed her company. I'd built Sutton Industries from the ground up; I could figure out how to be friends with Sloan.

> **Me:** Lobotomies are surprisingly effective

> **Me:** Went to my parents' house today with Xander—consider us even

A couple of minutes later, a call came in from Sloan. She never called me.

"Are you guys okay?" she asked without saying hello when I picked up. "Xander is always a little down when we leave the house."

"Yeah, we're fine. I just dropped him off at his place." Why did she call me instead of him? "Did you talk to Xander?"

"No, I just wanted to check. I usually give him space after our visits." I could hear a sigh of relief. She was the reason Xander got through the worst of it. "Are you okay?"

She called out of concern for Xander, not me. I had to keep reminding myself of that fact. "Yes, Sloan. I don't know if I ever thanked you for—"

"You don't need to thank me. He's my best friend. If you *want* to thank me, don't leave again. It was really hard on him."

"I won't."

"Thanks for talking to Henry."

"You don't need to thank me. He's my best friend," I teased, and she laughed. A pleasant and familiar warmth filled my chest at the sound. Then, the gnawing that always seemed to follow returned.

Once I stopped denying the feelings were there, I spent too much time trying to figure out why.

Why was she stuck in my head?

Why was I always thinking about her? Why was the idea of keeping her at arm's length still better than being an ocean away? Especially when being away meant I wouldn't have to feel *everything* as intensely?

Sloan and I talked about nothing in particular for a few minutes before she had to go. I hung up and tucked my phone back in my pocket.

Originally, I thought it was our shared interests that endeared her to me. Or that she was always looking out for the people she loved. Over the years, she'd been the one to steadily chip away at the pain and help us heal. She was the one to subtly, and sometimes not so subtly, make us face things we didn't want to.

I realized something today. I wanted her to be happy, and I wanted to be the one to make her happy. I wanted to ease her pain and let her ease mine.

She wasn't stuck in my head.

She was stuck in my heart.

Shit.

Chapter 16

SLOAN

I can't believe you came to this thing," CeCe whispered to me over her third mimosa. Society dictated that we all be pickled drones of happy housewives, and CeCe took the pickled part very seriously. "I almost didn't show up, and I have literally nothing better to do."

"Yeah, last time I make that mistake." I laughed as I tried to read the document on my phone, covertly placed beneath a napkin fort.

I can't believe I had to take the day off for this.

Now, into the second hour of a planning committee brunch for the Manhattan Society Junior League, I rechecked my phone to see if the paperwork for the Burton merger came through. We were in talks with the Securities and Exchange Commission to see if the acquisition would hold up to governmental scrutiny. Penelope went to D.C for the week to help smooth things over. I was supposed to go too. But I was needed here, sitting still and looking pretty.

I looked like society Barbie. The tweed Chanel jacket was itchy. The pearl necklace bothered my neck, the earrings felt too large, and I hated it all. My purse was large enough to hold a change of clothes if the embarrassment of being in this ridiculous outfit became too much.

The Junior League selected the venue and confirmed the details for this year's debutante ball. As a chair of the committee, I was required to be here. My mother generously gave me the seat in one of her attempts to help me feel like I fit in.

I couldn't even blame her. I spent so many years trying to fit in these rooms in some ridiculous attempt to be the granddaughter her parents might want to meet. When my mother recognized this unrelenting desire, she took it as a duty to give me every shot. Years after my debutante ball, I realized how much I didn't care what they thought about me.

The rejection still hurt, though.

"At least the cake is good," I said as I stood at the end of the meeting, making no attempt to hide my phone.

"And the champagne is top shelf," CeCe said, giggling.

CeCe, an amazing woman in her own right, came from a long line of heiresses. Her lineage traced back to the Livingston family. They were old money from European nobility. The type of old money that scoffed at the Rockefeller family fortune. CeCe was nothing like that, however. She was a deeply caring individual with a huge heart.

We turned in our ballot sheets and walked out of the ballroom. "I'm heading downtown; want to come along?"

She shook her head. "Drinks later? I have day-date plans."

"Yes," I agreed, and hailed a cab. Another cardinal sin. I should have been in a town car.

* * *

SINCE I HAD a couple hours before I needed to rejoin CeCe, I decided to see my grandfather. I didn't make a habit of going to the Amari Global building anymore for the same reason I hated society events.

Nobody liked the reminder that they weren't someone's first choice.

We may not have been as close as I was with my late grand-mother, but I wasn't going to see him until after I got back from London. I felt like I *should* see him. My relationship with him could be summed up by that sentiment. I always wanted to see my grandmother, I always felt like I *should* see my grandfather.

"You look well." He smiled from his desk. "How is the pursuit of partner?"

"Almost in hand," I confirmed.

"I expect no less." His schedule was busy; we only had half an hour to catch up. We didn't have much to talk about. He was always happy to see me, but always wholly consumed with the company.

Mostly, we talked about my plans for work in London while I was there. I never had much to talk about with my grandfather. The only thing that ever really interested him was the company.

After a short conversation, I got up to leave, but stopped before getting to the door.

"Is there anything you need? I can help if it helps Henry."

They were clearly worried about Henry taking over, but the actual concern eluded me. My grandfather and father often underestimated Henry and me—that, or they expected too much. Either way, they had a way of making us feel like we needed to prove ourselves. I finally recognized that my unhealthy competition with Henry wasn't helping anyone. And my skill set was pretty similar to his.

I could've been useful. I wanted to help.

He opened his mouth and sat up a bit like he was going to say something, but then hesitated. "No, nothing."

That irked me. It felt like he didn't trust me with an important task. I hadn't proven myself yet. I felt it—the poorly controlled resentment about to sneak out.

There was no point in relitigating the past. There had already been far too many arguments about it. I swallowed the annoyance.

I put on my best smile and nodded.

* * *

I TOOK THE private elevator down to the lobby. In my annoyance, I forgot to change out of the terrible outfit.

"Sloan?" Henry's voice called. Distracted by my phone, I didn't realize I had walked right past him and Marcus. "What are you doing here?"

They must have come from a late lunch or something. It was nice to see them together. Henry looked happier, and Marcus looked . . .

Focus.

"Junior League event. Then I came to see Grandfather." I looked at Henry, but I could see Marcus's eyes fall on me. Marcus was meant to wear suits. Today's was navy. He was holding a to-go coffee. It made his biceps flex against the fabric. I wondered what it would feel like to run my hands down those arms. Or be lifted by them.

Henry looked at my outfit and smiled with pity.

"You look nice." Marcus's voice was kind, but his smile smothered a laugh.

The humiliation was nauseating. If he was joking, it was poorly executed.

"Well, this was fun." My voice sharpened.

I turned on my heels before feeling a hand reach out to my elbow to stop me. It was Henry's. "It's getting late, have Winston take you," he said, nodding in the direction of his driver.

"It'll take twice as long. I'm going to walk." I brushed off his hand and shooed him with my own. The sun had already set, and apparently, I wasn't trusted to walk alone at twilight.

"Why are you so stubborn?"

"It's not stubborn. Driving will take an hour," I snapped back.

"I'll walk her," Marcus cut into what would have been the heirs to the company sniping in the lobby. "The firm isn't far from my office."

The optics of the two of us fighting in the lobby would've been terrible, and Marcus knew that. Always a step ahead.

Henry sighed. "Thanks." He turned around with a long huff and headed to his office.

"Fine," I snapped at Marcus. If I was going to walk the streets of New York with him, I would not do it looking like this. "I need to take this jacket off."

Without waiting for his answer, I walked to the bathroom in the lobby.

Chapter 17

MARCUS

Sloan changed. It made me feel like more of a jackass for mocking her outfit. In my attempt to tease her, I offended her. Not the best way to try to establish a friendship with her, one that wasn't based on her relationship with Henry or Xander.

Or you're trying to push her away.

It would have been easier on me, but logistically, it was nearly impossible now that I was set on sticking around.

We'd made it a block past the building, and she hadn't looked at me once. "I didn't mean anything by what I said."

"Laughing at my outfit?" Sloan snapped. "You don't need to take etiquette classes to know that laughing at someone is rude."

"You just looked different," I blurted. That didn't help. Why was I so nervous? Nothing made me nervous. Yet, the words came out of my mouth, and I was powerless to stop them. "Still nice, though."

Nice? Fuck. Pick any other word.

I couldn't tell her she looked fucking devastating no matter what she wore.

She didn't say anything for a few minutes before looking up at me with annoyance. "I know I looked ridiculous. Nobody looks good in that disgusting jacket."

It was then that I noticed she was in a dress and probably freezing. I took off my suit jacket and threw it over her shoulders before she could stubbornly protest. "I'm sorry."

We walked in silence for another few blocks. I enjoyed the way she looked, draped in my jacket. The way it engulfed her lithe frame made my mind wander to what one of my T-shirts would look like on her. It stirred a possessiveness I'd never felt before. One I had no business having for her.

She stopped at an intersection and turned to me. "I'm not going to the firm."

"Where are you going?"

"I have plans to get drinks." She fidgeted with her fingers.

I ran the last twenty minutes back in my head. She changed clothes. Maybe it wasn't because of what I said. If she wanted to look sexier, she certainly did in that dress. The implication dawned, and the molten envy followed, covering my skin in a cold sweat.

I tried to swallow the annoyance. "A date?" I asked plainly.

You're not allowed to be bothered by that.

But fuck, I was.

"Why? Are you going to gossip about it with Henry?" she mocked.

"It's worth gossip? Embarrassed of him?" The same look she'd had since my comment on her clothes was etched on her face. My tone softened. "I won't say a word. Scout's honor."

"You were a Boy Scout?" A smile tugged at the side of her cheek.

"No." The furthest thing. I spent the morning completing a hostile takeover of a small biotech company. After months of bleeding their capital dry, we convinced the board to vote on a sale. Venture capitalists were fickle creatures, especially when you drained their profits. Morality was in the eye of the beholder, or in that case, the shareholder. "But it sounds nice."

She laughed. The warm, feathery softness wrapped around me in the cold air. I wanted to hear it over and over again.

Sloan didn't answer my original question. Instead, we walked awkwardly in silence.

"Visiting your empty office?" I asked. She had said she went to visit her grandfather, but I needed something to cut the rest of the lingering tension.

She had an office on the executive floor of Amari Global waiting, should she ever take her family's offer of joining the ranks. Despite her bickering with Henry, it seemed like it was never truly something she wanted.

"Oh, that," she began. I hated how much it bugged me that she had been there. I couldn't get the image of Preston Scott hitting on her out of my head. "No, I like reminding Henry that he's one misplaced insult away from a coup."

I chuckled despite myself. She was kidding. She had to be. There was no way she was still truly vying for control of the company.

She grinned and looked up at me, a mischievous glint in her eye. "What makes you think I'm joking?"

I couldn't tell if she was serious. My heart sank at the possibility that she was.

I didn't answer.

She rolled her eyes. "I'm kidding. Jeez, lighten up."

Sloan gestured in the direction of the street she wanted to turn onto, and I followed a step behind her. Seeing her wrapped in my suit jacket made the realization that I was walking her to a date cut deeper.

It wasn't long before we got to the bar in question.

She turned to face me again. "Don't worry, I won't stay out too late." A sly grin grew along her face. "CeCe is pretty strict about the three-date rule."

CeCe. CeCe Cummings. Female.

Relief flooded me. I took a deep breath, and the vice grip around my chest finally eased. Sloan looked victorious, and the sly smile grew into a friendly one.

Sloan turned to the door and waved when she saw CeCe inside waiting for her. "Thanks," she said, and handed my suit jacket back over to me.

"Give me your jacket." My command was pleasant. She cocked her head in amusement, opened her bag, and gave it to me.

"You don't look ridiculous." I threw it over her shoulders. Honestly, she looked cold. "You look pretty."

It was a terrible compliment, but what I really thought wasn't suitable for a public setting.

She rewarded me with a small laugh, clearly unconvinced. "Thank you for the company." She grinned and pulled me into a hug before saying goodbye.

I held her a moment longer than I should have, breathing in the scent of lavender in her hair. I had to remind myself to let go. It was easy to hold her, almost like I was meant to.

You weren't.

"What are friends for?" I watched as she disappeared inside, then turned to head back to work. The unwelcome jealousy served to unearth a memory I'd been searching for.

When I realized a shift had occurred.

It was a couple of years ago. Xander was throwing a party to celebrate buying his house in Southampton, technically a housewarming.

Of course, Sloan was in attendance. I arrived early the day of and spent most of it with her. While the party staff prepared, we lounged around Xander's palatial new home. She was attractive, sure. Spending most of the morning with her at the pool affirmed that.

The hours passed like seconds with her. We spent the morning and afternoon lost in conversation, but I didn't think much of it. She was up for junior partner at the time, the youngest at the firm, and was rightfully excited. I was enraptured. It wasn't until the party that I realized it.

The party mainly centered around the pool and drifted out to the beach. I remember looking for her at some point when I saw Xander spin her around in a tango before handing her off to her boyfriend at the time. It was her ex.

The next ten seconds felt like they happened in slow motion. He whispered something in her ear. She threw her head back in a laugh, leaned up, and pulled him into a kiss. I recoiled and felt winded. That's when it all dawned on me.

The sound of her laugh and the terrible gnawing in my chest stayed with me the rest of the night. I decided that I had to get some work done and left early.

The feelings only grew over the next few months. I wanted to spend more time with her but put space between us instead. I understood the boundaries I wasn't supposed to cross.

My feelings for her stirred up everything else I buried. It became too much to get a handle on, so Sutton Industries' rapid expansion was the perfect way to remove myself from it.

Recent revelations didn't change anything. They only put a finer point on what I was up against. Plenty of people ignored those types of things. There were books filled with those stories, albeit mostly tragic, but that was a minor detail. It was a puzzle, and I would have to figure it out.

Once I did, everything would go back to how it was.

Chapter 18

SLOAN

I broke in to Xander's place.

Technically, I had a key. It was early and I hadn't expected him to be awake yet. I needed to steal something. I was crossing the kitchen when I was caught.

"Where's my picture?" he called. He walked out of his bedroom and stopped in the hallway.

Xander had a photographic memory. For him, it was a gift and curse. Not that you needed it to notice what I'd taken. While most people looked at him and saw a handsome banker, they often didn't recognize that there were deep undercurrents of brilliance beneath.

"Hmm?" I gave myself up. He knew I was there, and I knew taking the framed photo of the four of us from his hallway would be noticed. I was hoping I'd be halfway to the firm when it was.

He walked into the kitchen, poured a cup of coffee into a mug, and turned to face me. His dirty blonde hair was neatly coiffed, his gray suit fitted perfectly, and his emerald eyes narrowed on me before they glanced down at the framed photograph wrapped in my arms.

He raised an eyebrow.

"Consider it photo-napped." There wasn't any point in hiding my intention; he knew it by now. "It'll be at Sutton Industries if you'd like it back."

He rolled his eyes and groaned.

Xander was one of the most understanding people I knew. He'd forgive Marcus's absence with time, but I had a vested interest in that being sooner rather than later. I was leaving for London in a few weeks, and I needed to know he was okay before I left. Holding on to anger always manifested in destructive ways for him, hence the rare violent outburst at Thanksgiving.

"You know, you don't need to fix everything." His eyes were soft, but his tone prickled with annoyance.

I brushed past it. "Any more complaints?"

He tilted his head and looked around, surveying what else I may have disturbed. "Stop moving the refrigerator magnets," he added. I moved one about an inch lower than its original position. Xander liked things in his home orderly, in his slightly compulsive way.

He handed me a cup of coffee and gestured for me to sit. "What's up?" I asked, putting the photo beside my Birkin.

"Are we going to ignore that you and Marcus are going to be in London at the same time?"

He seemed disinterested, but also like he knew something. He couldn't have; it was the one secret I managed to keep from him. Letting that bit of information loose was dangerous. It would change things for our entire group. It was too complicated.

Besides, nothing was happening. Unless you counted the X-rated dreams.

"Does it matter?" I asked. Marcus hadn't seen me once when he visited over the last couple of years. Being in the same city meant we might see each other. I was sure Henry and my grandfather would ask him to check in on me, but other than that, I probably wouldn't see him till we were back in Manhattan. Or whenever Xander came to visit. "We probably won't see each other."

I pushed past the acrid stab of disappointment. We may not have been all that close, but he was one of the few people who truly knew me. It wasn't enough to make him want to see me.

"I guess." Xander rounded the counter and sat beside me. "Make sure he comes back this time?"

I laughed, squeezed his shoulder, and pushed myself up.

I was taking the photograph to Marcus's office, and Xander could go get it when he was ready. That way, I knew they had to talk again. It was a way to force them together when they were too stubborn to do it themselves.

That was the only reason. It wasn't that I wanted to see him and needed an excuse.

* * *

MARCUS

I looked at my emails to see we'd just completed another leveraged buyout of a German nanotech company. It took longer than planned. Something about being back was distracting me. I was yanked from my thoughts by a familiar voice on the other side of my office door.

"Is he free?"

My mood lightened.

The door opened. Sloan walked in, and I got up to shut the door behind her. Her hair swept back and brushed forward with the door's movement.

"I didn't know Carter worked for you. We went to high school together," she said offhandedly. Her arms were wrapped around a large frame. The picture, however, was pressed against her, and I couldn't see it.

"Who?" I asked, suddenly annoyed. She must have seen someone she knew.

Over the past few weeks, I was confronted with a lot of annoying little truths I'd forgotten. One of them was that Sloan was a magnet for high-society assholes. Every man at the Augustus club between the ages of twenty-five and forty found it appropriate to ask me or Henry if Sloan was seeing anyone.

It was maddening, and choking the life out of every single one of them was largely impractical. I had to deal with it.

She laughed when she turned to me. "Nobody of any consequence."

"You look nice." I flinched at the word. She looked like a force of nature that threatened to destroy every shred of resistance I had. *Nice* felt more appropriate.

"Jeez, you and that word." She rolled her eyes and took a seat in front of my desk.

"How was the date?" I asked.

"CeCe says hello."

As I walked past her, she handed me the frame. "You stole this." I resisted the pull at the side of my cheek and sat down at my desk. It was a picture of the four of us after Sloan's law school graduation.

There were some memories I could hardly recall, but others were etched deep into my mind. For some reason, Sloan's law school graduation was a day I remembered with perfect clarity.

"Borrowed," she corrected. Her smile brightened the room. "He'll get it when he's ready."

We all had a copy of the small four-by-six photo that Sloan's mother took. She must've assumed mine was lost somewhere.

Sloan had hers and Xander's enlarged and framed. I was holding Xander's.

"That's why you stopped by? Ransom?" I ignored the disappointment. Why else would she have stopped by, if not for something Xander related?

Things were getting better with my little brother. I didn't expect him to forgive my absence overnight. But he needed a push, and Sloan was often the one to administer those. She did things like that a lot—everything she could to keep our little group together. I was sure it was for Xander's benefit; nobody handled monumental changes well, and least of all him.

She shook her head. "Well, that's not the *only* reason I came by."

"No?" An unfamiliar excitement shot through me.

"If my coup is going to work, I'll need a head on a platter to present to the board." Our eyes locked, and a sly smile grew along her mouth. "Yours would do."

"How generous of you."

"No queen can stage a coup without keeping her military generals happy. And the board would be mine. No better way to win their favor than giving them our biggest competition."

"That's big talk," I teased and leaned back in my chair. I tried not to picture all the ways she could convince me to give up my company. "You'd have to either convince me to step aside or force me out."

"I can be persuasive."

I swallowed hard. If she wanted to persuade me, fuck, I'd let her. "Oh?"

"Besides, what makes you think it's *you* I'd try to convince?" She stood and looked around the room with a devious grin.

"Who else would it be, Counselor?"

"Xander." She walked to the bookshelf, her eyes gliding past the book spines. "If I had to guess, he probably has almost as much stake in your company as you do. Even if he doesn't know it."

She was right. When I started Sutton Industries, I gave Xander almost half of my stake in it.

"What makes you think that?"

She flicked her glance over her shoulder. "I know you."

"You do," I agreed calmly, despite the thundering in my chest. I didn't know what we were doing, but watching Sloan piece together exactly how she'd take me down was the sexiest thing I'd ever seen.

"Mmmhmm," she continued, her gaze fixed on scanning the books on the shelf. "Buy out Xander. Find a few weak links on the board and any other stakeholders I may need. Maybe force their hands or bribe them. You know, normal stuff."

"You've got it all figured out." I couldn't have planned it better myself.

She released a contented sigh and walked back to her seat. She dropped back down into it with a victorious smile. "All hypothetical, of course."

"Of course." I folded my hands on my desk and leaned in. "That's an excellent plan to supplant Henry. One problem, though." I paused, and she leaned forward in her chair. "You did just tell it to his best friend."

She feigned a disappointed sigh. "Classic supervillain mistake."

"You're the villain?"

"Anyone who questions my grandfather's grand plan is the villain." She shrugged. "I guess that's me."

We couldn't tear our eyes off each other for a few heavy seconds. She broke first and glanced around the office.

"Why didn't you—" she began. Her eyes darted along the floor. Her tone lost the slyness it adopted for our faux coup scenario.

"Sloan?" I asked after a few quiet seconds.

"You visited Henry and Xander," she murmured. She clasped her hands together tightly on her lap. Her lashes swept up, and her gaze lifted to meet mine again. "Why not me?"

Wanting her, and waiting for that feeling to eventually fade, burned. But hurting her seared every nerve ending in my body. Sloan was only ever vulnerable with Xander, on occasion Henry. Never me.

"Seeing them made me miss home. Seeing you would have made me stay, and I had work to do." There was a moment, a flash, where the confession felt like I was finally stopping to catch my breath. Her chest rose, and her eyes went wide with my confession. *Shit.* "You're the glue that holds our little group together."

It was true. There was more to it, but that small part was still true. It was as close to the whole truth as I could ever give her.

Her eyes were glassy for a moment before she blinked it away. Her face brightened, and a laugh cooled the scalding guilt. "It's always 'you look nice' and never 'you're the glue that holds us together.'"

"I'm sorry."

She nodded. "Don't do it again." Her command was low and soft. My phone buzzed against the desk, and she jostled slightly. With a deep inhale, she smiled and got up. "I should get back to the firm."

"Marcus," she called, as her body was halfway out the door. The sound of her softly saying my name echoed in my mind. "Xander and I are going out for dinner tonight. If I invite Henry, will you come along?"

I nodded, and she smiled again.

Chapter 19

SLOAN

The next few weeks passed like seconds. Before I knew it, it was Christmas.

Christmas was one of the few holidays we didn't spend with the Suttons until after their parents passed. After that, we'd visit on the day of. The visits turned into the four of us having our own sort of holiday. My parents grew accustomed to it and never expected to see us on the actual day.

With Marcus gone the last two years, Henry moped and worked through the holiday, and Xander and I did our own thing. This year I planned to do the same, but in an attempt to regain some semblance of normalcy, I thought Henry would join if I asked, and I was sure Marcus would too. He was being extra accommodating to help placate some of the wounds Xander sustained in his absence.

My place was minimally decorated, with a tree in the corner dressed in some lights and ornaments, a wreath on the door, and some stockings pinned onto the mantel. I wasn't big on decorating.

Henry arrived an hour or so before Marcus and asked every few minutes how he could help, even though Xander and I were seated comfortably on the large couch day drinking and clearly doing nothing.

"Does he need a kidney?" Xander whispered when Henry went to the bathroom after spending ten minutes telling me how proud he was of me.

Before I could answer, we heard the door open and close and the lock click. Xander and I turned to see Marcus walking in with a familiar pastry box wrapped with kitchen twine.

I jumped up and ran to him, opening it to see my favorite treat. Jalebi, from a place close to his office. Before he left, he'd occasionally bring me some. It became mandatory around the holidays.

"I remembered," he said, as if reading my mind. My heart skipped.

"Did you break Henry?" Xander looked back to his brother while I took the package from Marcus, rewarding him with a quick hug before going to the kitchen island to open it. "He's been kissing Sloan's ass all day."

"I may have overcorrected." Marcus's wry smile made me look away. I needed to rein it in. He took my seat on the couch next to Xander. I handed him a glass of wine and nestled into a new corner spot facing the Sutton brothers, jalebi in hand. "I meant well, sorry."

"It's better than all the moping around he did last year." Xander laughed as Henry reentered the room.

"Not too mopey to kick your ass at FIFA." Henry plopped down on the armchair across from us.

"It was a fluke. Xbox is upstairs if you want proof," Xander reminded him, referring to one of the guest rooms he had claimed as his own.

"Since when do you play FIFA?" Marcus looked mildly perturbed that Henry and Xander had forged a friendship in his absence. It was odd, but nice. They would occasionally get drinks after work.

"Since you ditched me for two years, I realized your brother was more fun than you."

Xander and Henry exchanged looks and raced upstairs.

That left Marcus and me on the couch.

"If it makes you feel better, your brother *is* more fun than you are," I teased, scooting closer to him. Something about how he looked at me in that moment drew me in and made me nervous at the same time. "But you brought jalebi, so I won't ditch you."

"How kind of you." Marcus's gaze softened, and a few moments passed. "How do boyfriends feel about Xander being here so often?"

I blinked a few times in surprise. We never really talked about our relationships. Everything I knew about his relationships was secondhand from Henry or Xander. Not that he ever had any. His dating history was a list of conquests, not relationships.

"Nobody would ask that question if Xander and I were both women," I reminded.

"Fair enough," he conceded. "So, they're all fine with it?"

I pulled my legs off the floor, folded them in front of me, and faced him. "They don't love it," I admitted after a long pause, and shifted a bit. The fact was, most of the guys I dated hated it. They were all threatened by Xander, and I guess I should have been more cognizant of that. I always felt it shouldn't be my job to fix their self-esteem. "But Xander is a part of the deal. I'm not going to pretend he's not a huge part of my life. If they can't handle that, that's not my problem."

His mouth quirked. "Their loss."

"Were you seeing anyone while hiding out from your real life?" I asked. If he was going to ask me about my personal life, then his was fair game. "I'm sorry, I meant working."

"Are we playing twenty questions? Because I know better than to play any sort of game with you," he teased.

"I answered yours."

He paused. "I wasn't seeing anyone seriously."

"What does that mean?" I knew what it meant. I wasn't a nun. A part of me wanted to hear him say it. Maybe then I'd be shaken out of the delusion my mind kept drifting to.

"I'd explain, but someone might question your honor." His voice was low, and his eyes flickered over my face. The cool tone sent shivers skittering up my body. I felt feverish. Goose bumps one minute, a cold sweat the next.

We were dangerously close to flirting. I didn't know what we were doing, but I liked it.

"You forget, Xander and I often witnessed your and Henry's . . . antics." I laughed lightly and ignored the sting of jealousy the memory gave me.

He winced.

I didn't mean it in a judgmental way. The years preceding his time away were pretty quiet, or at least I didn't bear witness to him with a different girl every weekend as I had in the past. Work took up more of his time.

He paused again before answering my original question. "Nothing past a few dates, and before you ask why, I was working. I didn't have time for a relationship."

I nodded for a second, thinking about that. It must have been lonely. I felt a little sad for him. And a little annoyed. Why hadn't he visited if he was alone?

It wasn't until that moment that I felt his thumb stroking a pattern along my wrist. The slow movements sent an electric hum through my skin. Our arms lay lazily on the back of the couch, overlapping slightly. He looked like he didn't realize he was doing it.

A bolt of courage ran through me, and my heart beat palpably in my chest. "Why did you bring me jalebi?"

"You're going to waste one of your questions on that?"

I nodded.

"You like them, and before you burn another one—that's what friends do." His expression was marbled with thought.

"You waited in line for them." Imagining Marcus in line for anything was just ridiculous. Marcus and Xander didn't grow up in the elite world we did, but they fit right in once they both made their way into it. Considering how successful Marcus was and the team of people taking care of most of his mundane tasks, I relished knowing he did this for me himself.

"I have the ability to be nice," he reminded lightly.

"Oh, I know." I leaned in, careful not to jostle my arm. The heat from his touch was addictive; I didn't want it to stop. "The world sees you very differently than we do. Don't forget that."

The world saw the solitary billionaire. The wunderkind whose meteoric rise was documented in financial journals and business schools across the country. They lauded his cold, calculated demeanor.

I saw Marcus. Really *saw* him.

I knew the caring, almost to a fault, man beneath the façade. The vulnerable one he locked away. The glimpses I caught made me yearn for more. If only to prove to him that he didn't need the walls he'd built.

Not around us. *Me.*

Having spent my life wishing to be seen for who I truly am, it hurt me that he didn't covet that fact like the treasure it was.

He nodded. The air became heavy again.

"Well, thank you," I croaked. I didn't know what to say. He was touching me, and it was driving me absolutely crazy. He couldn't have realized he was doing it.

Just as he was about to say something, he was interrupted by raucous yelling from upstairs. Henry and Xander were screaming at the screen.

I didn't bother looking in the direction of the noise. I knew what it was and had become accustomed to it at this point. "I think Xander stole your best friend."

He looked up in the direction of the staircase, and then back at me, flashing a smile that sent a flutter through my stomach. "Then I guess the only fair thing to do is steal his."

His thumb traced the same slow pattern on my wrist.

Chapter 20

MARCUS

Xander and Henry leaving Sloan and me alone on the couch an hour ago was the best Christmas gift I could have received. I found myself thinking about her constantly. She was a habit I couldn't break.

"I saw that." Sloan noticed when I glanced down at an incoming call and ignored it. I should have taken it privately. It was a board member. Normally, I would have interrupted to take it. "Did you just ignore work?"

I also couldn't seem to stop myself from gently nudging the boundaries of what was appropriate between friends. I told myself that the line would be wherever she pushed back. We hadn't gotten there yet.

I shrugged. "I guess it is Christmas."

"If you take a day off, how will we mere mortals be reminded of your superiority?" she mused.

"I can arrange for reminders."

Her eyes sparkled when she laughed. The sound made the possible loss of a board vote seem like a minor inconvenience rather than the giant roadblock it would be.

"So . . . you're just going to live your life alone then?" she asked, looking down at her lap. Her lashes swept up, and she looked at my puzzled expression. Where the fuck did that come from? "Earlier, you said you weren't in any serious relationships because you were working. You're always going to be working."

"Yeah . . ."

"Then, by your logic, you'll always be alone."

I shrugged. Why did any of that matter? "Seems unavoidable."

"You could *choose* to make time."

"Why would I do that?" The future wasn't something I planned—not my personal one, anyway. Why plan for something that could be ripped away at any moment? I could control Sutton Industries; that was the future I planned.

"Won't you feel lonely?" Genuine concern papered her face.

"I'm fine."

"Fine isn't really a feeling, though."

"This *feels* a little like an interrogation."

"Oh, good." She grinned. "I was scared I was being too subtle."

"I thought you weren't a litigator."

"Doesn't mean I'm not great at it." She leaned back into the couch with an arrogant smile. It was fucking adorable.

I needed to change the subject. She threw me off balance. I would slip up and say something I shouldn't.

"Once you become partner, what's next?" I asked.

She crossed her arms. "I wasn't finished with my questions."

"I'm changing the terms, something *I'm* great at."

"Managing partner," she answered in a huff, defeated.

"That's what you want?" Sometimes I wondered how much of her drive was fueled by expectations or the rebuking of those expectations. She was defiance personified.

"At the firm, I can be first. I can be heard. I have a real shot at it," Sloan continued. She looked down, and some of her thick black locks fell forward. "I know it's a childish reason."

"It's not childish." Without thinking, I tucked some of the hair behind her ear. It felt good. Intimate. Her luminous brown eyes met mine, and something passed between us. Like a circuit finally clicked into place. For a moment, we were frozen.

She blinked and jolted back slightly, as if waking from a dream, and crimson ran along her cheek. I took note of the boundary I clearly crossed.

I had to get better at adapting.

I couldn't be away from her, that much was clear. I'd have to find the edges of what was appropriate and stay within bounds. I could reel it in and stop myself from being lulled into a fantasy.

I could ignore the adorable way she filled the silence with a sly joke. Disregard that her laugh lifted my mood. I could pretend that I didn't feel the way I did. I'd been doing it for years, and practice did make perfect.

A few seconds later, I heard the sound of a door swinging open. Sloan fell forward and released a frustrated groan. Her head leaned against my chest for a moment. My blood heated at the brief contact, reminding me to start putting space between us, at least physically. She pulled back as quickly as she had leaned in.

"They're in the wine cellar." Her tone was disinterested, as though it was a daily occurrence. She stood. "We should probably stop them before they break something."

The night devolved from there. I don't think anyone ate any real food—just desserts. And we all drank too much.

Things between all of us were starting to feel like they did before I left.

I'd been hoping for that since the gala.

Why did that hurt so much?

Chapter 21

SLOAN

Packing for six months was proving to be more difficult than I thought.

I had two weeks until I left for London. I would fly there on the Sutton jet with Marcus, an interesting development we squared away on Christmas. I kept running that day through my head in an attempt to make sense of it.

Marcus was different. Forward. It didn't make any sense. There were times when it felt like we were flirting. I didn't mind it, but the implications made me crazy. Was he just indulging me? That would mean he probably understood I had a crush on him and was being nice. It was humiliating to think about, especially since it was starting to feel a lot deeper than a crush.

"I have to go to the Hightower New Year's Eve party," I told Xander as I tried to concentrate on the task at hand. I looked at a black sequin dress that wasn't long enough to cover past mid-thigh and tossed it to the side. Xander re-evaluated my choice, overruled it, and threw the dress in the suitcase. "Do you want to come?"

Xander sat on my bed next to the open suitcases as I packed the items to take and tossed others to the side.

"I have plans." He got up for a moment, walked into my closet, and pulled out a few more similar dresses.

"You can bring your own date. I'm going with Ashton Carmichael," I said. He was a friend of one of the senior partners at the firm; we'd met on a few occasions after work. He was nice enough, a perfectly suitable date for a party I was essentially required to attend.

"Who?" He sat back on the bed in front of the open suitcase, suddenly interested. Xander was particularly interested in my love life lately.

"He's a friend of a partner." I shrugged. There was nothing remarkable about him. "Easy to talk to; there isn't any heat there."

The truth of the matter was that there wasn't a lot of heat anywhere. Unless Marcus was around, in which case, there was too much heat in inconvenient places. That whole situation was something I would normally run by Xander if it weren't so complicated.

"Then why bother?" He laughed and turned his attention to the pile of books beside the suitcase. My refusal to adopt using an e-reader made packing light impossible. "If you're going for strictly platonic, I'm sure Rohan or Tristan would go with you. At least that way, you can have a decent dance partner."

As lovely as being the sad friend who couldn't get her own date sounded, I passed. Besides, I had a feeling both had better ideas of how to spend their New Year's than with me.

"Oh, I meant to tell you. Remember Jay Sachi?" I asked. Xander's head shot up from moving the books aside. "He's in London. He texted me, asking to get together to catch up."

It was a bizarre text that came in on Christmas Day. I was distracted, or I would have responded then. I still hadn't. His messages sat in my texts and awaited my reply.

> **Jay Sachi:** I hear you'll be in my city soon

> **Jay Sachi:** Let's catch up when you get here

"How does he know you're going to be in London?" Xander's eyes lit up, intrigued. He walked back to my suitcase.

"No idea. I'm guessing someone told him."

Xander snorted a laugh. "Given he's wanted to get into your pants since you met, probably not Henry."

Jay was a gorgeous investment banker who had graduated the same year Xander did. We all knew each other from college. He and I only saw each other at parties, first in college and then at events where our circles ran together. He was one of those impossibly charming people, similar to Xander. He slept with almost all the women in the class. Despite his record, you'd be hard-pressed to find anyone to say a negative thing about him.

Being one of the few girls who didn't fall for his charms was a feat.

Xander saw another dress I had tossed to the side and picked it up. I'd decided not to pack it, but Xander threw it in the suitcase. "Seriously, Sloan, I say this as your friend. Are you planning on being a nun for the next six months?"

I finally decided to evaluate everything Xander added to the suitcase. Most of the additions were short dresses. He was trying to pack me a social wardrobe when I was going there to work. "Why are you so interested in me getting laid?"

"You only have work clothes in here," Xander pointed out. "You don't plan on going on a single date? All I'm saying is you being hard up and then seeing someone like Jay is a recipe for sex."

I skated past that visual. "Is there a reason you're so interested in my dating life lately?"

"I don't know. You seem different, is all."

"Different how?"

"I don't know!" Xander gave an exasperated laugh. "Are you seeing someone?"

"No," I said emphatically.

He raised an eyebrow. "Why do you have *that* face?" His finger drew a circle in the air in front of me.

I crossed my arms. "This is my face."

"You know what I mean. It's that 'I'm sleeping with someone I shouldn't be' face."

I rolled my eyes and walked back into the closet. I was terrible at hiding things from Xander, and he was a like a drug-sniffing dog when it came to rooting out my secrets.

"Oh god, it's not another fucking Grimaldi, is it?" He stood and followed me into the closet. Xander may have been the one to stop me before I could make a colossal mistake with a member of the royal family of Monaco.

"Who is it? Come on." He continued to probe. He ducked his head to try to catch my eyes. He knew I couldn't keep a straight face, and he'd interrogate me until he got close. "Remember when you set me on fire last summer?"

Trading guilt for secrets, he took a page out of my mother's playbook.

I whipped around. How many times did I need to apologize for that? "You were fine, and I put you right out."

I had set Xander on fire. Accidentally.

Who knew glitter bombs were combustible?

I didn't.

He was the one who stood too close to a lantern.

I switched to offense. "What are these plans you have for New Year's?" I asked.

He paused, caught in a trap of his own making.

"Paris," Xander grumbled, and released a heavy sigh. Suddenly, he looked serious. Another I-owe-you bit the dust. "Drop it."

I complied and changed the subject. But I tucked the little evidence I had in my mind for whenever I had more.

> **Me:** Hey. Yeah, I'll be in London for a while. How'd you know?

> **Jay:** I have my sources. See you soon, love.

I pushed my phone into my pocket when I heard the doorbell. To my surprise, Cece, Tristan, Rohan, and Jackson had come to my place to see me off. Xander planned an impromptu get-together before the long stretch of time away.

Settling on the couch, an assortment of food sitting on the coffee table between us, we planned how we would celebrate when I finally became senior partner. And we arranged the annual trip Xander and I took every summer.

My heart ached at the thought of leaving my merry band of cohorts for half the year. They were the family I'd chosen. It would be a flash before I was back, and everything was back as it was.

The only difference? I would be a senior partner.

Chapter 22

MARCUS

The Hightower New Year's Eve ball in SoHo was something to experience, an opulent event to ring in the New Year. Victor Hightower, the rising CEO, invited me, so my attendance was mandatory. In addition to being in the energy business, they had a monopoly on some coveted shipping routes that I needed access to.

Thankfully, I got him to agree to allow Sutton Industries access, so I could enjoy the party or leave. I would have chosen the latter, but I brought a date, so I was stuck till midnight. With a bored sigh, I took a sip of whiskey and looked around the room for her. She was wearing something blue, or green, maybe red. Before I could waste another brain cell thinking about it, she reappeared, drink in hand and smiling.

She was . . . fine. An editor at *Vogue*, she was intelligent and amiable. I only asked her to this event in a desperate attempt to clear my head. Luckily, she found my company to be just as tedious as I found hers and left me to my thoughts.

Ones I shouldn't have had. I headed to the bar for another drink when, as if summoned by those thoughts, I heard a familiar laugh. Like melted caramel, it was soft and warm. And stuck to every part of my soul.

My heart raced. Was Sloan here? A warm tingle ran up my spine.

The pleasurable sensation didn't last when I finally caught sight of her.

I never considered myself violent. Growing up, I'd been in a few scraps, but nothing compared to the overwhelming urge I had to beat the life out of the man who pulled Sloan in closer to him. Their bodies pressed together as they danced. He was forward, and she didn't seem to mind.

The glass in my hand nearly shattered under my grip. My blood heated at the sound of her soft, feathery laugh when he dared to get close enough to whisper something in her ear.

That laugh. The one I loved. *My laugh.*

My molars ground tightly. I put the glass down.

I watched him closely. If his hand slid any lower, I would rip it off.

I was momentarily distracted from the building rage by Sloan herself. She wore a floor-length, strapless, form-fitting black dress. A diamond necklace dipped provocatively just above where her dress began. Regal, refined, and so damn tempting. Unlike at the gala, her hair was down in loose waves, sweeping along her back as she danced.

She was stunning. And he was a dead man if he tried *anything.*

Having to watch her with someone else was torture. A few agonizing minutes later, I was finally freed of it when the song ended and the pair walked toward the bar. The one in my direction.

"Marcus!" She immediately pulled me into a hug. Her arms wrapped around my torso. If the contact wasn't rewarding enough, the surprised look on her date's face almost made having to see her with him worth it.

Almost.

Sloan sputtered as she stumbled through an introduction. His name was Ashton Carmichael, and that was all I heard. I got distracted by the hand he placed on the small of her back after she returned to his side.

It moved lower, and I snapped.

"Get your hand off of her," I barked. I could barely hear my words over the blood rushing through my ears. I wasn't raised in high society, I didn't go to etiquette class, and if he didn't follow orders, he'd find out just how unrefined I could be.

In that moment, every valid reason I had to conceal how I felt about her vanished. I didn't care.

I leaned in. "Or not even a dental record will identify your body." The lethality in my voice wasn't well hidden. It wasn't meant to be.

Sloan took a sharp inhale. Her eyes widened. She didn't react past that, though. I was expecting defiance. Instead, she smirked.

She smirked.

She fucking smirked.

An uncomfortable silence wrapped around us. "I'll get us a couple of drinks," Ashton said, and made himself scarce.

"That might be considered a little rude." She stood looking amused. Her bright red lips puckered for a moment, then grew to a smile.

"Where do you find these people?" I asked. The fury suddenly dissipated.

That guy? Really? The idea of Sloan with one of those society types always bothered me.

She closed the distance between us and patronizingly tapped my chest. "You're welcome to pick my next one."

"What are you doing here?"

"I had to come; half the firm is here." She gestured around, as if I would know what the partners at her firm looked like. "Hightower Energy just closed a deal with the firm. The Hightowers are one of the hosts of the event."

I nodded.

"What are *you* doing here?" she probed.

"I was invited."

"Where's your date?" Her tone pressed while her eyes disarmed. She may not have been a litigator, but her interrogation techniques were effective. At least, they were on me.

"No idea."

"Why did you run off mine?" Her eyes flashed with intrigue, the same look she got when she was about to win a game.

"I did no such thing." He left of his own accord. It was probably best if he wanted to remain a man with two arms and a pulse.

"So, you wouldn't mind if I go back and find him?" she asked, probably knowing it would provoke me. When I didn't answer, she raised her eyebrows and turned to find him, only to be stopped by my hand on her arm.

"Counselor," I warned slowly. I was jealous, and she knew it. She giggled with delight, knowing she had won, and turned around. She gestured to a bar opposite from where her date had skulked off to.

An hour later, I had successfully stolen her away from her date and found a secluded corner where I had her all to myself. We sat on a plush tufted chaise in the hallway outside the ballroom, her back leaning against the corner. My arm was draped casually around her waist; wherever the appropriate line was, I had pushed it about a mile further.

She didn't seem to mind. In fact, she encouraged it.

We were both available, and my assumption that time would cure me of these feelings was dead wrong. The boundaries I wasn't supposed to cross seemed trivial when I was this close to her.

"How do you stomach going to so many of these?" I tucked a strand of hair behind her ear. She didn't flinch this time. I couldn't stop touching her or finding ways to be close. I ignored the facts that hurt and leaned into what felt good. She felt good. "At least tonight I have some good company."

"Well, Xander and I have a game we play at these things."

"Do I want to know?"

The corners of her mouth tipped up. "It's called Sip and Seduce. I pick someone for you, and you do the same for me. Whoever has sex with their mark first wins."

My body went rigid. *I'm going to kill Xander.*

What the fuck kind of game was that? I didn't even want to think about what the score was.

"Wanna play?" I couldn't tell if she was serious. In some moments, her eyes told me everything I wanted to know. The next, they were an abyss.

We'd fallen into a pattern whenever the conversation lulled; one of us threw the other a loop. I would push a physical boundary, and she would push all the others.

"You're not serious," I informed her flatly. She would have gone back and found her date if she had been. "You're trying to bait me."

"Oh?" A competitive smile crept over those alluring red lips. It took every ounce of willpower not to press my own against them and swallow every sassy retort she had ready. "Why would I do that?"

"Probably the same reason I ran off your date." I ran my finger along the side of her necklace. Looking back up at her lustrous brown eyes, I drew closer to her and felt her hand gently tug on my lapel.

A soft moan slipped out of her lips as mine brushed over them. We were shaken from the moment by a commotion in the ballroom, and then the countdown. She looked over to the doors and sighed. "Well, I should probably go find my date. New Year's kiss and all."

"Not a chance." I wrapped my arm tighter around her waist and pulled her in for a peck on the lips. It was short—far too short. She pulled closer, her lips begging to be kissed again. A real kiss. It was impossibly tempting now that I knew her lips were as soft as they looked.

After a moment, she smiled, making no attempt to part.

"Happy New Year, Sloan," I whispered.

"Happy New Year, Marcus."

I had never loved hearing anything more than the sound of my name on her lips.

Chapter 23

SLOAN

I woke the next morning to sunrays streaming into the room, burrowing like knives into my eye sockets. The terrible thumping in my head kept getting louder.

The pain was quickly forgotten and replaced with panic when I opened my eyes and they began darting around the unfamiliar room.

Where am I?

I tried to piece together what I remembered from the night before and recalled the distinct memory of getting in a town car with Marcus. A different concern popped into my mind before I realized I was in a guest room. I was in Marcus's guest room. I let out a loud sigh of relief. Nothing had been done that couldn't be undone—or no one, to put it more aptly.

A change of clothes sat on the dresser. I carefully pulled myself out of bed, steadied my uneasy gait on the nightstand, and walked over to change.

I somehow got out of my dress last night, but that was probably me—no way Marcus did it. My mind drifted to last night and remembered the hours we spent in seclusion. It was intimate. I wanted more.

Then I tried to remember how I got so drunk, and it dawned on me.

Wife, Daughter, or Mistress. A game where we guessed the relationship status of the many guests in attendance. We played, or more specifically, I played, much to Marcus's amusement right after we kissed.

The kiss. If you could even call it that. It was a peck. Sweet and innocent.

What it did to me was the furthest thing from innocent. The feeling of being held tightly in his arms, the desire that pooled in my body and begged for more. All of it replayed over and over in my mind. My dreams were filled with how his lips would feel on my neck, my inner thigh . . .

Something shifted last night.

I changed into what felt like my clothing. I looked in the mirror and realized it was my clothing. I must have left it behind after he drove me back to my townhouse.

Although, every woman in Manhattan society had a pair of Brunello joggers and a Loro Piana pullover.

I shook off the bizarre thought and tried to pull myself together before I went downstairs. Thankfully, I had some makeup in my clutch to touch up what had smeared, and my hair looked great. Day two of a blowout was easily the best day, hair-wise. I ran my fingers through it, gave myself a once-over, and walked out into the hallway.

Marcus's TriBeCa townhouse was enormous. It was clean and airy, with large windows and high ceilings. I reached the top of the staircase, from where I could see most of the dining room and living area below. Marcus sat at the head of the dining table with his laptop open. He was seemingly switching between reading the paper and working.

I descended the staircase slowly, trying to ignore the waves of nausea and the hammering in my head. "She lives," Marcus said.

He didn't look up from his laptop as he took a sip of his coffee. The sunlight streamed into the dining room and washed over him, casting devious shadows on the shirt he wore. I was dizzy again, but this time it had nothing to do with the alcohol.

"Are these mine?" If he gave me another woman's clothes, I would kill him. My mind wandered to all the women who must have passed through this place. I used all my power to walk steadily from the staircase landing to the seat beside him at the table where a place setting awaited me.

"Yes." He still didn't look up, but he did his best to suppress a smile at my expense. He knew why I asked the question. "You left them behind in the car after Thanksgiving."

Right. At least the jealousy faded. The humiliation, however, mounted.

I gripped the cup of coffee in front of me. "How bad was I?"

"You were a perfect lady." He put a pastry on my plate and nudged me to eat something.

His voice was soft and welcoming. The more time we spent together, the more I got *this* Marcus. The one whose laugh was joyful, whose serious façade was easily broken with a sly joke, the one who went out of his way to care for me. It was making it more difficult to extinguish the sparks that threatened to set our lives alight.

I grinned uncontrollably and grasped the coffee mug with both hands. "How dare you, sir? I've never been accused of such a thing."

He smiled, turned back to his laptop, typed a few things, and closed it. He *finally* looked at me. Upon closer inspection, his gray eyes had the most enticing flecks of green.

"Does this mean I get to call in a favor, no questions asked?" His eyes sparked with envy. Was he jealous of the I-owe-you game

I had with Xander? He was being *different*, and it made everything in my body short-circuit.

"What exactly do I owe you for?" I put the coffee down, folded my legs onto the chair, and turned my body slightly to face him directly. "I thought I was a perfect lady."

"Well, if it weren't for me, you'd have probably gone home with Ashton." There was an almost possessive undercurrent in his tone.

"Maybe I wanted to go home with him."

"No." He smiled wryly and leaned in. His eyes searched mine, and his voice lowered to a whisper. "You didn't."

My mouth went dry.

Dammit, he was right. That was obvious now. At least between the two of us. I honestly couldn't pick Ashton out of a lineup. My only regret from last night was drinking too much. Maybe if I had my wits about me, I would have woken up in Marcus's bed, feeling satisfied and not hungover.

"Yikes. I just ditched him, didn't I?" I winced at the thought. Ashton was a perfectly nice man with whom I had no chemistry. It was bad form to leave without at least acknowledging him.

"Don't worry. I gave him your regards." His smile radiated a knowing arrogance. A shiver sailed up my spine.

That was when I saw a familiar brown journal at the corner of the table, hidden.

It was the one I got him years ago when Xander and I were in Paris. Marcus was impossible to shop for; he didn't want anything. The journal caught my eye because it reminded me of the ones their mother wrote in. I saw it and instantly thought to get it for him. I expected it would be on a shelf collecting dust. Marcus would never throw away something any of us got for him. Instead, they'd get neatly tucked away out of sight.

I wondered if he remembered I got for him. "You still have that?" I wondered aloud.

He looked down to the journal in question. "There are still blank pages." He shrugged. "I have to do some work. Are you going to be okay?"

I nodded. "You can't steal me away from all my dates. You know that, right?"

"I guess we'll have to see." He got up from the table, stopped behind my chair, and rested his hands on either side of me. His hot breath skated across my neck when he leaned down and whispered in my ear, "Feel better, Counselor."

My toes curled beneath the table. My entire body trembled as his footsteps receded down the hallway.

* * *

I FELL ASLEEP at the table.

I couldn't help it. I never slept well when I drank, and the soft upholstery on the dining chairs was surprisingly comfortable. The combination of the two quickly lulled me to sleep.

My head rested in my folded arms. I didn't know how long I had been sleeping, but I was awoken when someone's hand ran slowly up and down my side.

"Sloan," a hot breath said in my ear. The heated tickle along the hollow of my neck made me regret the hangover even more. That would have been nice to wake up to.

I could tell by the way he said it that he was smiling. Marcus drove me crazy, and he knew it. His large body loomed over me.

My eyes stayed closed, and I savored the feeling. "Mmmm."

He chuckled softly. "Henry will be here in twenty minutes."

I sprang up and nearly hit him in the process. The banging in my head returned tenfold.

"Relax," he went on. "I told him you were exhausted and stayed here."

"That was mean." I rubbed my head and wondered what Henry

could want. Then I reminded myself that they were, in fact, best friends and had their rituals just like me and Xander.

He sat back in his original seat. "Feeling any better?"

I yawned. "I could have used a longer table nap."

He laughed again. *That* smile made me glad I was already sitting. The time we spent alone diverged from the atmosphere when we were with Xander and Henry. He was relaxed and affable. It made me wonder if this was what it would be like if I woke up here more often.

There was something about our back-and-forth that gave me a surge of confidence. "Why don't I see that smile except on these rare occasions?"

He shrugged. "I guess I save them."

For me?

It didn't last long. His face changed the second we heard the door open and Henry being let in. His entire demeanor morphed, as if all the playfulness in him left his body. Maybe he was saving it for the next time we were alone.

Henry arrived at the table, took in my slightly disheveled appearance, and chuckled. "Drunk at a work event?"

Henry took a seat across from me.

"It was a party, and I was a perfect lady." I looked over to Marcus. His serious and faux uninterested countenance was almost broken with a smile. "Right, Marcus?"

"Something like that."

"So much so that you needed Marcus to take you home?" Henry countered.

Maybe Marcus wanted to take me home.

As if he read my mind, Marcus shot me a look. Fine, I wouldn't say that.

But I wasn't going to bite my tongue. Not my style. "Since you seem concerned about all the people I've inconvenienced, which is more of an imposition in your mind: me waking up in Marcus's guest room or my date's bedroom?"

Neither of them liked that. Two birds, one saucy comment. I was proud of myself.

"Henry, leave her alone. She's hungover." Marcus's voice remained disinterested.

"You're too nice to her," Henry said offhandedly, as if I wasn't there and couldn't hear him.

It was met with an indifferent shrug from Marcus.

I suffered through them talking about work for a few minutes before deciding to head home to recover. Marcus's gaze lingered on me as I left.

Chapter 24

MARCUS

A few days after the New Year, I met Sloan at the airport's private hangar to take my jet to London.

Sloan and I hadn't spoken outside of a few texts to coordinate travel. I wasn't sure what to expect. But as we boarded the jet and engaged in idle chitchat, it seemed like she wanted to ignore what happened on New Year's Eve.

The memory of her in that dress replayed on an endless loop. That, and the sound of her whispering my name. My mind wandered to all the ways I could make her call it, moan it, scream it until her voice was hoarse.

She remained quiet and sent a flurry of texts from her work phone as the crew readied for takeoff. I found myself wishing to be interrupted from my work with sly banter.

"Oh, I forgot." Her voice soothed the anxiety that began to mount that whatever we had going on was over now. She looked at me and clicked her phone screen off. Her eyes gleamed with playfulness, and a devious smile stole whatever air was left in my chest. "Thanks for the ride."

There she is. I heaved a sigh, mostly of relief, at her terrible joke. "Not your best."

"I'll keep trying." She winked and looked back at her phone.

* * *

WE'D BOTH SETTLED into the flight and began working, occasionally interrupting the other with a brief conversation or a proactive comment. That was largely Sloan. She was being more forward.

We were working quietly when we hit a patch of turbulence. I didn't pay much attention to it, but from the corner of my eye, I saw Sloan fidgeting. Looking up from my work, I could see she was shaken; the anxiety was evident in her eyes. Her skin grew pale.

"I don't love this part of flying." Her voice squeaked.

"It'll level out soon," I assured her, as if she hadn't flown before. She'd been all over the world, and the turbulence wasn't all that bad.

She nodded.

I didn't think much of it, and I went back to work when there was another dip. A bigger one this time.

I looked over to her. Her face held a quiet terror. "Sloan?" I closed my laptop and put it away.

"I used to take something for it, but haven't needed it in a while." Her voice was shaking. "I thought I was cured." She laughed nervously, and her chin wobbled as she swallowed hard.

She was trying not to cry. I winced at another hard rattle, less intense this time, but her veneer of calm was crumbling. Pride competed with fear. A kick of protectiveness rattled in my chest. I got up, sat beside her, and felt completely useless.

Dammit, if Xander were here, he would know what to do.

Her hands gripped the seat so tightly that her knuckles were white. I rubbed the top of her hand with my thumb. I watched her closely for the next few seconds as the brief turbulence seemed to have stopped, but as I stroked her hand, I could feel her pulse still racing.

"Well, in the absence of a pill . . ." I carefully rose, poured a glass of wine from the secured bar cart, and placed it in front of her.

"I don't want to drink." She looked at me sheepishly. "I'm worried about what I might say."

I was a little thrown by her honesty. It made me want to wrap her in my arms. "I can assure you I've heard worse." From her. She cursed like a sailor and was rather handsy the last time I witnessed her drunk.

An unsure smile lifted and fell along her mouth.

"What would Xander do?" I almost begged. Seeing her that distressed pulled on my heart in a way I'd never felt. I needed it to stop.

"He'd tell me things to keep me distracted."

"What do you want to know?" That was a bad idea. But fuck, I would do just about anything to make her feel better. "No holds barred."

She paused a few moments in surprise. "You're going to regret that, Sutton." She laughed nervously and took a large sip of the wine. Her other hand moved from gripping the armrest to my hand. I clasped it immediately. I never wanted to let it go. "Why did you leave? And don't tell me it was only work."

I sighed. I knew this one was coming.

"It was easier than dealing with things I couldn't control." It was the truth. I left out the part about what I couldn't control—my feelings for her. No better way to ignore something than to remove it from your view. A small smile grew on her face. She got the most honest answer to that question so far, and she didn't press on.

"Do I get a question?" I asked. The plane settled out, and the two attendants brought the bottle of wine over.

"I guess." She took a sip of wine.

"Do you really want the company?" I hoped the answer was no. "You seem like you'd hate it."

It was only recently that I realized how much it stuck with her. My meddling with the board affected her too.

She didn't answer, only shrugged. "You wouldn't get it."

"Explain it to me."

She gave a small sigh, closed her eyes, and leaned into the seat.

"You won't get it because you can't. Everyone expects you to succeed—you're annoyingly perfect." Her eyes opened and met mine. It seemed like the turbulence was forgotten, but I may have made things worse. "For me, the expectation was heinously low. I didn't get the chance to know if I wanted it."

The plane rattled again, and she flinched. It had mostly settled out past the small rough patch, but the anxiety was probably in control now. She poured herself another glass and took a large sip.

"Why aren't you and Xander together?" I asked.

The words came out before I could even think to stop them. I wanted to pursue her, obviously. And I had spent the last week thinking of all the ways to get around the reasons I shouldn't. The only one I hadn't found a workaround for was Xander. Every time it popped into my mind, I pushed it back. If there was even a chance, they could—

When I realized just how deep the feelings were, I knew I needed to ask Xander about it, but I wasn't sure I'd want to hear the answer. If it was the one I feared, that would slam the door shut on the fantasy. For a while, I wanted to live in it.

She gave me a stern look. "You know why. We're friends."

"You need a distraction. Plus, you'll be too annoyed with the question's premise to remember you're anxious."

I didn't want to know. But fuck, I had to know.

She chewed the side of her lip, deep in thought. She knew precisely why I asked the question.

"Okay." She sat up, crossed her legs, and tucked them beneath her. My hand felt an emptiness when she pulled hers back to tuck her hair back behind her ear. "We tried . . . once."

My heart sank into my stomach. I motioned for the attendant to bring me a glass of whiskey, expecting I'd need it by the time this story was over.

"After law school, the guys, CeCe, and I went to Paris over the summer. We were at a vineyard for a wine tasting and everyone had to pair off. Xander and I paired off, and the staff assumed we were together. We played along, no big deal. There was this old couple asking us questions about our relationship. We made things up. They refused to believe we were together, no matter what we did or said. They said we didn't have any chemistry."

Suddenly, I felt much better. She smiled widely and had a happy, faraway look in her eye. She looked out the window and then back at me. The story wasn't over.

She continued. "That night, we got all kinds of drunk, determined to prove them wrong. We'd been getting questions about our relationship for so long that we thought we would see what happened. We tried for probably an hour to kiss each other. It was awful. Keep in mind, the goal was to have sex."

I physically flinched at the words and took a large sip of the whiskey, hoping it would wash the bitter jealousy from my mouth. She giggled, ignoring the mental turmoil I was going through as I sat through the story.

"Don't worry, it gets better." A knowing smile swept across her face. "We got as far as a prolonged, very awkward peck on the lips. Anyway, we bagged the idea. We are *not* attracted to each other. And that is why we aren't together. And will never be." She took a large sip of wine and put the glass down. "You were right, that helped."

I tried not to let the relief look too obvious. All the bumps had leveled out; the plane was flying smoothly.

"See?" That was all I managed to spit out with every word in my vernacular tangled in my chest. Thankfully, the story was over and had a better ending than I expected. "Feel better?"

"Yeah, I do." She paused. "And you took it like a champ." She bared her teeth in a teasing grin. "The story, I mean, even the parts where you looked like you were going to pass out." She leaned over to give my leg a patronizing pat.

Sloan slept for the remainder of the flight; she was cute when she slept too. Despite having to sit through that story, it gave me the answer I'd wanted for so long.

I spent a lifetime giving Xander whatever he needed without a second thought.

My childhood room, my bike, half my company.

I never cared. He was my baby brother; it was my job. I wanted him to have everything he needed to be happy, whatever happiness meant for him. For a time, I thought that meant Sloan. Thankfully, it didn't.

She was *my* happiness.

Mine.

Chapter 25

SLOAN

The cold London air must have done something to cool the blustering tension between Marcus and me because I hadn't heard from him since the flight. It had only been a couple of days, but I didn't expect to feel so dejected by the change. We occasionally texted about administrative things, scheduling, and other mundane tasks, but nothing social or remotely flirty.

Marcus liked a challenge. Once he accomplished something, he'd get bored and move on. He knew that as well as I did. That fact made me sure he'd never actually make a move in our risqué chess match. He never cared to be in a relationship, and while he didn't seem to care about most people, I was on the short list of exceptions. He wouldn't hurt me.

That knowledge provided little solace. He may be attracted to me, but that was all. And certainly not enough to implode our world. The only commitment I could get out of a Sutton would be an unbreakable friendship with Xander.

I blinked back to reality and addressed the partners at the London office during our first strategy meeting.

"We shouldn't have any hold-ups, just a few banking-related regulations on the U.S. side," I said. "I could use one of the associates in finance to get through the red tape."

Luckily, my work was enough to occupy my thoughts during the day. Penelope and I got settled in our offices that week and began getting briefed on the current client roster and cases. The first and most important one was the Burton merger.

"Fine, take whomever you need." Van der Baun motioned to the other side of the room at one of the firm's senior partners with the finance group. "We need this done quickly."

I nodded, noting the annoyance in his voice. The timeline was not ideal, but it wasn't something I wanted to push—better to close a deal slowly than not at all. Two large banks merging was going to get attention, and not the good kind.

"Don't fret about the timeline." Penelope and I gathered our things after the meeting. "Men push timelines recklessly, lose deals, and it's just business. We do it, and we're unfit."

"Can't win." I sighed. "I have to get back to my office; I'm meeting with the head of Burton's investment division. He's handling the UK side of the merger."

She nodded. "I met him earlier. Watch out, he's a charmer."

Great.

I'd never met the Burton executive who would be my point of contact. All I knew was to expect them in a few minutes. I didn't realize how fast I was walking until I was stopped. It felt like running into a brick wall.

"Ooompf" was the attractive sound I made when I was stopped so quickly I may have suffered whiplash. My phone flew out of my hand and landed a few feet away on the floor. I landed on my ass, as did the unfortunate victim of my careless sprinting. "I am so sorry."

I looked over to see a familiar set of mahogany eyes. It wasn't until I assessed the golden-almond skin, strong jaw, and devilish smile that I realized whom I had assaulted.

"Well, don't let my existence stop you," he said in a smooth British accent, laughing as he stood and helped me up. He walked over to where my phone landed and handed it back to me.

Jay Sachi. Just as handsome as ever.

"I have to go," I blurted and turned to walk back to my office.

"I know." He followed behind me at my breakneck pace.

"What?"

"I'm your next meeting."

I stopped for a second. The pieces fell into place. "Is this how you knew I'd be in London?" I wondered aloud as I walked to my desk and took a seat. He invited himself in and took one as well.

He was the client. Interesting.

I made a mental note to text Xander. He would, at the very least, get a good laugh out of it.

"I didn't know Sloan Amari was some hotshot at this firm." He didn't answer my question, but that was all a part of his schtick.

Marginally annoyed that he was going to waste my time trying to charm me instead of the task at hand, I changed the subject. "We need to talk about the timeline."

He nodded. "But first, we need to catch up, properly."

I sighed. *Of course*, we did. Men never had to deal with this type of crap.

The meeting was a courtesy I had extended to familiarize the company with who would be handling matters at the firm. "That would be inappropriate," I reminded him.

"Old friends catching up hardly seems inappropriate."

"Why the sudden interest?"

"It's not sudden," he reminded me. I knew his interest in me was purely curiosity. Being one of the few girls who had never fallen for his charms made him want to check me off a list of conquests. "You know that."

"And yet the answer will remain the same."

"For now. It's been years. I am bound to wear on you," he boasted.

His confidence was unmatched. If my mind wasn't consumed with the memory of Marcus's breath on my neck, I may have fallen for it.

"Tell you what. You stop trying to sleep with me, and we can be friends?" I offered with no actual intention of following through. I didn't need a contact at the company for what was left of the merger, just a few signatures once the work was done. "The kind that keep their clothes on."

He refused. "Love, this isn't a negotiation."

"Then what is it?" I crossed my arms.

"Flirting." He was being presumptions, thinking it was bold and charming. It kind of was, along with being mildly insulting. "Come on . . . you know you missed me."

I scowled.

"I'm sure a part of you did," he continued. "But I'm not sure which part."

I flinched. "Is that all?"

"Think on it." He pulled himself up from the seat and made his way to my door. Finally, an exit. He looked at his watch. "Well, look at that. I've given you back twenty minutes."

"Or wasted ten."

"This is going to be fun, I can tell." He winked. Not long after he left, I looked at my phone to see he'd texted.

Jay Sachi: That doesn't count as catching up.

Jay Sachi: Let's get drinks. No charm, I promise. It'll be so appropriate that you'll hate every second of it.

I sighed and rolled my eyes, deciding to ignore it.

Penelope came in and I told her about the bizarre exchange.

"I can deal with the client updates if it makes it less awkward." She stood in front of my desk and paged through the latest merger negotiation documents.

"Nah, I'll be fine," I assured her.

"I think you should go. It could be fun."

A part of me considered it, out of sheer boredom. Xander would never let me live it down; I would be teased endlessly. "Maybe."

* * *

THE REST OF the week dragged along without incident, and to my surprise and delight, I had an unexpected visitor after lunch.

Marcus sat in my office, in one of the chairs in front of my desk. He wore a beautiful navy suit. His elbows rested on the armrests of the chair, creating a delicious outline of his biceps against the fabric. He was responding to emails as he waited for me. I strolled across his line of vision and stood at my desk. "Marcus."

"I don't think I've ever seen you at work before, Counselor." His eyes roved from mine down to my hips and backed up to meet my gaze again like he was seeing me for the first time.

"Thoughts?" I asked.

"Your desk seems"—the corners of his mouth tipped up—"sturdy."

I didn't know what we were doing, but I liked it. "I don't know." I gave it a little shake and looked at him with faux concern. "I may need to test it out. Know anyone who could help?"

Got him. Genuine surprise papered his face. I won that round.

"To what do I owe the pleasure?" I asked, as I sat after a moment of soaking in the victory. It almost made me forget that we hadn't actually done anything physical.

"I got you something." His eyes looked down at the beautifully wrapped rectangle I hadn't noticed sitting on my desk. "And I hadn't seen you in a while."

I skated right past the fact that he admitted he missed me. That's how I heard it.

"You wrapped this?" The butterflies in my stomach went into a frenzy. The sheer glee that he gave me a gift and wrapped it was apparent.

"I'm good with my hands." His mouth quirked.

My stomach dipped. He said it with all the casualness of telling me his coffee order.

I didn't respond. What was I going to say to that?

Are you good with your tongue too?

I already knew the answer, and the answer for the other body parts that had starring roles in my dreams.

Instead, I unwrapped the gift with the grace of a toddler. I could hear a low chuckle from Marcus as he watched. My hands trembled slightly as I pulled the gift out from the beautiful wooden box it sat in.

Then, after some inspection, the realization of what he bought me only made the trembles more pronounced. The soft, worn restored leather felt like butter beneath my fingertips. It was a copy of *Don Quixote*, but not just any copy; it was from the time of original publication, from what I could tell. I read the Spanish text and realized it had to be at least a few centuries old.

"It's a first edition." He looked happy with himself—the satisfaction of giving the perfect gift. My mouth fell agape; I couldn't think of anything to say. "Apparently, some of the old Spanish can be read as Catalan. Changes the meaning of a few of his adventures."

It was on the night of the gala that I realized I still had a physical attraction to Marcus, but it wasn't until that day in my kitchen that I realized it was probably something more. Few people would politely listen to me drone on about old books. Even Xander would beg me to stop at some point. But Marcus listened to me like he was eagerly awaiting my next word. It was unnerving and exhilarating.

He chuckled again, this time at my astonishment. "You okay?" He gave me *that* smile.

My entire chest swelled with emotion. I was, most certainly, not okay.

Grinning uncontrollably, I tried my best to control the thrill his gesture created. Reading an old book and finding the parts of the translation that may mean something different was a niche hobby. One that not many people knew about me. The only other gift that had ever come this close to perfect was one my parents gave me for my birthday last year—a collection of old court proceedings.

He opened his mouth to say something when the sound of Penelope walking in stopped him.

"Did you end up going on that date with—" She stopped dead when she saw Marcus sitting in one of the seats in front of my desk. "Sorry, I didn't know you were in a meeting." She registered my warning glance and promptly excused herself.

My heart dropped. Marcus tensed and turned back to me, his expression changed from the earlier softness. He wasn't angry. He looked amused, and maybe a little annoyed. Okay, he was definitely annoyed.

"You have a date? With . . ."

"Nobody." My mind kicked back on and reminded me that he may know Jay. Henry did, and they may have met at some point. "I haven't agreed to go."

His expression became unreadable.

"I'm not going to go," I corrected myself and held the delicate book a little tighter.

"If you want to go, you should go." He looked slightly more bothered. He gripped the sides of the chair and pushed himself up. "If you do, we'll get a chance to test your theory."

I didn't follow. The confusion must be evident because Marcus looked satisfied.

"Your theory that I can't possibly steal you away from all your dates," he continued as he leaned over my desk. His warm breath glided across my cheek. "I like my chances."

He winked.

At me.

Proving that he could have been this charming the whole time but chose smug and mysterious instead. I wished I had something clever to say, but his smile and swagger left me speechless.

"Thanks for the book," I shouted a little louder than I should have at the office. The sound of his laugh, deep and rich, filled me with a sensual buzz.

Chapter 26

SLOAN

I put a few files into my bag at the end of a long day. In addition to getting situated with how things ran here, I spent some time looking into the Amari Global board. Henry seemed suspicious about the eventual change in leadership, and my first thought was to shore up the board.

Nothing seemed out of the ordinary. I started by looking into about half of the board members I wasn't familiar with. But that could wait. I was exhausted.

I decided to head back to my family's London property. Staying there felt weird. It had been remodeled and decorated recently, so it didn't feel as old as it was, but being there made me feel like a kid again. We had only stayed there a handful of times, when we visited my maternal grandparents. Tense memories came with being there.

Deciding to channel my nervous energy into something productive, I stopped at the market on the way home and indulged in a favorite pastime.

Once I got home, I started cooking. Between work and social obligations, I went out too often to ever make cooking at home feasible. Growing up with cooks, I never really had memories that revolved around the kitchen as so many others did. One thing I did have was my grandmother. She was originally from northern India. She had grown up with a love of cooking and everything she made was heavenly.

My mom, being a socialite, never cooked much, but she tried to learn since Henry and I loved the food so much. My grandmother would teach her random dishes whenever we went over.

And I watched.

Cooking felt like therapy. It was by no means nearly as good as my Nana's, but it always made me feel at home. Like I belonged.

I sat on the counter, scanning my social media feed as I waited for the parathas to cool. My mindless scrolling was interrupted when I heard a knock at the door.

My eyes met Marcus's as I opened the door. "What are you doing here?" I gestured for him to follow me into the house.

"Checking on you." He walked past me with a taunting smile. He inhaled deeply and looked around as he took off his coat. "I didn't know you cooked."

"I don't cook." We walked from the foyer to the kitchen. I didn't love the idea of being known to cook, not that I would be, but I had other talents I'd rather people focus on. "This never happened." My hands gestured in a circle in front of a stove.

"Understood." He rounded the counter and peeked into the pan. "Trying to impress the date?"

"If I were trying to impress him, I wouldn't use my cooking." My heartbeats picked up. He was jealous, and "checking on me" meant seeing if I ended up going on that date. "I turned him down."

His shoulders relaxed, and his features lightened. A victorious grin spread along his face. He had done more to prevent the date than anyone else. He existed and made me feel things I couldn't understand or stop.

He leaned against the counter and crossed his arms. "When you don't cook, do you always make this much?"

I graciously allowed the pivot in conversation. "Usually Pen or Jax would come over and make something with me if I was cooking. Everyone else is usually good for an expensive bottle of wine."

"Sounds about right."

He looked comfortable, like he felt at home. Over the years, I had noticed that making him feel genuinely comfortable was a feat. He was always a little formal, no matter his surroundings. He took the bottle of wine chilling in the fridge, poured two glasses, and handed me one.

"It's weird here." I looked around. Marcus began putting down place settings on the kitchen island. It was endearing watching him silently invite himself to dinner. I leaned on the counter and looked around. "I have cousins, and they live here. I have never spoken to them."

"Things were that bad?" He knew what I was talking about. Henry didn't talk about it much, but he had told Marcus about the drama with our maternal grandparents over the years. They cut ties with my mom and didn't attempt to change that until well after Henry was born. We never really knew that side of our family.

"I don't remember too much of it, honestly. Just fragments." I placed the serving dish with the parathas on the kitchen island. "I remember Mom would cry a lot whenever we'd visit. Even when she agreed to come to London, she wouldn't go see them. My dad was the one who took us to see them. They were civil to Henry and me, though."

He didn't say anything. Instead, he nodded, silently nudging me to continue.

"For so long, I wanted them to like me. I tried to be a person they'd accept." I sighed. "A part of me blames them. They were the ones who kicked off a lifetime of being a chameleon. It's exhausting."

His brow furrowed.

I let out a small laugh. He didn't get it because he'd never had to do it. "It's this feeling, that I am always code-switching based on who I'm with."

A wave of anguish crashed over me. The weight of the unrelenting pressure to conceal parts of myself bore down on me. To friends, colleagues, and boyfriends who didn't want to see all of me, just the parts they could relate to. The excruciating feeling that nobody wanted to see me as I was, that I, in my entirety, was something that needed to be hidden.

"It's like walking around knowing that at any moment, you need to determine what someone is comfortable with and pull out any part of yourself they may not understand. All the time. Every second of every day."

The jokes that I wasn't *really* one or the other stung the worst because they were often delivered as well-meaning. I spent my entire life feeling like I was straddling two worlds but belonged in neither. Half of each. I felt tears begin to pool around my eyes. I swallowed hard to stop them when I felt strong arms wrap around me, a blanket of comfort. I hadn't even noticed him get up.

A soft exhale was the only reaction he offered. I looked up to find him looking straight ahead. I rested my cheek on his chest and felt an immediate calm once I was cloaked in his warmth. His thumb gently stroked my shoulder.

We stayed like that for a few moments.

"Poor little rich girl." I laughed and tried to introduce some levity as I wiped the few tears that fell. I pulled away and looked up at him. He kept his arms wrapped around me tightly. "For the record, I've never felt that way around you or Xander."

He smiled.

Maybe it was because I'd known them for so long. Maybe it was because we met when I was a teenager and most of who I was today formed alongside them. Whatever it was, I never felt the need to wear a mask, code-switch, or hide any part of myself.

They'd been there for it all. The Amari Diwali parties, Thanksgivings, summers in the Hamptons, every experience that made up the kaleidoscope of who I am.

Chapter 27

MARCUS

How I found myself at Sloan's house was a mystery.

Well, not a complete mystery. I spent the better half of a week consumed with stress about if she ended up going on that date.

I was so consumed that I missed a meeting with a small Swiss biotech I was trying to acquire. Technically, they weren't looking for buyers, not that it mattered. I missed the CEO while he was in London. I'd have to find some time to meet him in Zurich.

The more time we spent alone together, the more she pulled me in, dangerously close to our event horizon. I knew so much about her, but then there were times, like tonight, when I felt I hardly knew her. I was drawn to every facet. Her mind, her body, her soul. I wanted it all. The parts she was proud of and the parts she tried to hide.

Sloan ignited something in me that had lain dormant for years. A deep desire to feel *everything*. If only to know her just the slightest bit more.

She perked up for dinner.

"What's this?" I asked. Sloan and I finished dinner and began to clear the dishes when I noticed something reflective on the end table leading into the kitchen. I thought I saw my name on it, and after picking it up, I found I was right.

It was clearly a book. No points for creativity.

"No!" She tossed the towel in her hand and attempted to yank the gift from me. She may have been tall, but I was much taller. I pulled it back quickly and stretched my arm above my head. It dangled just out of her reach.

I laughed at her attempt to overcome my arm span. "It has my name on it, Counselor."

"I wanted to come by your office and deliver it." She shocked us both with her confession. There are a million things I adored about Sloan. One was how she could be confident one moment and wholly disarmed the next.

"You can still visit me. We're . . ."

Fuck.

She smiled victoriously and tucked her tongue at the side of her mouth. "We're . . . what?"

"Sloan." My warning was flimsy at best.

"Answer the question."

Instead of answering her question, I brought my arm down. I couldn't think of any answer that would satisfy me. Except for the one where I took her to her bedroom. "What's in this?"

She could have pressed me on it. My hopes fell slightly when she didn't try a little harder to get me to finally cross the line.

"Fine. Open it."

Her hand landed on my chest as she steadied herself after attempting to jump for the gift. My heart thundered beneath it. She left it there for a drawn-out pause, sending electricity through us. The sound of her shallow breath became a siren song that drew me in.

Kiss her. Take her to bed.

I pulled away and moved my line of vision to focus on the gift wrap. She took a step back and watched as I opened it. There was a shadow of disappointment in her eyes.

"*The Count of Monte Cristo.*" I smiled. She picked a good one.

"It reminded me of you. Successful, handsome, calculated, a little morally questionable. Major Edmond Dantès vibes."

My heart dipped. She called me handsome. With her, I was a man starved but would live on the breadcrumbs she dropped.

"Morally questionable?" I scoffed. I was a fucking saint. I hadn't bent her over her desk, even though it was all I could think about.

"I'm only teasing. You may bark, but you don't bite. Not me, at least."

I might.

I was beginning to think the references she'd toss into conversation were meant for me. They were always obscure, like she meant to keep them from anyone else in the room who might catch on.

She stacked the deck so only I could win.

Win her. All I had to do was play.

"Edmond Dantès was a lunatic," I mused. Great story, not one you'd want to happen. He didn't get the girl, either. Not the one he wanted.

"It's a work of fiction, not a biography. But it can teach you something." Her hand brushed over the leather binding and my fingers. Electricity skittered up my arm.

"Teach me what?"

She knew, to some degree, how I felt about her. That knowledge lit an intrigued spark in her eyes. "Running from things doesn't work. They might catch up." She walked to the couch, grabbing our glasses on the way.

"Who says I'm still running?" My voice dropped low. "Maybe I'm chasing something."

She glanced up but didn't say anything.

We settled on the couch, watching TV with wine and a short struggle for the remote. Sloan sat beside me, leaving no space between us, her legs draped over mine. Her head rested on my chest, occasionally popping up to take a sip of wine or change the channel. Neither of us acknowledged it. We let it be.

She scrolled over to the entire Fast and the Furious movie collection and started it from the beginning. "It's thrilling," she mused. As if that were the reason. She didn't pull her eyes from the screen for even a second.

For the record, I was not jealous, but I was not interested in indulging her fast car kink. Not right now, at least. I grabbed the remote. "No."

She turned. Her hand pressed on my chest to push herself up. "Fine, you pick." She laid her head back down, and I found myself running my finger along the length of her neck. I had no idea what movie I picked. Instead, my thoughts were consumed with what to do.

It was pretty fucking clear what was going on. I needed to make the decision and act on it.

I'd never taken so long to make the wrong decision.

I stupidly decided to wait till the end of the movie. By the time it was half over, so were any chances of anything happening tonight. Trying not to take the fact that she fell asleep on me too personally, I picked her up to put her in her bed—alone.

She stirred briefly, and then settled when I laid the blanket on her.

"Marcus?" Her voice was heavy with sleep. Her eyes opened to meet mine. I was frozen in place. She let out a deep, tired exhale. "Are you chasing me?"

I swallowed hard. Technically, no, I was supposed to be figuring out how to be her friend. But every muscle wanted to crawl into bed with her. "Am I allowed to?"

She nodded and smiled. Her eyes closed again. "I'm not running. Just waiting to be caught." She turned over and drifted back to sleep. I didn't regain control of my mind or body for another minute. I got lost in watching her sleep.

I left a note on the kitchen counter before I left.

I owe you dinner

* * *

I SPENT MOST of the following morning waiting to hear from her. I woke up early to distract myself so I wouldn't think too much while lying in bed. I worked out and got to the office early to keep my mind occupied. I was reduced to someone who constantly checked their phone for a text.

Around 9 a.m., I got the text I was waiting for.

Sloan: You owe me dinner?

My smile was wild. I cursed the things that woman did to me, then took a second to think about everything I wanted to do to her.

Me: I do

Me: Saturday, 7. My place.

This back and forth was agonizingly gratifying, but it needed to end. If she wanted to be caught, I was going to catch her. And I was never letting go.

Sloan: I'll bring the wine

Me: I'm cutting you off after two glasses

Sloan: I thought I was a perfect lady

Me: That's what I'm trying to avoid

Chapter 28

SLOAN

Giddy.

Schoolgirl-level giddy.

I knew I was supposed to keep whatever the fuck was going on with Marcus a secret. But I couldn't contain the sheer exhilaration from my nonstop texting with him, especially when Penelope kept catching me doing it. It was nearly constant, through meetings, strategy sessions, everything.

I couldn't focus. And I didn't want to.

All I wanted was to drown in that feeling.

"Ooh, saucy." Penelope leaned over my shoulder and saw the latest texts. She was invested in us getting together after reviewing almost every text that came through. "Flirting, inside jokes . . . I might venture to guess someone is having some sex this weekend."

Finally.

An excited gasp escaped me at the thought, and my office filled with our laughter.

* * *

SATURDAY NIGHT FINALLY arrived, and I spent more time than I'd like to admit trying to figure out what to wear. The one thing I was sure about was the red lace La Perla set that I had waffled over packing.

My mind raced over what was to come.

The thought was enough to send excited shivers down my spine. If the months of foreplay were any indication, the sex would destroy me in the best way.

Penelope warned me not to overthink it, as if I could help it. Crossing this line was something we should have talked about more, or at all.

Was it cavalier to run headlong into the unknown? Probably.

But I didn't care; I wanted to give in to something that felt so right.

I found an outfit, one that was easily removed, and got a suspicious text.

Xander: You have a surprise waiting for you on the porch

Chapter 29

MARCUS

I was never nervous.

I had stared down life-altering deals and risked more than I was willing to lose on multiple occasions. None of that gave me any anxiety. In fact, it was a thrill.

A date with Sloan was giving me a stress ulcer.

I wasn't exactly a good cook. So, the chef I hired had just left, and any trace he was ever here was gone too.

This entire week was a blur. I had never been so unproductive at work. My mind was entirely fixated on Sloan. The days-long marathons of texts between us were getting wildly out of hand and didn't make it any easier to focus. I found myself texting through board meetings and hearing my phone vibrating when it wasn't.

It was almost seven. I paced the kitchen a few times, annoyed with time for moving slowly and myself for getting so worked up. The nerves probably stemmed from the fact that we hadn't discussed what was happening. Instead, we let our hormones take charge. It wasn't the best time to come to that realization, although it wasn't going to stop me.

At this point, nothing was.

I heard the door and my phone buzz at the same time. The anticipation of seeing Sloan was far more appealing than checking my phone.

I swung the door open, and it was not the Amari sibling I was expecting.

"Henry?" I choked out after a second. I stood there, momentarily frozen in surprise.

"Surprise." He smiled widely. He began saying something, but I didn't register any of it. "Since you're not hopping around the world, we decided to visit."

He walked in, and we began to catch up. My mind raced to figure out what to do.

I needed to tell Sloan. I grabbed my phone before Henry could see the texts that came in.

Sloan: Xander is here

Fuck.

* * *

JUST MY FUCKING luck that Henry decided he wanted to be a better brother *now*. He and Xander concocted the visit over drinks one night. I probably would have been happier to see him if I wasn't so annoyed with the night they intruded on.

It wasn't long before we heard the door open and another two voices fill the foyer. Xander laughed loudly at whatever Sloan said and casually strolled into the kitchen. Sloan was right behind him, mustering a smile.

"We're going out," Sloan announced. She wore a short cocktail dress that ended at mid-thigh.

Xander and Henry filled the air with the story of how they planned a surprise visit for the weekend, finding only a single night where their schedules would align. They took the Amari jet in and

were here for the night, flying back midday tomorrow. In my mind,
I was already planning a re-do of tonight's scuttled plans.

Sloan's expression remained the same, exactly as mine. Happy
to see them, disappointed at the evening that was lost. In wanting to ensure a surprise, they booked rooms at the Four Seasons
rather than stay with either of us, a fact I noted for later consid-
eration.

The conversation drifted to work, as it so often did between
the four of us. I couldn't help but enjoy the way she looked in that
dress. The black fabric clung tightly. Long beaded sleeves wrapped
her delicate arms. The hem sat on the honey skin of her thigh,
beckoning to be touched. Being more cognizant of how often my
eyes roved over her, I attempted to pay attention. She clocked my
lingering gaze and waited until a lull.

"Are you wearing that out?" Sloan asked Xander with mild trepidation. She looked from his feet to his eyes, slowly narrowing hers
as she did. Henry and Xander ambushed each of us directly after
deplaning, and both were dressed for comfort. Their things had
gone directly to the hotel.

"Oh, good call." Xander looked himself over, then nodded to
Sloan. "Want to come hang while I get ready?"

Henry had no such question for me, and I was mildly annoyed
with Xander's. The question was inherently innocent, but I wasn't
in a sharing mood. It didn't matter; I knew the answer.

Sloan walked further into the kitchen and leaned over the stove
to smell the pasta. "Why don't we meet you there? I'm dressed and
hungry, if Marcus is willing to share."

It was good enough for them. They went on their way with a
plan to text us wherever they decided to go.

"I see what you did there." I smiled at her. She bit her lower lip.
"You look . . ." I looked to the door after it clicked to confirm that
both Henry and Xander had left.

"Nice?" she teased.

"Fucking lethal."

"So . . . will you share?" she asked. Not waiting for my response, she grabbed a bowl, scooped some pasta, and sat on the counter to eat it. The already short dress moved higher up her thigh.

"Does this still count as the dinner I owe you?"

She let out a faux resigned sigh, with a hint of disappointment in her eyes. "Sure."

I closed the space between us and resisted the temptation to move her knees apart so I could be even closer. I took the bowl, placed it at her side, and met her gaze. My hands gripped either side of the counter. I leaned in closer. "Then no."

She beamed and playfully swatted my chest. She didn't flinch when my hand rested on the bare skin above her knee. My other hand ran my fingers through her hair, tucking some behind her ear, drawing her closer.

"What will you make me next time?" She ran her finger up and down my chest. Her scent enveloped me, making anything other than the thought of having her right now nonexistent.

How much time do we have?

Probably an hour and a half. I tried to prioritize all the things I could do to her in ninety minutes.

"What do you want?" I whispered. My hand ran up her thigh to the end of the dress, and my fingers played with the hem. I could feel the goose bumps on her skin. She uncrossed her legs, letting me a step closer.

"I think you know," she breathed. The air shifted from light to dangerously volatile; any movement would trip the fuse. Ignite our entire world.

My lips brushed over hers. "Was this dress for me?"

She shook her head. "No, but what's underneath is."

Fuck. The resistance crumbled.

I gripped the back of her neck and pulled her forward. My lips pressed against hers, and I skimmed my tongue across her lower lip. She tugged at my shirt and granted me access. I swallowed her soft moan as my tongue stroked and sparred with hers. She tasted like everything that plagued my dreams.

The kiss became heated in an instant. My hands roamed her body, claiming every inch they touched. I slowly pulled her forward. My hands slipped beneath her dress, stopping when my fingers found lace.

She wrapped her legs tightly around my waist, grinding herself against my hard cock. The feel of her hips bucking against mine shot liquid fire up my spine.

Mine.

I looped my fingers around her panties. She moaned into my mouth, louder this time. Her hands, lost in my hair, yanked gently. I pulled away and found the enticing spot on her neck and dropped kisses there before a hard nip. "Marcus," she panted softly.

That sound drained any remaining hesitation or resolve. Pulling back, I looked at her for a moment. She nodded, flicked her gaze to the hallway, and then back to me.

"You're mine," I told her, and pulled her back into a kiss. I lifted her off the counter. Her legs tensed tighter around my waist as I turned to take her to the bedroom. We were stopped by the sound of her phone buzzing madly against the countertop. It rang through the lust-filled cloud.

Sloan jerked back slightly in surprise. We both looked to the source, seeing Xander's name light up on the screen.

She looked back at me and dropped her head in disappointment. I felt a soft whimper against the crook of my neck.

"I'm going to kill him," I growled. It was almost poetic that the one thing that stood between us and a night of passion was our brothers.

I put her back down on the counter, and she unhooked her legs from my waist.

"Pick this up later?" she asked, catching her breath. I nodded and pressed a kiss on her lips. I sighed and turned around to go change.

"Hey, Xan," she said. I smiled as I walked away and heard her attempt to control her breath.

Chapter 30

SLOAN

We took a town car to the bar. Marcus and I kept our hands to ourselves so we would look presentable. Mostly.

"We should probably talk about that." I fidgeted nervously, twining my fingers. He sat beside me with his arm draped over my shoulders. "Right?"

He nodded, turned to move closer, and ran his hand up my thigh. His fingers began stroking the skin beneath the lace of the La Perla set I wore for him.

"What color is the lace?" His voice was gravel in my ear. He dropped his lips to the hollow of my neck.

I struggled to fill my lungs. "Marcus." The trembling made it to my voice.

"I need something to picture until I can get you into my bed."

I couldn't think. He stole any logical thoughts and replaced them with sinful fantasies. "Red."

A pleasure-filled groan entered my ear. His fingers pressed desperately on my hip beneath the dress. "Don't get drunk," he commanded.

I inhaled sharply when his hand moved from my hip to my core, and he gently stroked his thumb over my aching clit. I arched away from the seat with a gasp. My body lit up with arousal.

"I don't want to put you in the guest bed again," he whispered.

How was I supposed to get through a whole night if he kept talking to me and touching me like *that*? My head fell back when he continued his strokes for a bit longer. Every nerve ending in my body hummed for him.

"You can't do things like *that* for the rest of the night," I warned, knowing he needed to stop, but wishing he wouldn't. His low chuckle was enough to put me over the edge the way everything south of my naval was throbbing. "I can't keep it cool and collected like you."

"I'll behave." He lingered for a second, then pulled back slowly. Almost immediately, he looked unbothered and composed, not like he had his hand up my dress the second before. His focus made me nervous in a thrilling way—it promised pleasure, sin, satisfaction. "We can tell Xander and Henry when there's something to tell."

I nodded, reminding myself not to let Xander rope me into a drinking game.

* * *

WE RELIED ON Penelope to choose a place to meet. She was the most familiar with London. Luckily, she was available tonight when I called her from the car. She was surprised to hear that Marcus and I were going out on the town, less so when she found out who was visiting.

The night began to follow a familiar track. Xander and I bopped around, talking, dancing, and catching up on the last couple of months. Henry and Marcus were deep in conversation.

It felt like it used to.

Except for occasionally sneaking a few sultry glances at Marcus; that was a delightful new addition.

I had been so distracted with Marcus the last few weeks that I forgot how much I missed Xander. Seeing him was like being reunited with a part of myself. A fun and silly part. It felt like a dream or passage to an idyllic past that never actually existed.

Either way, it was an exceptional night.

Until it wasn't.

At some point in the night, something shifted. Marcus no longer met my occasional glances, avoiding them for the most part. It didn't make any sense; we left his place in a tizzy. Something over the last couple of hours had affected him. His playfulness around me was gone.

"Sloan, why are you seeing Jay Sachi?" Henry looked at me with an almost judgmental curiosity during a lull in the conversation. We'd all settled at a table, and I was distracted trying to backtrack and figure out what was wrong with Marcus.

I could practically feel the thud in my chest. Marcus's eyes narrowed on me. I didn't look in his direction.

Instead of answering, I looked at Xander in shock that he would ever disclose anything about my dating life to Henry. He put his hands up in defense. "He was there when you texted me."

"She's not seeing him," Penelope scoffed before I could answer. She was the only one fully aware of what was going on between Marcus and me, and she knew what tonight was supposed to be. "He's a client. I was there too."

"Why would you just assume?" I snapped. As if I needed the night to take another unexpected and unwelcome turn. I woke up this morning expecting to be having sex with Marcus by this point. Instead, he could hardly look at me. And now, my brother was berating me about a client. I kept my voice steady and tried not to ruin the night by unleashing my pent-up aggression on Henry. "Do you think I'm too stupid to know he's a walking red flag?"

"That's not what I meant. I'm sorry." Henry course-corrected immediately. "I was just surprised."

"Who is this?" Marcus finally spoke up. His tone crackled with annoyance. I looked over at him and he finally made eye contact. He was angry. But, as always, composed.

"He's someone I went to school with," Xander said, his eyes darting suspiciously between Marcus and me. "He wasn't really friends with Sloan." That was partly true. Whatever Xander picked up on, he immediately went on defense for me.

"If I remember correctly, he was only interested in one thing with you." Henry laughed, not realizing how unfunny he was. "And it sure as hell wasn't friendship."

"As interesting as rehashing every person that works with Sloan is, I'm already sick of the first one," Xander groaned loudly and pointed to Penelope. She rolled her eyes. "Can we move on?"

Xander looked at me with some disappointment. He knew he was missing something and hated being left out of the loop. Not missing a beat, he changed the subject. He knew something was going on.

We called it a night an hour or so later and decided we would meet for breakfast before they left the next day. Henry and Xander headed back to their hotel. That left Marcus and me for what was shaping up to be a very different car ride.

"What's wrong?" After a few minutes of awful silence, I finally asked as we rode back to my place.

Tension radiated off him. His jaw was tight, and he looked forward. "Sloan, that can't happen again."

A part of me was expecting it. Knowing that alleviated some of the disappointment, but it did little to blunt the painful sting of it. The building irritation from the entire night, mixed with my anger at him for suddenly turning on a dime, was getting dangerously close to boiling over.

"Is this about Jay?" It came out sounding patronizing. I didn't mean it to, but the rejection hurt. And the hurt quickly became spite.

"No," he spat, almost offended that I would assume he was jealous. He'd spent the last few weeks running off any possible date I might have. It was a safe assumption. Although, thinking back to the night, his mood darkened before that conversation ever came up.

"Then what the hell is wrong?" My voice was noticeably louder, with no indication of coming down.

"You can't be this shortsighted." His voice was strained with frustration. The accusation only added to the anger seeping into me like poison. "We can't fuck up fifteen years."

He wasn't talking about us; he was talking about his relationship with Henry. And mine with Xander. In my anger, I chose to ignore that he had a point. We hadn't talked about any of this, and we probably should have. But I felt rejected. To pile on, he had the audacity to call me shortsighted. As if I was some silly heiress who didn't think anything through.

"I'm shortsighted?" My tone was sharp enough to draw blood. All the heat in my body had found its way to my face. "I'm not the one who felt up my best friend's little sister before thinking about how it might affect him."

His eyes were alight with emotion, but he maintained his stoic demeanor. "Sloan," he warned, the coolness in his voice adapted a razor's edge.

I felt like I was spinning out, and his ability to control his anger made me feel like a child for letting mine loose.

"Just to make sure we're clear—I'm good to go ahead and sleep with Jay?" My hypothetical got just the reaction I wanted. His eyes flashed with anger, and his body went rigid like the words hurt to hear. "Or anyone, for that matter."

"Stop," he commanded firmly.

"You're fine with that? His hands up my dress, his lips between my thig—"

"Sloan." His voice boomed in the confined space of the town car. It was the first crack in his façade. I could keep going and let this thing boil over, or I could stop.

I let out a deep sigh and tried to maintain control. If it didn't hurt him, I wouldn't allow it to hurt me. I gripped my hands together tightly on my lap and held my tongue. After a minute of silence, my heart rate slowed to something closer to normal.

"You're right," I yielded. I didn't want to. I wanted to fight.

I wanted to see every pent-up emotion finally make its way out so he could be a mere mortal like the rest of us. But I couldn't continue at this clip and keep my emotions in check. I knew, in my anger, that my response wouldn't be proportionate. There was no way to take back the awful things I knew I'd say.

"I'm sorry. I never wanted to hurt you." His eyes filled with pain. I disagreed with his reasoning, but I had to accept it. I could have used his sincerity as a place to call a truce and make the steps forward easier. It was the mature thing to do, no matter how much it hurt me.

I didn't do that.

Instead, I let out a short, condescending laugh. "There's a short list of people who could hurt me." I looked straight ahead. "You're not the Sutton that's on it."

We sat quietly for the rest of the awkward ride. I politely thanked him for making sure I got home safely. It was a sad attempt to maintain the little dignity I had left.

The second my front door closed behind me, I slid to the floor. My legs weren't able to take me any further, and I exhaled in shock.

The Marcus who bought me *Don Quixote* was gone. The one who left for two years was back.

I wanted something to pacify the overwhelming humiliation. I needed it, so I sent a text I probably shouldn't have.

> **Me:** Sure, sounds good. Let's get drinks.

> **Jay:** I knew I'd wear you down

* * *

I DECIDED TO skip breakfast the next morning, claiming I drank too much and wasn't feeling well. In reality, my eyes were puffy and I looked awful. I was not in the mood to be seen.

Xander refused to believe that and stopped by before he had to leave.

"You want to tell me what's going on? Because you don't look hungover." He invited himself over, made himself a pot of coffee, and waited until I was finished filling the air with anything other than what happened last night. I just ran out of things to say.

"Nothing." I sat on the couch with a coffee cup Xander forced into my hand. He could tell something was up. The extent of it, I couldn't be sure.

He sat next to me and paused for a moment. He leaned forward and looked ahead. His elbows rested on his knees. "You look like you've been crying."

His voice bubbled over with concern, unsteady like I hadn't heard it in years, and I couldn't get myself to speak. I would cry, and he would get upset. It would be bad. Few things could shake his gentle and even temper, but I was one of them. That was a power I had to wield very carefully.

"The guys can be here just as soon as Tristan's jet can be ready. CeCe too." He was only half joking. He leaned in and cupped my face in his hands, forcing my eyes to look into his. The seriousness of his voice dulled. "Who are we messing up?"

"I'm fine." I hiccupped a laugh and pulled myself back. I wanted to tell him, but I couldn't. This was the exact situation all this hurt was meant to avoid.

"You're not."

"Istanbul."

I looked down at my cup, too scared to gauge his reaction. It was a card Xander joked I wouldn't use until I needed help cleaning up a murder. He'd be surprised, and probably more concerned, now that I had used it. I stood and turned away from him. I walked to the kitchen, needing a second where he couldn't see me, to gather myself.

You're fine. It was nothing. Move on.

"Seriously, it's nothing," I said, turning back to face him. His emerald eyes were a sea of worry and disappointment.

A long silence passed before he sighed. "Okay."

He ran his hand through his hair, stood, and wrapped me in a hug. "We always end up telling each other why we used them. You'll tell me eventually."

I snorted a laugh in his chest. "I know."

Xander dropped it, and we chatted about his next trip to London, the one I knew about and had been planning. He didn't have much time before meeting Henry to fly back home, so our conversation was short.

"You know." Xander stopped in the doorway and pulled me into a final hug before heading out. "Nothing changes you and me. You don't need to worry about that."

I nodded. "When you come back to visit, take me dancing?" I laid my cheek on his chest. I couldn't look him in the eye; my emotions would spill over. He was a constant force in my life, something I couldn't and wouldn't lose.

"Duh," he assured. "One foot in front of the other."

Chapter 31

MARCUS

I turned my phone over in my hand again and again.

She needs time.

The mix of alcohol and lust that hung over yesterday escalated tempers.

Last night was an overt reminder of what was at stake—being away for so long dulled some of the memories of Xander and Sloan. She relied on his friendship for so much more than I ever realized. He was one of the few people in her life that saw her as she was and demanded nothing more. I couldn't be the reason she lost even a part of that.

Then, there was Henry. Spending an evening out with him reminded me of why I avoided my feelings for her in the first place. Henry was my closest friend, practically a brother to me. We'd spent the better part of ten years keeping guys like us from dating her. Lying to him about the board was one thing; sleeping with his little sister was another. Forgiveness for the former would take time, but throwing an affair with Sloan on that was suicide.

It would, at best, irreparably change the relationship between the four of us. The one Sloan tried so hard to maintain over the years.

Fuck.

How, in the span of a few months, had I forgotten *all* of that?

I was roused from my thoughts by a loud banging on the door. "Marcus!"

Fuck.

Xander's eyes narrowed when I opened the door. "We need to talk." He pushed past me through the doorway, making sure to clip my shoulder on his way in.

He paced like a caged animal in the living room.

I shut the front door and followed him. "Why is Sloan upset?" he asked. Direct. No banter, no double entendre, nothing. "And why did she use 'Istanbul' this morning?" he whispered to himself.

His line of questioning continued. "Why do you look like absolute shit?"

Asking what Sloan had told him was a terrible idea, so I stood there at a loss for words.

"Xander." I ran a hand down my jaw and let out a deep exhale. How did I even start explaining it to him?

"What happened?" he demanded. The silence made it clear.

Then, the continued silence became an insufficient answer. His tongue clicked.

"I have seen a lot of shitty people try to hurt her, and I picked up the pieces when some of them managed to do it." Xander's voice grew louder. The anger radiated off him as he took a few determined strides to stand toe to toe with me. "You were the one who *wasn't* supposed to fuck it up."

"What?"

"Come on, Marcus," he said in a sardonic drawl and rolled his eyes. His shoulders relaxed for a moment, and he took a seat in the armchair across from me. "You two, last night?" he continued with a soft chuckle. "Yeah, I caught on. I caught on at the gala, too. And I saw her this morning."

"Is she okay?" I sat down. Guilt had singed my chest all night. She never looked at me like she had yesterday.

"Yeah, she's doing great. That's why I'm here screaming at you."
He rolled his eyes. "Tell me what happened."

I told him everything from the start.

Xander sat silently for a few moments deep in thought. "Look, I understand your reasoning. But think about how that sounded to Sloan."

"What?" Genuine confusion plagued me all day. My head was pounding from the stress of what had happened and the lack of sleep. Sloan was incredibly intelligent; she knew the risks of starting something as well as I did.

"Sloan has spent her entire life in second place. With the company, hell, even half her family treats her like she doesn't exist. She is never good enough for any world she's in, always consumed with not being accepted. If she's going to put aside her overwhelming fear of rejection, it'll be for someone who puts her first. And you just put her dead last."

Fuck. "That's not how I meant it." I raked a tired hand through my hair.

"Well, I'm sure that's how she heard it," he said with a heavy sigh. "As for the relationship, you need to figure out if you want an *actual* relationship with her. One where she comes ahead of work and everyone else for good. Because if it's anything short of that, it's not worth it, and it's better that you guys stop it now."

"You don't have a problem with us being together?" I asked.

"If I had a problem with it, I wouldn't be here. I would've let you fuck it up." He smiled. "Of course I'm fine with it."

"Henry's gonna—"

"He'll get over it," Xander interrupted. "Don't be the guy to validate his concerns. If this is actually endgame, that shouldn't be a problem, right?"

"Right."

He grinned. "Go get her."

Chapter 32

SLOAN

I had drinks with Jay after work today.

It was childish of me to have texted him when I was upset; I knew that. I wanted to feel better and less rejected, and I knew one surefire way to do that. Xander's words taunted me when I did it.

All I'm saying is you being hard up and then seeing someone like Jay is a recipe for sex.

At first, I thought it would remedy my terrible mood. The best way to get over someone was to get under someone else . . . or something like that. But now, four days after the kiss, being out with Jay did little to lift my spirits. All I wanted to do was go home. Alone.

He was great company, though—the same devilishly charming man he'd been in college. But he wasn't the company I wanted. Over drinks, he invited me to a party in celebration of Holi in a few weeks, as friends. I loved the holiday, so I was tempted to go.

Maybe it would get my mind off Marcus and having to pretend I was okay with going back to the way things were.

I made it all the way home before collapsing into tears. It was a mixture of anger, the hell of the past weekend, and missing Xander. We hadn't spoken since he left.

The entire past week was spent trying to wrap my mind around the steps forward. The last few months felt like a dream, and now it was time to wake up. I had to figure out a way to get on board with Marcus's request, and it was torture.

He'd called and texted all week, asking to talk. I knew it was to figure it out and pretend it didn't happen. I needed time to at least act like I was okay with it.

I decided to settle in with wine for the night.

I walked to the living room, bottle in hand, and dropped onto the couch. The box holding the copy of *Don Quixote* that Marcus bought me sat on the coffee table. It was wooden and lined with silky fabric to protect the old book. The box looked familiar . . . and then I realized something.

My heart rate ticked up.

The bottle of wine made a loud thud when I placed it on the coffee table and picked up the box instead.

I inspected it, and then flipped it over. The engraved logo at the bottom of the box was branding from a rare book dealer. Goose bumps swept down my arms. I'd seen that exact logo before.

It was on a box containing the first edition print of a group of excerpts from the Old Baxter Sessions. The original publication was in a museum. A small batch of first editions were in circulation, but incredibly rare. I owned a set. It was a gift from my parents on my last birthday.

Or so I thought. I never actually asked them about it.

When it arrived at my place by courier, it didn't have a note. They often sent gifts without a card to Henry and me, so I assumed it was them.

Old Baxter was the central prison in Boston. The Old Baxter Sessions papers documented the criminal proceedings between the 1600s through the 1800s. They were fascinating.

That should have been my first clue.

My parents knew of my love for those types of things, but now I realized it probably wasn't them. I never thought about it and never questioned any of the gifts my parents gave me; they never remembered what they got me anyway.

But *that* gift. It was from Marcus. It had to be.

My mind reeled. *All this time?* I could feel the emotion over the realization taking control, and I needed to know more.

My hands trembled violently when I reached for my phone. I called Xander for the first time since he left.

"I'm hoping this is good news." His cheerful voice only made the truth more repelling.

I exhaled deeply. "Xan."

"Fuck. Well, I already know everything. Unless something new happened in the last four days?"

"No."

"If he wasn't my only remaining family, I'd have kicked his ass." When he left on Sunday, I suspected he might stop and see Marcus. I guess he did.

"I'm your family," I reminded him. He was thousands of miles away, but I knew he smiled when I said it.

I tried to maintain some level of composure when I went through the heartache of the week. Xander listened quietly.

"What do I do?" I asked him when I finished explaining the entire mess.

"What do you want?" Xander asked. "And please, the PG version."

"I want him." I went over it in my head a thousand times. Each time, I wanted him despite the risks. It felt like something real, something rare.

Xander laughed on the other end of the line. "Yeah, I figured. Look, I'm not going to tell you everything he told me because I'm not getting in the middle. But he wants to fix it."

My heart fluttered. "He does?"

It was wonderful and terrifying. What scared me the most was how much I wanted to let him fix it. If he wanted to break my heart, I would probably let him.

"You two are exhausting," he groaned. "Yes, he does. Before you get all hot and bothered, just take a beat and make sure it's what you want too."

It is.

"Okay." I paused for a second and glanced at my copy of *Don Quixote*. "How long has he had feelings for—"

"I'm not answering that."

"Xan."

"Ask *him*. He'll tell you."

I sighed deeply. "The Old Baxter Sessions papers that I got as a gift on my birthday. Do you know where they came from?"

"The what?"

I laughed. "Nothing. I'm sorry you're in the middle of this."

"It's okay. Better me than Penelope."

"Thank you, Xan. You're always looking out for me." My voice hitched.

I could feel the tears welling in my eyes again. Xander was being Xander. Then there was the realization that Marcus may have been harboring feelings for years. And finally, the hope that we could be together. All of it was too much.

I could hear him take a deep breath. "Listen, about Istanbul—"

"I'm sorry I brought it up." It was easily one of the scariest weeks of my life. I had never brought it up because I never wanted to remind him of it. Xander had these moments in his life where he went completely off the rails. The first time was after his parents died. The second was during our trip to Istanbul. It never happened again, but the morbid anticipation of a recurrence kept the anxiety alive.

"Don't be. I'm glad you did. I'm okay now, and you don't have to worry about me all the time," he said. I opened my mouth to retort, but he stopped me. "We both know you still do."

"I love you, Xanny."

His laugh reset the tone of the conversation. "I thought we retired that nickname."

"I was feeling nostalgic."

"Don't punish him for too long."

"I won't." I wanted to hold on to my anger, but the desire to melt into Marcus's arms was so much stronger.

Chapter 33

MARCUS

It was Friday. It had been almost a week since our kiss, and Sloan still hadn't answered my texts or calls.

Her phone went straight to voicemail, again. I shoved my phone in my pocket, the vice grip on my chest tightening. Thankfully, Penelope was answering my calls. I could only pray my plan would work.

I should have waited until she was ready. I knew that. But the terror that I'd lose her made me question everything.

When I got to her office, I stopped for a moment to watch her from the doorway. She had her headphones on, her hair tousled from a long day. Her head bobbed adorably as she stood at her desk, reading the pages in her hands, glancing down to the ones on her desk, and scribbling notes.

Her mannerisms, her laugh, her voice. I missed it all.

Her eyes lifted. She froze before removing the headphones.

Silence smothered the room.

"Marcus," she said as she placed the papers on her desk neatly. "What can I do for you?"

"Can we talk?" I took several steps into her office, and her expression softened. Her eyes darted around in thought.

I wanted to pull her into my arms. Instead, I took a few more cautious steps closer to her. Having to be even arm's distance away from her felt like torture. "Sloan, I'm sorry, I thou—"

"Amari, love, I thought you were lead on the Burton merger," a voice interrupted at the doorway.

Love?

A cold wave of possessiveness rippled through me. My grip nearly crushed my phone in my hand, the one I'd stared at all day hoping to see her name.

He stood at the doorway, stealing her attention from me. Whoever he was, he looked oddly familiar.

"Jay Sachi, this is Marcus Sutton," Sloan said. He took a few steps into the office when Sloan gestured to me. Recognizing the name, my eyes narrowed, taking in the guy she was apparently too smart to go out with.

"Pleasure." His voice was grating and polite. I was sure nobody would miss him if he disappeared.

I didn't say anything. Fury rumbled low in my chest.

"Sutton? You know Xander then? Small world," he added jovially. My jaw flexed. An awkward silence fell in the room. "Terribly sorry if I'm interrupting something—"

"You're not." Her eyes finally met mine again and stayed there. "He's Xander's older brother. Just checking in on me."

I flinched. *Xander's older brother.* That's all?

"Right." His eyes moved between the two of us. "I'll ask Ms. Astor."

"Good. Pen is running point," she said, not breaking our gaze.

"Pleasure to meet you, Sutton, the elder." Jay gestured, tipping a nonexistent hat, eliciting a little giggle from Sloan when she flicked her eyes in his direction. "Let's get drinks again, love," he called as he walked down the hall.

The furious rumble became deafening. She drove me crazy, and

I didn't care. I wanted to be the one who made her laugh, who felt the warmth of her smile.

Before I could say anything, she walked to the door, shut it, and turned the lock. My hopes soared. She could kiss me or kill me; at that point I was fine with either scenario.

She turned back to face me. "He's a client, the Burton merger."

"Why did he call you—"

She rolled her eyes. "He's British. They call *everyone* that."

"Drinks, *again*?"

Her eyes darting to the ground cut deeper than any blade could. "We went out for drinks, as friends. I went home alone and sober. Nothing happened."

"This isn't a game, Sloan."

"I know," she spat, tension lining her lithe frame. "You were the one who—"

"If you want it to be," I said, closing the space between us, "fine. Game on." My eyes searched hers. "I'll chase you. Around the fucking world if you want." Every drop of indignation that bathed her body evaporated. Her shoulders relaxed. "I'll play by whatever rules you set." My hands landed on her waist and pushed her softly against the solid mahogany door. "For as long as it takes."

Scarlet stained her cheeks, and her breath shallowed. She laid her hands on my chest. "Marcus," she breathed.

"When I catch you, and I *will* catch you," I whispered. My forehead dropped against hers. "I'm never letting you go."

Before she could deliver the defiant retort I knew was coming, I kissed her.

Chapter 34

SLOAN

Relief shuddered down Marcus's body when I kissed him back. He kissed me like he was pouring every ounce of restrained emotion into me. It was nothing like the kiss we shared before. This one was filled with a deep and slow passion, one that would wait a lifetime if it had to.

He held my head between his hands. His fingers played with my hair, and his scent filled my lungs. Musk and spice. I couldn't tell whether a minute or an hour passed when we parted; hell, I was barely able to stand. My entire body trembled blissfully. My chest seized with emotion when we parted, and I could see the storm in his eyes had finally quieted.

"The Old Baxter Sessions excerpts?"

His nose nuzzled into my neck. "How did you know?"

"Same book dealer. You're off your game."

"You seem to be the exception." He pulled back, and his eyes searched mine. I didn't know what the power I had over him was, but it was probably the same one he had over me. "I thought you'd like them. And I knew you wouldn't question your parents about it."

He knew me. Like a book he'd memorized in secret over the years.

"You were going to let me think you sent me those stupid cookies for my birthday?" I remembered the excitement that ran through me on my birthday when something was delivered from him. Then, the crushing disappointment when it was an offensively generic gift.

"You have a sweet tooth," he reminded me.

Ever calculating, he knew he couldn't be the one to give me such a meaningful gift. It would have raised flags.

"I liked the Baxter Sessions more."

"I knew you would."

I traced my finger nervously up his chest, and he wrapped his arms around my waist to pull me closer. "You've been pining for me."

He nodded. "Something like that."

I nodded and pressed a short kiss on his lips, hoping to soothe the pain I knew he'd silently endured.

"Why'd you wear that red dress to the gala?" His thumbs stroked either side of my back.

I grinned. I wanted him to see me in it. I wanted him to want me the way I wanted him. "Maybe you're not the only one who's been pining."

His light chuckle eased all the pain of the last week. I chewed on my lip and asked the question he still hadn't fully answered. By now, I knew. "Why'd you leave?"

He swallowed hard and looked down. "Work." He exhaled a large sigh. "And I couldn't watch you with anyone else. Everything became easier further away. I figured it would pass."

My chest ached at the truth of it all.

"Don't do it again." Tears welled at the sides of my eyes, and he kissed them away.

"If I knew back then that you—" His voice shook for a millisecond before he reined it in. His hands moved back up my sides to cup my face. "I am never letting you go."

He kissed me again. This time, his arms supported the weight of my body when the trembling became overwhelming. It went on for what felt like hours. We only stopped when we heard a couple of knocks on the door and a note slipped underneath.

The self-assured smirk that made me melt was back. He gave me a final peck. We parted, and I leaned down to read the note.

Things are covered here. Have fun.

Pen

"Penelope cleared your schedule; you're done for the day."

The grin that spread across my face refused containment. "Where are we going?"

"Not far."

* * *

THE CAR PULLED up to the airport's private hangar, where I saw the Sutton jet ready to go. "Not far?"

"Not far, relatively speaking."

"Relative to?"

"The moon?" The lightness in his voice made me laugh. He pulled his arm around me and kissed my head.

"You're really not going to tell me?"

"Sloan, please." Marcus was being unreasonably patient, even after I bothered him about it between kisses in the car. He kept the kissing tamer than the last time we were in a town car together. His hands stayed on my hips or caressed my face, but nowhere else. I was getting impatient, and he was finding way too many ways to postpone sex. "Relinquish control for a few hours."

"Have we met?" I flicked a glance up at him as we walked to the jet. "And are you really one to talk about control?"

He smiled. "You're right."

"You're being very *patient*." We got on board, and I took the seat beside him. He pressed a kiss against my lips and didn't attempt anything more.

He read my deflated expression. "It's *killing* me. But I want to do this right."

I knew what we had was different than the short flings of his past, but hearing it helped pacify the insecurity.

"What if I didn't come with you?"

"I'd try tomorrow." His voice was heartbreakingly vulnerable. "And every day after."

Chapter 35

MARCUS

We landed in Brussels ninety minutes later.

After we landed, it was mayhem. Sloan was impossible when she wasn't in control. I hoped she would close her eyes and let me lead her twenty steps so she didn't spoil it for herself. She, of course, refused.

We stood at the entrance of the Spa-Francorchamps instead of in the McLaren pit, as I had planned. Watching her as the pieces started to fall into place was incredible.

But this car, on the Spa-Francorchamps, that's the dream.

I took her hand and began leading her through the corridors, following one of the engineers. When we walked into the pit, she saw one of the McLaren team cars, suitable for two, being prepared.

"No." She inhaled sharply. The realization of what was happening slowly poured into her. Her eyes went wide.

"You can't drive an Artura on this track, but the team was able to spare one of their cars."

By spare, I meant I bought it. The look on her face was worth it.

She stood in stunned silence for a couple of seconds. "I can drive that"—she pointed to the car—"on the track?"

I nodded.

"What's all this for?" she squealed.

As if it weren't already obvious. The look in her eyes was everything I was hoping for.

"Marcus, I can't believe you did all this." She wrapped her arms around my torso and rested her head on my chest. "Thank you."

"Have fun," I said, remembering the ground rules, just as she turned to run to the car.

I grabbed her hand and pulled her back. She bumped against my chest, and I wrapped my arm around her waist. My chin dropped to rest on her shoulder. "This isn't without guardrails. If you want to go any faster than one hundred miles per hour, you're going with him. And he's driving. Any slower, you can drive the lengths, not the turns."

I pointed to a man standing next to the quarter-million-dollar car. Since it was during the F1 season, the team couldn't exactly spare their driver, so one of the backup drivers was persuaded to fly in from Bahrain.

"He's cute." She turned around and smiled.

"That's not funny." Did I love the idea of another man taking her around her literal fantasy? Hell no. I certainly didn't love that I was the one who set it all up. But I wasn't ever going to put her in harm's way. "He's there for your safety, he so much as touches you—"

"Relax, I prefer my men completely unavailable for *years* first." She grinned, gave me a quick peck, and walked ahead in a hurried excitement.

* * *

About an hour later, the McLaren was back in the pit. When I planned this excursion, I assumed I would use the time to finish some work. But seeing Sloan rip through a racetrack at over a hundred miles an hour was unsettling.

I also realized why Sloan never dragged Xander to anything related to racing. It brought up terrible memories.

The agonizing anxiety finally ceased when the car was parked and Sloan got out of the driver's seat.

She scanned the pit to find me and darted over once she did. "That was amazing! Thank you, thank you, thank you." Jumping into my arms, she wrapped hers around my neck.

That smile made my heart dip.

I leaned my head against hers, and my arms looped around her waist.

"Are you finished being a gentleman?" Her brown eyes sparkled in the late afternoon light. I wasn't one of the society types she'd dated in the past, I had every intention of making that difference known.

"Sloan." I leaned my head against hers. "Gentle is the last thing on my mind."

My resolve diminished to nothing, and I dropped to cover her lips with mine. Catching her off guard, she jerked back slightly but quickly warmed to it. With a soft moan, her head fell back, and she pulled down on her arms, holding me tighter.

Delighted in how her tongue swept against mine, I kissed her deeper, gripping the back of her neck, my fingers laced in her hair, allowing me control. Her hands got lost beneath my shirt, and her fingernails pierced into my back as she let out a soft moan.

Fuck. I wanted her. I breathed in the scent of lemons and exhaust.

"Do we . . . do we need—" Sloan pulled away breathlessly. "To go back right away?"

"No," I said softly in her ear and brushed my nose against her neck. Hoping today would go well, I had a suite at the Warwick and a weekend bag Penelope packed for Sloan. "I have plans for you."

Chapter 36

SLOAN

Marcus was unsurprisingly composed when the town car stopped at the hotel's entrance. Things got heated in the car and escalated quickly. Luckily, the ride to the hotel was short. The mixture of anticipation from months of foreplay and the sincerity of his gesture made me want to do all types of things to him as soon as possible.

He held my hand and led me through the hotel. He didn't dare look at me until the suite door shut behind us. I turned to face him. My breathing slowed with heavy anticipation when I heard the lock click. He looked at me with the intensity of a lion stalking its prey, his features darkened in an unbroken stare as he silently prowled to me.

If a look could make me orgasm, that was it. Unwavering focus. Everything about him was commanding, and God, I wanted to comply.

His eyes glided over my body, as if trying to decide what to do first. Marcus looked down at me and ran his finger across the side of my neck. Pushing the hair back, he leaned in and dropped a soft kiss there. "Sloan," he whispered.

Moisture gathered between my legs. He never said my name like *that* before.

My legs nearly buckled. His arm wrapped around me to take my weight when I arched into him.

"Tell me to stop and I will." His voice was low and graveled in my ear. The feel of his breath sent goose bumps all over my skin. My nipples hardened beneath my bra, aching to be touched.

A firing squad couldn't stop me.

"No." My voice shook. He swallowed hard. There was no turning back from here. It wasn't just sex or a fling. It was a different beast entirely.

He brought his lips to mine for a tentative kiss at first, pulling away to run his hands up my shirt and pull it off me. He unhooked my bra, threw it to the floor, and met my lips again.

I moaned into the kiss when his hand found my breast, and his thumb rolled over my hardened nipple. The other hand ran down my side, resting at the small of my back. He held me tighter against him, allowing me to grind against his thick arousal.

The desire that pooled low in my stomach began to scream for attention. Months of waiting made me impatient.

"I need you," I rasped, breaking from the kiss momentarily. I tried desperately to suck in some air to abate the way his touch made my head spin.

Marcus leaned his head against mine. "I hope you know, you're not sleeping tonight," he warned, crashing his mouth back onto mine. This kiss was different. It was unrestrained and demanding. His fingers dug possessively into my skin, and any tenderness vanished.

His tightly leashed desire was finally allowed its freedom, and he took it. His mouth, teeth, and hands all did things to my body that I didn't think possible. He wanted to claim every inch of me, and I wanted to succumb. In one quick motion, he hooked an arm under my thigh and picked up my entire body. My legs snapped around his waist.

I gasped at the feeling of his cock grinding hard against my core. He groaned loudly into the kiss, backing us into the wall.

"You've been torturing me, Counselor." His lips pulled away, and he sank his teeth possessively into my neck. He ground his hips against me with each bite. "For months."

Oh God. "Marcus." I bucked against him desperately.

"For *years*." He groaned against my neck and brought his mouth back to mine. He carried me to the bedroom. The sound of him kicking the door open was the only thing I remembered before my back hit the mattress.

He broke our kiss to stand up and remove his shirt. I'd seen Marcus without a shirt at the pool or the beach, but seeing his sculpted body before it claimed me was *hot*. I sat up on my elbows and took a moment to enjoy him. His sculpted arms, muscular chest, and washboard abs were all for me. My pulse ticked up wildly. His pants went next, leaving him in his boxers, and the pulsing between my thighs grew stronger.

He smirked as he watched me take him in.

Marcus unzipped my pants and hooked his fingers around the waistbands of them and my panties. They were off me in one quick motion.

He paused and let out a low, controlled growl. His hungry gunmetal eyes roved from my legs to my hips, and finally met mine. He crawled on top of me, and our lips met again.

"Fucking lethal." He broke away and breathed into my ear. My lungs desperately searched for air. He moved his mouth to my neck, and he pushed his body hard against mine. The feel of it, pressing me into the mattress, sent sparks dancing along my spine. "And all mine."

I pulled him back to kiss me. My hands dug into his back when his palms moved up my thighs and splayed at my navel. He was teasing me. His hand moved down my navel slowly, and he finally pushed a finger into me while his thumb caressed my clit.

My heartbeat went from fast to crazed.

"Marcus." I arched away from the mattress. His smile was wicked. I needed more. I was desperate for it.

"Fuck, you're wet." His voice was strained, he added another finger. "Were you this wet on New Year's?"

Yes.

All I could bring myself to do was whimper and buck at his fingertips as they put on a show inside of me. Their cadence hastened to a maddening pace.

"I don't think we can be just friends." I let out a small laugh. The pleasure mounted; I was so close. I didn't know why I said it. Maybe a part of me was still nervous about it—not the ramifications, but seeing Marcus so intense and focused on me was unnerving.

"Just friends?" He groaned in my ear. As if to punish me for that statement, Marcus withdrew his fingers. He stood to remove his boxers. I inhaled sharply, taking in the sight of his long, thick arousal already slick with anticipation. Waiting breathlessly as I heard foil ripping open, I swallowed hard at the thought of him inside of me. He was *big*. He walked back to the bed, his gaze penetrating mine, and positioned himself at my wet entrance.

"Do your friends do this to you?" He teased me with his tip. I panted in response. "There's only one right answer."

"No" was all I managed to get out, lost in a cloud of lust. He groaned loudly as he pushed himself fully into me, his size stretching me to my limits.

I let out a small cry, but was so turned on by that point that he slid in without resistance. He leaned forward and brushed his lips against mine. "Just me." He lifted my trembling legs to his shoulders and slowly picked up his pace. "Only I do this to you."

Biting my lip, I adjusted to his size. He looked down to assure me. "Don't worry, you'll get used to me."

I nodded in compliance, and the prickle of pain melted into pleasure as my body began to accommodate him. He pulled out of me slowly, only to push back in at the same torturously slow speed. I whimpered and bucked against him for more.

"Tell me what you want, Counselor." He looked down at me, smug. I was entirely under his control, and he *really* liked it.

I moaned softly.

"No." He smirked and pulled himself almost completely out of me. "Sloan Saanvi Amari." Dominance drenched each syllable as he slowly pushed back into me. "Tell me what you want."

"Fuck. Me. Marcus," I commanded through gritted teeth.

He slammed into me hard, once, restraint warring with desire. "Almost." Only one of us could be in control, and right now, it was going to be him.

"Please." I heaved a heavy breath.

He ran his thumb down my lips before returning his hand to my hip. "Good girl."

He rewarded me with harder, faster thrusts. My breaths became shallow, and the moans got louder. Usually, any inkling of control over me felt like barbed wire. But with Marcus? I wanted him to take me, fuck me, make me his, turn me around, and do it again.

Every ounce of defiance left my body when he entered it.

Heat coiled at the base of my spine until he hit the spot that made my entire body quake. "Marcus. Please."

The last bit of resolve in his face faded, and his strokes became more savage.

Rough. Powerful. Uncontrollable.

The sound of our bodies colliding filled the room as the tension built at my core. My moans became an unintelligible mix of panting and desperate sobs. The sound of his heavy breathing was the last thing I heard before it finally shattered. My body was electric with waves of satisfaction.

"Marcus." I moaned his name loudly when I came.

My breath was ragged, my body trembling with nearly overwhelming gratification. I sighed when Marcus lowered my legs from his shoulders and leaned forward. His arms were bracketed on either side of my body. My hazy eyes registered him as he dipped his head and kissed me softly.

"You were meant to scream my name," Marcus grunted on my lips. His movements slowed and became more sensual. I moaned again, still coming down off the high of a powerful orgasm.

"How are you doing this?" I gasped out between kisses. How could it be *so* good?

"I'll let you interrogate me later," he said and kissed me again. It was lazy and soft for a moment when he broke away. "You're mine, Sloan."

He began to thrust a little harder, and I moaned in agreement.

"No." His mouth went to my ear, and his voice turned jagged. "Say it."

I cupped his face in my hands and pulled him to meet my gaze. "I'm yours."

The tenderness reappeared for a moment before the gray flashed back to midnight.

He pulled me into another kiss, stronger and more lustful this time. His hand found its way to my clit and rubbed it roughly, sending new sensations in all directions.

He pulled away from the kiss and began to snap his hips against mine with more force.

The tingling gathered in my lower half again. "Please—" I could only moan as he thrust harder and harder into me.

The next orgasm built as quickly as the last. I clawed at the sheets, his back, his hair, anything to hold on to as I lost myself in bliss.

Years of repressed longing found their release in each of his unrelenting strokes. His tempo became rougher and more primal. All the restraint drained from him, and he ravaged my body mercilessly.

I writhed beneath him as another climax rocked my body. This time, I heard a guttural groan in my ear. His grip on my waist tightened and he jerked forward, feeling the full force of his orgasm. He leaned down and groaned into my neck before laying a kiss there. A final, delightful, shudder ran up my spine.

I lay there in stillness, enjoying the euphoric cloud I was lost in. My fingers absentmindedly ran through his hair as he kissed his way along my chin and down my neck.

Marcus got up momentarily, then crawled into bed beside me. He pulled me into him. We lay on our sides, legs interlaced. His fingers stroked the locks of my hair. "You okay?" His eyes were closed, and his forehead leaned against mine.

"Mmm" was all I could really muster—that, and a contented sigh and uncontrollable smile. "I don't think I've ever—" I said softly, mostly to myself. I only now realized that my sex life was missing something if it was meant to feel like *that*. He wasn't my first, not by a longshot, but he may as well have been. "Wow."

He chuckled softly and placed a kiss on my forehead. His arm looped around my waist from beneath me and pulled me in even closer. "I'm not done with you tonight."

I bit my lower lip in anticipation. He looked happy, not just post-orgasmic happy. Truly happy. It made my whole chest fill with warmth. "Oh no?"

"I need to hear you moan my name more."

We remained like that for a few minutes in comfortable silence. The way he looked at me made me want to surrender my heart to him forever. The sex was primal. The way he held me, kissed me, stroked my hair. It was something else entirely. It felt like love.

We'd both harbored these feelings for a while . . .

I wanted to ask him, but my insecurity stopped me.

I shifted at the uncomfortable hold the thought had on me.

"Do you ever think about that night, if they hadn't visited?" I laid my head on his chest when he turned onto his back. My fingers idly drew circles on the taut ivory skin.

"Constantly." His thumb stroked my shoulder in the same pattern over and over again. I looked up at him. "We would have had dinner. I would have flirted with you, and then—"

"All's well that ends well?"

"You wouldn't have slept in the guest room, that's for sure." He turned slowly at first, and then, all at once, I was beneath him.

The air suddenly became charged. His hand pinned my wrists above my head. He dipped down and captured my lips into a slow, sensual kiss.

He had warned me. I wasn't going to sleep.

* * *

THE NEXT MORNING, after very little sleep, I woke to the feeling of Marcus's arm lying over my waist. His sleeping form lay beside me, and his body wrapped mine in warmth. I could hear my phone buzzing. I had heard it a few times overnight, but Marcus kept me busy. Taking a few more minutes to bask in the warmth of the bed, I closed my eyes.

Another buzz called me, and I sat up. Marcus's arm fell onto my lap. He looked different when he slept; his features were less sharp, and there was a softness about him. The intimidating demeanor and all the pretenses were stripped away. What was left was the real man I was beginning to see more and more. I glanced around the room, smiling at the trail of clothing leading from the hallway and strewn about the room.

I looked over to see what woke me. Xander had texted me a few times throughout the night. I could tell him we'd finally resolved things.

Seven times. Memories of last night made my face heat up.

I skimmed the messages.

Marcus's arm found its way around my waist and pulled me back into bed. The phone dropped back on the nightstand. He pulled me in and pressed me firmly against his chest. He dropped a line of kisses along my neck.

"Morning." His voice was gruff and scratchy and so *damn* sexy.

I turned to face him.

"Mmm, good morning." I arched up to kiss him.

His thumb stroked my cheek. "Last night was—" He looked over to the nightstand as my phone buzzed against the wood.

"Perfect," I finished for him, and ignored the call. Marcus kissed me and rolled me onto my back. His body weight prevented me from moving to see who was calling.

"Why don't we order some room service for breakfast?" His lips moved down my neck to my breast, taking a hard peak into his mouth.

I yelped slightly at the contact, arching away from the bed, into him.

Another loud buzz.

"Who is that?" Marcus growled.

"I'll give you one guess." I rolled from my spot to the other side of the bed, sat up, and attempted to retrieve my phone.

"Ignore it." He followed and settled on wrapping his arms around my waist and laying lazy kisses on my neck. It was an attempt to wear at my resolve, and it was working.

"It's the third call; he'll think something is wrong." I tried to put some distance between us so I didn't get tongue-tied. Marcus pulled me back with ease. Xander and I had a rule, three missed calls were a code for danger. Originally, it was born of my own anxiety after he spun out the first time. Now, it was a just a rule we followed.

I picked up the phone and exhaled deeply to regain composure. "Xan?"

"Why are you ignoring my calls and texts? Are you okay?"

"I . . . I am . . . sorry, hold on," I stammered. Marcus was now fully committed to making it impossible to have this phone call. He moved his hand from my waist to between my thighs. I tried to conceal a small cry. I looked back at him as a warning, to no avail. It only enticed him.

"Uhhh," I began again, but swallowed hard when one of his fingers sank into me. My body betrayed my mind and leaned back into him. "Can I call you later?" I managed to get it all out in one sentence, although the hitch in my voice and the sound of the sheets moving were audible.

"Are you talking to me while in bed with someone?" Xander laughed. We didn't toe the line of what was appropriate; we skipped rope with it.

Marcus looked at me, an eyebrow raised. "Someone? Who else would it be?" he demanded quietly, half joking, in my ear. He pushed another finger into me.

"Gross," Xander groaned.

Hardly composed enough to speak, Marcus seized the opportunity and grabbed the phone. He pushed the pads of his fingers against the spot that drove me crazy and stroked it masterfully, rendering me boneless. "Bye," he said into the phone, hung up, and tossed it into the bed for us to retrieve later.

My mouth was agape in a mixture of surprise and pleasure. "I can't believe—" Unable to think of anything but the mounting pleasure, I said the only thing that came to mind. "Marcus."

He didn't respond. His amused smile turned into something wicked. He removed his drenched fingers and shifted so he was on top of me, and pinned my hands on either side of my body while he laid soft kisses on my neck. "Mine."

"Mmmm," I hummed.

He got up onto his knees, pulling the sheets out of his way. His eyes were focused on me. "Turn around."

Yes, sir.

Chapter 37

MARCUS

Over the past five years, Sutton Industries became a behemoth. Due to this growth, I was expected at certain society events as a part of good business. I was often lucky enough to witness some of the greatest orchestras perform at the most distinguished concert halls around the world.

But no symphony was more heavenly than the one that came out of Sloan when she was moaning and, at times, screaming my name.

It was addicting; she was addicting. And I would do anything for that high.

Sloan was a firecracker. I don't know why it surprised me. She was never shy about getting what she wanted in any other aspect of her life. Why would this be any different? Luckily for me, it wasn't.

She was insatiable. We spent the weekend having sex on any object that would hold her inviting body. When I planned the weekend, I initially expected she'd want to go out during the day. I kept some things to do in the back of my mind. We didn't need them.

Our chemistry was explosive, and it certainly translated to the bedroom. And the kitchen counter, the shower, the couch, and anywhere else I could pin, lay, or bend her over.

I smiled at the memory, gently caressing her skin with my thumb as she slept peacefully beside me. She was curled under my arm, with her head rested on my chest. It was early. I had awakened a while ago but wanted to give Sloan some time to rest.

My mind replayed the last twenty-four hours with tantalizing detail until a low moan stopped it. We hadn't left the suite because everything turned into sex.

Like when she moaned in her sleep.

With great care, I turned her over on her back and laid a kiss on her neck.

She smiled. Looming over her, I continued until I heard a louder moan. "Mmmm." Her eyes remained closed, but her smile grew. "More."

I didn't need to be told twice. I got up and moved to the edge of the bed, then slowly pulled her to the edge as she began to wake. Getting down on my knees, I spread her legs apart and kissed my way up her inner thighs, moving closer to the wetness already pooling inside her.

When I finally made it to her entrance, I kissed it once. She let out a sharp inhale that quickly melted into a pleasure-filled sigh. "You like that?" I blew a puff of air across her clit. She arched up, and her breath hitched.

I smiled and blew a few more puffs of air. She arched again. Her hand raked through my hair and yanked at it. "Marcus." Her voice was irritated with impatience. "Please."

The weekend was filled with hurried, desperate passion. We were making up for lost time. But we had to leave later today, and I wanted to go slowly, savor every moan, and make her beg for more.

"I haven't even touched you yet."

She whimpered. I ran my hand up to her stomach and stroked her navel slowly; my fingers spread and caressed the soft skin. She groaned and pulled at my hair again.

I flattened my tongue and lapped across the smooth skin of her entrance, leaving a few teasing strokes below her clit. Her breath shallowed. I added more pressure with my tongue and slowly lapped it up and down.

"Marcus," she panted. Her hips began to buck.

My thumb began stroking her clit, and my tongue finally plunged into her, tasting the forbidden sweetness of body. She gasped and shook beneath my touch.

Her hands moved from my hair to the mattress. She clawed into it frantically. "Please," she begged again.

Hearing *her* beg for me was heaven. It made it nearly impossible to deny her. I spread her wetness over a couple of fingers and plunged into her. I curled them up slightly to reach for that spot I already memorized. I felt it and pushed back and forth as I rolled my tongue across her clit. Her hips shifted against my fingers. "Oh . . . God."

My hand pressed her down against the mattress when she writhed. Her moans filled the room, getting louder with each press inside of her. I groaned and continued, feeling her walls tighten against me. "Marcus," she moaned, and shuddered violently. I continued until the shudders ceased, dragging her orgasm out as long as I could.

I got up and looked at her, panting; her eyes were glazed over. She lay there, legs spread wide, a goddess at my mercy. Her eyes met mine. "More," she said between pants, coming down from the orgasm.

"That's my girl." I bent over and pressed my lips against hers. "What do you want, Sloan?"

"Fuck me." Her eyes closed, and her breathing was still ragged. "Again."

I quickly got off the bed and fisted my hard cock. Once I rolled on a condom, I returned to her, caging her body between my arms.

"You taste better than I could have ever imagined." I pulled her into a sensual kiss.

She pulled away and cupped my face in her hands. "You feel better than I ever dreamed," she whispered. My lips pressed back onto hers, and I kissed her more deeply. A low hum rumbled up her throat. It stirred something in me, something possessive. I pushed into her slowly, her walls pressed tightly against me. Her eyes closed as the pleasure mounted.

"Don't close your eyes," I grunted. I wanted to see the look in them when she came for me. I waited a moment to let her adjust, and then began. I dragged myself out slowly, teasing her, only to slam back against her with more force. The sensation with each movement coiled the pressure tighter at the base of my spine.

It took every drop of restraint to hold back and continue at a slow, sensuous pace. Watching her writhe beneath me was almost too much.

With every thrust, her brown eyes baited me for more. "Harder," she begged through gritted teeth.

My mind played the countless times I wanted to rip off her clothes and make her mine. The *years* I'd dreamt of her, only to wake up disappointed with someone else. The memories of having to sit by and watch other men pursue her made my will to tease her slip.

I wanted to fuck her. Hard. So hard she'd never remember anyone before me. I would own every orgasm, every moan, every scream.

Every inch of her was *mine*.

Ruthlessly plunging into her at a frenzied pace, she moaned beneath me. I fought the urge to come at the sound of her. A sound I couldn't live without now that I'd heard it. She dug her nails into my back. Her body shook with pleasure as she tightened around me.

One last moan was all she could offer as she came again. I

couldn't hold on any longer. I let the release wash over me, and in a blinding rush, the warmth took over.

My lungs struggled to find air. I pushed myself up, keeping her body between my arms so I could watch her in her afterglow. Her skin flushed with a hint of crimson spread across her cheekbones. She was radiant. Her fingers ran through my hair for a moment, and I finally rolled over and kissed her.

When I pulled away, she cupped my face in her hands again. Her eyes were filled with emotion. She paused. "I don't want to leave."

"We can do all of this at my place."

This weekend was just a preview of what was to come. I had every intention of spending the next few months making up for lost time. I would happily spend the rest of my life memorizing every inch and facet of her. That's what you did with great art, and she was a masterpiece.

"Mmmmm." She smiled and closed her eyes. "But all day?"

I wasn't the only one addicted.

* * *

WHEN WE BOARDED the jet, Sloan slyly said something to the cabin staff while I settled into the seat beside her. She sat down with a look in her eye that was quickly becoming my favorite thing about her. "I told them we wouldn't need anything for the flight." She leaned in and laid her hand on my chest.

Her hair fell forward, and I swiped it back. I leaned in to kiss her neck before whispering in her ear, "I've been thinking about fucking you on this plane for months."

She bit her lip and ran a finger down mine. "We'll see if we can fit that in." Her finger continued down my chest to the uncontrollable bulge in my pants, begging to be freed. "After I finish what I have planned."

We spent the ascent kissing. Early this morning, before Sloan awakened, I made sure our flight path and time would be free of any weather. I didn't want any turbulence stopping what was about to happen. Once we were at cruising altitude and we'd leveled out, she got up and straddled me on the seat. Her mouth dipped back to mine for another kiss.

I gripped her hips tightly when she began to swivel and rock them.

She was practically a professionally trained dancer with all her years of instruction in different styles. She knew how to move her hips, something I'd finally confirmed firsthand this weekend.

Fuck, it felt good. And she was never dancing with anyone else ever again.

I wanted to take control, but it seemed she enjoyed taking the lead. And it felt fucking fantastic.

"Thank you." Sloan sighed and pulled back from the kiss. My palm pressed the small of her back, wanting to keep her pressed against me. The look of happiness mixed with wanton desire made my heart surge and my pants feel even tighter. "For this weekend."

"Anything for you, Sloan." I gripped the nape of her neck, weaved my fingers into her hair, pulled her forward, and found her lips again. Her hands moved down my chest, and her long fingers undid my belt and pulled down the zipper. I kissed her harder when she stroked my length.

She broke the kiss and got on her knees. My hand gripped tightly to the armrest of my seat while the other stroked her hair.

She bit her lower lip and looked up at me with those lustrous brown eyes as she ran her tongue along my length while stroking me with her hand. Her eyes never left mine. I could've come just from the fucking sight of her.

Agonizing chills ran up my entire body. My head fell back

against the seat. "Sloan," I groaned as she began to take me into her mouth slowly.

She giggled. *Fuck.*

She took almost my entire length in her mouth while her free hand stroked my balls. She pumped, sucked, and even grazed her teeth along my shaft. My hand tightened its grip on her hair. The pleasure was dizzying. I couldn't remember my own name.

"Fuck." I groaned louder that time. Both my hands got tangled in her hair and pushed her deeper as she bobbed up and down. Watching her move up and down my shaft, coupled with the feel of the back of her throat, nearly did me in.

"Sloan," I warned between heavy breaths.

Our eyes met again. A sly smile tugged at the side of her cheek. That smile, those eyes, all with my entire cock down her throat. *Fuck.*

She began to suck harder and deeper, her mouth taking all of me in. Her pace increased wildly, and she let out a long moan along my cock, the vibrations the final act to do me in. Every nerve ending in my body erupted with sensation. I released hard in her mouth. "Sloan," I grunted loudly, my hand gripping her hair tighter.

She didn't pull away. Instead, she bobbed up and down to draw every bit out of me. After a moment, I got a handle on my frantic breath. Her gaze locked to mine, and she swallowed all of it. Then, she smirked and released me.

I leaned back into the seat and closed my eyes for a moment. I hated to relinquish control, but Sloan could have it whenever she wanted it.

When I finally regained some power over my senses, I pulled myself together enough to look, at the very least, fully clothed. I reclined in my seat and looped my arm around her as she brought herself up to rest her head on my chest.

"Well look at that, the great Marcus Sutton, under my control."

She laid a kiss on my neck before looking up at me. I was finding it impossible to keep my eyes open.

I laughed and kissed the top of her head. I was under her control long before this weekend.

"Marcus?" she said after a few minutes of quiet.

"Mmm?"

"We still need to talk about what happens if this doesn't work out." My body tensed. She looked straight ahead and chewed on her bottom lip.

"You can't ask serious questions after doing that to me, Sloan." My head was still spinning from that explosive blow job. I wanted to know how she got so fucking good at that. And then kill the bastard.

"It's called leading. Asking questions in a certain way to get the answer you want." The seriousness lifted.

"Mmmm?" My eyes closed for a moment, still fully lost in the afterglow of what she just did to me. I didn't want to think about her question. I didn't want to think about a scenario where I wasn't waking up next to her. Where she wasn't wrapping those plump lips around my cock at thirty-five thousand feet. Where she wasn't mine. "And, what is it you want, Counselor?"

"I want you to tell me it won't happen." Apprehension slipped into her voice. The sound nearly broke me, bringing back the memories of her voice the night we argued. I never wanted to hear it again.

I lifted her chin, and her eyes met mine. "This is endgame, Sloan. I wouldn't have started this if it wasn't."

She brought me to my knees in every way, even when she was on hers.

Chapter 38

SLOAN

After coming back from Brussels, I was distracted in the best way.

I found myself daydreaming about my boyfriend, then giggling to myself at the idea that Marcus was my boyfriend. That conversation was quick and painless. He wasn't going to share and neither was I.

"Amari?" I was shaken from a particularly sultry memory of Marcus cornering me in the kitchen this morning.

It was Van Der Baun. He looked angry. Or happy? I couldn't tell.

"Amari," he repeated, and invited himself into my office, taking a seat in front of my desk. "Why can't we get the Burton deal done sooner?"

"Regulators have their timeline. We have ours." I sat at my desk and leaned back instead of sitting up attentively. Watching powerful men my whole life, I had picked up a thing or two. "We push and they dig in their heels. We don't need that kind of scrutiny."

He didn't say anything, and his eyes narrowed for a moment. "You and Astor have been instrumental in these past couple of months."

That was his way of accepting my terms.

"We're a good team and exceptional at our jobs." I learned early on that if I wanted to get the same respect as the men, I had to exude the confidence that even the mediocre ones seemed to have. I never said thank you, I kept the conversation moving. I didn't apologize. Instead, I offered solutions.

"And modest," he said, chuckling to himself. He rarely lightened up, even with the partners he'd known for decades. The lightness in tone did nothing to quell the annoyance at his comment. He would have never said that to any of the male partners.

"Modesty is for the mediocre."

"I knew I liked you." Another chuckle. "What do you think about the London office being yours? Partner, then managing soon enough?"

What?

My heart got caught in my throat. But I pulled it together. I couldn't let him see me sweat.

"The deal was New York," I countered, my tone firm. I wasn't even licensed to work in the UK. There had to be an angle here. My heart sank at the possibility that Reese wouldn't hold up his end of the deal. It wasn't like him. He was my mentor and wouldn't have promised it if he couldn't deliver.

"And it can be, but this is global reach. All the firm's power, every large merger deal in the world, under your watch."

"I can do all of that from New York," I reminded him. I needed confirmation or some recognition that the terms of the deal hadn't changed. I would rain down hell if it had.

"Don't be so skeptical, Amari. This is what I look like when I'm impressed." He was stoking the flames of my anger with his refusal to answer my concern. "Think about it. This is just hypothetical for now. We still have months to see if you can handle it."

It should have been good news. It was all the power and recognition I deserved. It was everything I wanted. *Right?*

Despite having worked myself ragged the past few years, I had never stopped to think about whether it would make me happy. After all these years, this was the goal. What was I left with if I didn't have a remarkable career?

Just me.

My entire body filled with an unfamiliar joy. I hadn't given it much thought in those terms. Just me felt like enough.

I was going to be senior partner, though. Nobody double-crossed an Amari.

* * *

MY OFFICE DOOR was seldom closed. Usually that was because I was always in and out, so it was largely impractical. But between the nonstop texting with Marcus and all the work I needed to catch up on, it was better to do that privately.

"Thank you, Cecilia. A year would suffice." I ended the call when I heard the door open. I assumed it was Penelope.

"Pen, let's go to lunch. I want to hear about the whole ex—"

I stopped when I realized it wasn't Penelope at the door. Marcus stood leaning casually against the doorframe, his arms crossed. His dark gray suit mirrored the swells in his eyes. Knowing exactly what laid beneath the perfectly crafted fabric made my body fizz with excitement.

He had that look in his eye.

"What are you doing here?" My heart beat erratically in my chest.

"I thought we could test the desk," he said plainly, as if he'd actually come to complete some mundane task. Keeping his eyes fixed on me, he turned the lock to my office and closed the space between us. He rested his hands on my hips and backed me up against the desk. "Make sure it is sturdy."

My mouth went dry.

Sex at work. That was new.

I nodded. "So concerned for my safety."

I jumped to sit on the edge. My hands had a mind of their own as I pushed his suit jacket off his shoulders, unable to break his heavy gaze. Time slowed. I took my time unbuttoning his shirt, surprised by his patience as he let me do it at a tantalizingly slow pace. His eyes fixated on my chest when my breathing became erratic.

His hand lifted my chin and stroked my cheek gently. The calm before the storm.

"How do you want it?" His voice was low and controlled. The gentility was lost. He wanted me with an intensity that made me shiver.

"I'm all yours." After the past weekend, I knew exactly which buttons to push. "You can decide."

"Now you're getting it." His mouth moved to my favorite spot at the base of my throat.

"Question is . . ." I pushed him back. I wanted to see the shift. When he went from tightly restrained to unleashed. My hands found his belt and began removing it. "When are *you* getting it?"

He grabbed the back of my head and crashed his mouth on mine. His fingers fisted in my hair. Making quick work of his belt, I tossed it to the side and undid his pants. He groaned loudly in my mouth and ran his hands up my dress to loop his fingers around my panties.

In one quick motion, he pulled down my panties and turned me around. "Brace yourself, Counselor," he commanded roughly in my ear. The graveled sound of my nickname nearly pushed me over the edge. My hands braced against either side of my desk.

He shoved my dress up past my waist.

"You came all this way for me." I bit my lower lip to keep from moaning at the feeling of his fingertips teasing my wet entrance.

"And soon, you'll be coming for me." I couldn't see his face, but

I knew that victorious smirk was painted all over it. He pressed his fingers into me, tentatively pushing against the sensitive spot inside.

"What if I was in a meeting?" My voice hitched.

"I'm a busy man, Sloan." His fingers begin to move at a fast pace in concert with his thumb teasing my clit. "You'd end it early. Because I needed to get something."

"And—" He pushed another finger into me. My breath got caught in my throat. "That is?"

"What's mine." Pulling his fingers from me and having the foresight to cover my mouth with his hand, he slammed into me in one swift motion. I moaned loudly. Thankfully, it was muffled. He kept his hand there as he began, removing it only when the pace hastened and I adjusted to him.

Once I had, his hand fisted my hair, pulling roughly with each thrust.

Oh, God.

Sex with Marcus switched between sensual and animalistic. I didn't know which I liked more. But when he turned me around and pulled my hair, *that* was almost too much.

"Marcus," I whimpered. I tried my best to control the volume of my moans. I had never been a screamer in the past, but sex with Marcus made every past sexual encounter pale in comparison. With him, it was a five-alarm fire making everything else seem like a poorly lit match. "Oh, God."

"No, but—" He leaned into my ear. His hands moved to my waist, and with each thrust, his fingers gripped harder into my hips. "You're welcome to get on your knees and worship me."

His thumb moved to press controlled circles along my clit. My nails sank into the desk. I was getting *so* close. "I'll keep that in mind."

He groaned, and his strokes became increasingly erratic. The pressure finally became too much. I bit my lower lip to keep from screaming. The orgasm ripped through me, tearing me apart and piecing me back together.

My climax spurred his. He cursed under his breath, and his body became rigid momentarily. He slowed to stillness and leaned forward; his arms braced him alongside mine.

"Desk holds up," he said with a chuckle while catching his breath, a casualness returning. He pulled away from me, getting dressed as he normally would if he were home. "Let's test mine next."

I turned to face him, flushed from the high he had just given me. I pulled up my panties and adjusted my dress. I was amazed at how quickly he could go from the animal that bent me over my desk to the calm and collected CEO.

It made me want to pull those clothes off again.

He adjusted his tie and pressed a short kiss on my lips. "I'll see you tonight."

I collapsed into my chair. The annoyance of the day had been fucked right out of me.

Chapter 39

SLOAN

Dating Marcus was like dating a stranger I'd known my whole life. The walls he had built over the years were hardly all the way down, but I didn't have to wait for a rare occasion to peek behind them anymore. He was a little more himself to me every day.

Discovering little things about him was a thrill, like how he would absentmindedly trace the outline to the fleur-de-lys when he was lost in thought. His mother was a French history scholar. It seemed to be a relic that stuck with him. I never asked about it, but it felt intimate to know.

I was quickly becoming accustomed to his gentleness when we were alone. How he stroked my hair while we watched TV, or how his hand would rest on the small of my back whenever we walked together. I never wanted any of it to end.

Marcus texted me that we'd be going out tonight, but that was the only hint he gave me. After work, I briefly returned to my place to get some clothing and a few other things, and then made my way to Marcus's. I had stayed there every night since Brussels.

He refused to tell me what we were doing until we got to the building and the elevator doors opened to a demonstration kitchen.

"I thought a cooking class might be fun." We walked in to find Izan Decasta, chef and owner of the three-Michelin-star Spanish restaurant of the same name. He was there to teach us a private lesson.

"I love it." The things this man did to my heart. And every other part of my body. I pulled him down for a kiss. "Who knew Marcus Sutton was so good at planning dates?"

Every few nights, I would think of something I wanted to cook, and we would spend the night in the kitchen making it, occasionally getting distracted with other pursuits. It was a nice pattern we were falling into.

"I'm not. You're the exception," he whispered in my ear before the chef began to walk us through the recipe. We were making paella.

The whole endeavor took about two hours, and we punctuated the time with tapas and wine. Once it was done, Chef Decasta left us to enjoy the meal we had made together.

"I have to be in Zurich in a couple weeks," Marcus said. His arm rested along on my shoulders, and his fingers played with my earring.

"Really?" My heart picked up with excitement. I loved Switzerland. My grandmother and I used to visit Henry at boarding school there all the time when I was a kid.

"I'll be there a few days, maybe a week."

My hopes crashed. He was telling me he'd be away, not inviting me on a trip. It was a silly thought; it wasn't like I'd be able to go for a whole week anyway. I hated that I felt disappointed for no real reason.

His eyes moved away from me to the table. "It's the week Xander visits," he continued.

I tilted my head away from his hand. "You're going to miss Xander's visit?"

"No, I'll see him when he arrives. Besides, he's coming here to see you."

The last few weeks had been blissful; they felt like a dream. The reminder that Sutton Industries always came first for Marcus was a rude awakening. My irritation was more with that realization than his actual trip—the sudden realization that I was in second place again.

"Yeah, but I'm sure he wants to spend some time with you," I snapped.

"He'll be fine." Marcus raked a hand through his hair.

"Well, excuse me for looking out for him," I retorted, feeling my blood begin to rush to my face. *Don't say it.* "Someone should."

I immediately regretted it.

He tensed. It was a shot I shouldn't have taken. I knew how badly Marcus felt about abandoning Xander the last couple of years.

"I'm sorry," I said quickly, taking his hand in mine. I wasn't in the mood to get upset and argue. Besides, I couldn't make him want to put us ahead of his work. It felt like he was finally doing that on his own, like he didn't want to shut us out anymore. "I didn't mean that."

"I know," he said, taking notice of my clearly deflated expression. He leaned forward and pressed a kiss on my lips. "I'll be back to spend some time with him before he leaves too. I'm sorry."

I nodded and pushed past the foreboding feeling I couldn't shake. We finished our dinner in an uncomfortable silence.

"You okay?" Marcus finally ended the quiet when he noticed me rubbing my left wrist for probably the hundredth time that night. It always seemed to get sore when I lifted a heavy pan poorly.

"Yeah, my wrist gets a little tight on occasion ever since that nigh—" I stopped with a noticeably sharp inhale, mentally kicking myself. Falling into being so comfortable around Marcus meant my defenses were down. Occasionally, things I hid for a reason bubbled up, and I would forget who I was talking to.

Marcus put down his wine. He released a controlled sigh. "That night." He wasn't asking a question but telling me he knew what I meant to say. The night at the bar, the story I didn't tell him at Thanksgiving. Julian.

"Forget it. It's nothing," I said.

He agreed, but the mood shifted for the rest of the night, like a cloud lingering over us. The annoyance over the timing of his trip and my refusal to tell him about my wrist culminated to what was probably our first actual fight as a couple. Unlike arguments I had with past boyfriends, this was a war fought in silence.

The ride home in the car was uncomfortable. Marcus's arm was draped around my shoulder, his thumb stroking it in a familiar pattern the whole way. His turbulent eyes were deep in thought. When we got back to his place, we changed and got ready for bed, all without a word to each other.

"I'll tell you what happened." I sat beside him on the couch. I didn't want to play the game of who could ignore their issue the longest. In all my other relationships, I always felt myself rearing up for a fight. With Marcus, I wanted calm. I wanted this, us, to work. "You can't do anything about it now. And please keep in mind I'm fine."

He nodded in agreement, his hand resting on my thigh.

The story wasn't as exciting as all the secrecy made it out to be. "A little while after I broke up with Julian, I was out with everyone. We happened to run into him at a bar. He tried to talk to me, but I wasn't interested, so I kept close to the guys. Everything seemed fine. Later, when we were leaving, I walked past the hallway toward the bathrooms. He yanked me into the hallway, trying to get me alone."

Marcus's nostrils flared, his jaw flexed, and his grip on my thigh tightened. What Julian would have done, drunk and angry, I didn't know. It wasn't something I wanted to think about. I wanted to believe I'd have been able to fight him off. Luckily, it never got to that.

"He was drunk and wouldn't let go of my wrist. When I tried to pull away, he pulled hard and twisted. Something popped and it hurt *a lot*. Tristan saw him grab me, and he and the guys were there in seconds. Xander punched him, Tristan and Rohan dragged him to the alley, and they beat him senseless."

My skin beneath his hand could feel the fury-fueled tremble as he struggled to keep his word and not react. "Okay," he agreed.

"My wrist was sprained and splinted for a few weeks, nothing major."

"That's everything?"

"Yes."

He pulled me into his arms and kissed me on the head. A shutter of relief passed through him.

"Want to feel better?" I asked as I pulled forward and straddled him in an attempt to lighten the mood. I rested my hands on his chest and leaned down to lay a peck on his lips. "I called an old law school friend. He works at the office of Chief Counsel at the IRS. A couple of inopportune investigations into his family's financial affairs have rendered them insolvent for the foreseeable future."

A ghost of a smile tugged at the side of his lips. He tenderly ran a hand through my hair and pulled me closer. "I know you can take care of yourself. But you could have told me."

I rolled my eyes. "You're not really the prime example of being open and honest."

"What do you want to know?" His hands gently gripped my hips.

Everything.

His walls came down around me at times, but it was up to me to figure things out. He never gave up information on his own. I had to ask the right questions.

He knew why most of my past relationships had failed—I never felt seen. I knew nothing of his. "Why don't I know anything about *your* previous dating history?"

Over the last few years, there had to have been someone. I didn't want to know, but it felt like a secret. He knew all about my past, and his seemed to be shrouded in mystery.

A smug grin crept across his face. "Jealous?"

"A little." I was. My finger twisted around the fabric of his shirt. "Answer the question."

"They weren't serious. I didn't want anything serious."

"Why not?"

He paused and looked at me like the answer was obvious. "They weren't you."

The sentiment stole the breath I was about to take. "You can't do that." I playfully swatted his chest.

"Do what?"

"Say things like that when we're fighting." I pouted; all the anger of the night was lost. "It disarms me."

"It's true," he said, with a sincerity that washed away the bitterness from the night. "Besides, only a fool with a death wish would allow Sloan Amari to be armed."

I laughed, leaned down, and gave him a kiss. There were a million more things I wanted to know, but I was finding it delightful to stumble upon them at the most unexpected times. Somehow, it felt more intimate that way.

Chapter 40

SLOAN

We hardly ever spent any time at my London residence. Most nights were spent at Marcus's, and weekends too. It always felt a little off when we slept here. The idea of having nights filled with explosive sex in a house you most associated with awkward trips during your childhood felt weird at best.

But Marcus and I stayed here last night, because Xander flew in today, and he was staying with me for his visit.

We skipped the normal weekend ritual of staying in bed for a while after waking. I sat on the kitchen counter as the coffee brewed, fully dressed as we were expecting Xander any minute, when Marcus joined me. He pushed my legs apart and wrapped his hands around my waist so he could pull me closer.

"How long do we have?" His face was lost in my still-damp hair. He was missing the morning romp in bed he had become accustomed to.

"Not long enough for *that*." A new voice filled the kitchen loudly. We pulled apart quickly to find Xander grinning widely. "You guys have to lock your doors if you're going do that."

Marcus cleared his throat and took a step back. "Hey, Xander."

"Don't look so embarrassed." Xander walked through the kitchen, dropping his luggage in a corner. "I've walked in on her doing much worse."

"Careful," I warned, feeling Marcus's hand on my waist tighten its grasp. Shifting around him, I hopped off the counter and ran to Xander with the energy of a child seeing Santa. Xander laughed and stretched out his arms, awaiting his hug.

We all settled on the couch with coffee. It was the first time Marcus and I were a couple around anyone we knew, outside of Penelope. I was expecting it to be awkward, or at least a little odd, but it felt like we all picked up where we left off. Xander and I talked a mile a minute, while Marcus chimed in occasionally.

"You guys need to tell Henry." Xander's demand dampened the mood. Marcus's relaxed body tightened at the mention of my brother. It was bothering him more and more lately.

"I'll tell him." I let out a long sigh. I knew Marcus was planning to take the brunt of that, but it was probably better from me.

"You really think he's going to be that upset? He likes Marcus way more than anyone else you've dated."

"Don't underestimate the Amari temper." Marcus stood from his place next to me and pressed a quick kiss on my lips. "Stay out of trouble." He looked at Xander as he walked past.

Marcus was leaving for his Zurich trip later in the afternoon. I hadn't brought up the trip again. I couldn't pin down what exactly I was angry about. He and Xander made plans for after his return, and Xander seemed fine with it.

"Does he not understand that *yours* is the Amari temper he needs to worry about?" Xander grinned.

I rolled my eyes and laughed. "Let's go."

* * *

XANDER AND I spent the day at the British Museum, mainly because Xander loved to ask docents about how the museum came upon all those lovely artifacts. It was also an excellent place to get lost in quiet conversation. We had an over-under on how long it would take him to make the docent storm off. His record was three minutes. I guessed today would be about five. We were busy catching up, after all.

"I've been seeing him pop up in the tabloids again," Xander said as we turned the corner to the Benin vases, eager to ask the docent when the museum planned to return them.

Our conversation shifted to Henry and his latest round of bad press. He never had much luck with the papers. He was an easy target. As his ascension to CEO neared, it seemed like the old Henry, the one who used to get in all sorts of mischief with Marcus, wanted one last hurrah.

I ignored the prickle of jealousy at the thought of Marcus's debaucherous days, reminding myself that I had those too. Mine were spectacular and luckily sealed in secrecy with Xander. "How bad is it?"

"Not bad. But he's been going through models and ballerinas like Veuve Clicquot at a socialite's brunch. Tabloids are having a ball with it."

"How's he doing?"

"He's being more careful, fewer nights out." In Marcus's absence, Xander had taken on the role of Henry's moderator. "Marcus noticed too; he asked me to check in on him. Henry seems fine. I think he's just stressed, and honestly, a little lonely."

Thankful that Xander was there to help Henry, I ran my arm around his torso and squeezed him.

Henry hadn't taken Marcus's absence well. They were best friends, and I could only imagine how abandoned Henry must have felt. I could hardly go a few days without talking to Xander. I was positive that was why Marcus was so nervous to tell Henry about us. He and Henry hadn't really moved past his absence yet.

Marcus hadn't mentioned anything to me about Henry or asking Xander to check in on him. The feeling burned in my stomach, making it turn. "He didn't mention it."

"You know Marcus, god complex." Xander's laugh was forced. He could hear the trepidation in my voice. "Why tell you when he could just fix it for you?"

Xander was right. Being in an actual relationship with Marcus made that incredibly clear. It wasn't a problem most of the time, but I hated that he felt he had to carry some burdens alone, as though we wouldn't love to help him.

"About that," Xander began, his face becoming serious. "I'm happy for you both, I am."

"But . . ."

"Marcus doesn't really do relationships. Hell, he kind of sucks at the ones he has now. I worry, that's all."

"Yeah." I sighed, thinking about the Zurich argument.

"Oh no." Xander grimaced. "I know *that* face."

"It's nothing. Typical Marcus stuff." I wished I could shake the feeling he was hiding things from me. "He doesn't open up all that much."

"Wow, you mean sex didn't fix everything?" Xander tilted his head and dramatically smacked his hand to his heart. "Crazy."

"A girl could hope." I grinned.

He barked a laugh. "He bought you a McLaren after a kiss, so maybe?"

"I don't know." I sighed, and my grin fell. "Sometimes he's so clear about what he wants, and other times it's like deciphering a dead language."

"That's such a Sloan way to put it." Xander's chest shook with a chuckle. "Did you talk to him about it or are you expecting him to guess?"

"I told him." *Mostly.*

"Then give him time."

I blew out an annoyed sigh. He was right. I had to be patient; it wasn't my strong suit. "I hate when you're right about this stuff."

"You're the one who forced me into therapy." He smiled impishly. "It's not my fault I'm so good at it."

"What about you?" I asked. He had to know that was coming. He was particularly evasive as of late. The last time I saw Xander really serious about someone was while I was in law school. He was finally getting into a good headspace again. His breakup with Reina took him a long time to recover from.

He only told me parts of why it happened, but he was heartbroken for years afterward. And he never let anyone get close enough to do that to him again. I blamed and hated her for it. It was unfair of me; I didn't know the whole story. But I saw the fallout. I put him back together, and it was enough for me.

"What would you like to know, Sloan?"

"Is there anyone you're seeing?" I asked as we turned the corner and re-entered the large atrium. His arms retracted close to his sides, as if bracing himself. "I promise no judgment or opinions—"

He chuckled. "I should think not. You're sleeping with my brother."

"I just want you to be happy, Xan."

"I promise I am."

I didn't move when he tried to steer me in the direction of the next wing. I gave him a hard look. "Paris? We always end up telling each other why we used them."

He ran a nervous hand through his dirty blond locks. He sat at a nearby bench, and I followed. With a long exhale, he leaned forward and rested his elbows on his knees. His gaze was straight-forward and stern. Stern Xander always scared me. I never knew where that might lead. "I saw her."

My heart dropped into my stomach. I didn't need to ask who. The way he said *her* made me sure it was Reina. "When?"

"New Year's Eve." He looked at me with a crooked smile. "Closure. Finally." He whispered the last word.

She had a strange power over him. Like he was waiting for something that never came. His love life had been on pause until it was sorted. Maybe now he'd let someone in. I threw my arms around him. "I'm proud of you."

"I'm proud of me too," he said with a chuckle and stood. He offered his hand to me as I did the same.

He motioned to me and began in a new direction, heading into the Egyptian exhibits, his favorites for bothering docents.

* * *

WE SPENT THE rest of the day getting lost in a few pubs, discussing our plans for our annual trip. I spent the whole morning figuring out how or if I should tell Xander about Van Der Baun's pseudo-offer.

"Jeez, what is it?" Xander put his beer down and sighed. The sudden thud of the pint hitting the table shook me from my thoughts. We had settled into a booth at a small pub near my townhouse. "You've had a weird look all day."

"I got an offer for managing partner." His face lifted, and his chest rose in excitement. "But, it's here, in London."

And it fell just as quickly. "Oh." His eyes were suddenly lost in thought.

"I'm not going to take it," I assured him. I hadn't actually decided that I wouldn't take it, but I didn't want it. If I was completely honest with myself, I didn't think I cared much for managing partner in general. Getting caught up in the next goal was blinding at times. "I'm going to use it as a bargaining chip. London was never something I wanted."

He still looked down at his pint and watched as the beads of condensation tracked slowly down the glass. "Only if that's what you want." He sighed and mustered a smile. "You need to stop worrying about me."

That was easier said than done. After everything we had faced together, we felt responsible for each other. "It would be me alone here, a fancy job and nothing else. That's never what I wanted."

"Yeah?" Relief entered his tone, and his shoulders relaxed.

I nodded. "And I haven't told Marcus about it."

"He doesn't love Henry and me nearly as much as he loves you," he replied off-handedly. "He'd just move here."

Love. My heart skipped.

Chapter 41

MARCUS

I got back from Zurich last night and went straight to Sloan's place. Xander was still in town for another day, and I knew she was still upset I didn't spend much time with him. She didn't show it, though, and we ignored it when I got back.

It wasn't worth all the tension. My meeting with the CEO of the Swiss biotech was useless. He was dead set against selling his company, and it left me at square one. Normally, I would have spent the next few weeks figuring out a way to force his hand, but right now, all I wanted was to show Sloan that I *was* trying to put her first and be as open with her as I could be.

When I woke up that morning, I was alone. A few minutes later, I found her downstairs. She stood in front of the stove, her hair pulled up in a messy bun, giving me access to that enticing spot on her neck.

"I thought you didn't cook." I groaned. Wrapping my arms around her waist, I breathed her in. She leaned back into me, and I kissed the spot on her neck that usually got her to stop her task and give me the attention I craved.

No luck.

I trailed a few kisses up her neck and stopped at her earlobe. She laughed softly as her breath shallowed. I looked forward to weekends with Sloan. She had cured me of my inability to sleep past dawn. The promise of being wrapped between her legs when she woke was too enticing to pass up.

"She does for me." Xander's loud voice rang through the kitchen. I took a moment to enjoy Sloan's body against mine before turning to see my brother sitting at the end of the kitchen island, smiling.

"When did you get here?" I asked.

"Right around the time you were feeling up my best friend."

"I don't cook for Xander, he just happens to be around when I cook." Sloan handed him a plate with an omelet on it.

"Same difference." Xander smiled smugly. "Sloan's got you sleeping in?"

"I was tired." I grinned despite myself.

"Eww." Xander didn't look up from his plate. "You know, normally the new boyfriend tries to impress me."

Before I could respond, Sloan interjected. "Whatever this is," she said, wagging her finger from Xander to me, "I can hear you, and I don't like it."

We finished having breakfast before Sloan left for a spa day with Penelope. Sloan wanted to give Xander and me some time together.

I figured we could use the day to catch a soccer match.

We got to the stadium and settled in one of the suites. I realized how long it had been since we did something fun together, just the two of us. I figured he'd love to take in a match. He'd been playing soccer since he could walk and became a D1 forward, who quickly became a college star.

He lived for the sport until our parents died. After that, the commitment of it all seemed to put him off. He watched matches but never played.

"So . . ." He kicked his feet onto an empty recliner at his side, flicked his hair aside, and smiled. "How are things?"

"Good." My mind drifted to Sloan. Aside from the Zurich trip, it felt like a dream, one I never wanted to wake from. "She's incredible."

He paused for a moment before the grin grew and stretched across his face. "You love her."

I did. I'd known that for a while. But the idea of telling her and awaiting a response I may never get was enough to keep me from admitting it.

"You don't need to admit it, your face did it for you," he taunted.

I didn't answer.

"She loves you too. I can tell."

I had spent my life looking out for my little brother, considering him too fragile to trust certain things. It was humbling to have leaned on him the last few weeks. It made me feel worse about the timing of the Zurich trip.

"Yeah?" My heart surged at the thought of her saying it.

"She told me about the McLaren. And the books." His grin was smug. "Trying to raise the bar so high nobody can meet it?"

I froze. Nobody would come after me because I was never letting her go. She was mine. I had the scratch marks on my back to prove it. "Nobody's going to fucking try."

Unless she decides it's over.

Every second closer we got to the board meeting in July, the more I felt the dread. The looming crash. Every move I'd made when it came to her family's company was at the behest of her grandfather. I was helping. I kept telling myself that. The deeper I fell for Sloan, the more I knew she may not see it that way.

There was a chance it would all go off without a hitch and maybe she'd never know. Or if she did, maybe she wouldn't care?

She'll care.

Xander grew quiet for a minute. "Be honest with her."

"What?"

"I don't know what it is that's making you look like you're about to be sick. Just be honest with her. I promise you, it is better than the full force of her wrath."

I knew Sloan wished I was more open with her, and I did try to be, but it was like learning a new language. I didn't often try things I knew I'd struggle with. Sloan was the exception.

I tried to keep myself from ever wanting anything so much that it would hurt if I lost it, and for a long time, it worked. But Sloan made me want everything. A deep, intractable desire for a life with her. A home. A family. Everything.

"Yeah." I knew he was right, but I couldn't tell her. I couldn't risk losing her, not when the entire world looked different when I had her.

We got a few drinks at the half and settled back in our seats.

"There's one last thing." There were a few minutes before the second half started. "There's a Holi celebration Jay invited Sloan to. You should go."

Blood drummed in my ears.

He asked her out, again?

My body tensed at the memory of him in her office. All I knew for sure was that nothing happened between them, but that knowledge did nothing to blunt the barbed grip on my chest. "She didn't tell me she was going to see him."

The thought of her lying to me made it hard to breathe.

"She's not. She's not going to go." The uncharacteristic firmness of his voice provided some relief. "But that's because of you. Sloan loves Holi. She wants to go, but probably doesn't want to broach the subject because Jay is the one who invited her. She would love it if you went with her."

I was suddenly very thankful that Xander went with her basically everywhere. I knew Sloan loved the holiday, a festival to usher in the start of spring. She and Henry weren't religious, but there were holidays—like Diwali and Holi—that Sloan loved.

My stomach churned with guilt. She felt the need to hide something from me.

"When you go, remember Jay is friends with Henry. Keep that in mind." That was Xander's subtle way of telling me to keep my hands to myself.

"I will."

"Although, it provides a good cover for you to scare him off for good."

I grinned. A skill I spent years perfecting.

Chapter 42

MARCUS

I sent my assistant to find me a kurta for the event. Not knowing what to get, she asked Xander. All I needed was to look at least half as good as I knew Sloan would, especially since Jay would be there attempting to check her off his conquest list.

I quickly forgot the anger when I thought about how good Sloan looked in the dresses. Taking Sloan to celebrate Holi got me thinking back to all those Diwali parties her family threw. The memories of the blouse, almost always stopping right above her mid-back, sent a molten heat through me. The way the skirt would sit at her hips, drawing my eyes to her stomach, alluringly toned thanks to the Pilates she did religiously.

As if the lewd thoughts summoned her, Sloan walked down the hallway and smiled. My mind went blank at the sight of her in a tight, beaded silver bodice that ended just below where her bra would have. A colorful yellow skirt fell from just below her navel.

"*Fuck,*" I whispered to myself.

I was so entranced I hadn't noticed the look on her face. "I forgot how good you looked in these." She drew near, ran her hands up my chest, and clasped them together around my neck. Looking up to me, she let out a small, wistful sigh.

Excitement flickered in her eyes, as it always did when I tried to tempt her. Apparently just wearing a kurta worked. I tucked that piece of information away for later.

I dropped my lips to her ear, suddenly no longer in the mood to do anything but remove the outfit I was just admiring. "How hard is this to put back on?" My hands ran down her bare sides and rested on her hips.

She giggled softly. "Too hard." She pulled back, but my hands stayed put. I remained hopeful I could persuade her to be a little late. "But I will need help taking it off later."

She gathered a few things and threw them into a small purse. Sloan was uncharacteristically quiet. She twisted her index finger into the colorful fabric of her skirt. Her face was calm and stoic, but her brown eyes illuminated with thought.

"Hey." I walked over and pulled her back into my arms. "You okay?"

She didn't move, but she nodded. "Maybe we shouldn't go."

This was one of her favorite holidays. I had spent the last few days looking through pictures I asked Xander to send me of past events they'd attended. She was beaming in all of them and had been excited about this all week. What changed?

We stood in silence for a few moments. I couldn't fend off the gnawing feeling that I was the difference.

She looked at the floor and sighed heavily. "It's like, if I show up with you, I'm a cliché. But if I show up with someone like Jay, I'm the mixed girl who's trying too hard."

I tried not to take that personally and rein in whatever mix of frustration and pain came rushing through me.

I was the reason. She didn't want to go because of me?

"No! That's not what I meant." Sloan read the concern on my face. She put her hands on either side of my face and kissed me in apology. "It's nothing to do with you. I just mean, I don't know if I want the judgment."

"Judgment?" I never realized just how much things like that weighed on her.

"It's always so draining. Trying to convince everyone I belong there too."

I wondered if it was their judgment of her or her own of herself that was the concern. I knew better than to offer my less-than-experienced insights, and let her continue.

"My name isn't Sloan." She twisted the fabric of her skirt more intensely.

Living under an alias was not the direction I thought this conversation would take. I had so many questions, but she needed to get it off her chest first. I took her hands in mine and leaned down to kiss her forehead.

"I mean, it is Sloan," she clarified, "but it wasn't always. I was born Saanvi Sloan Amari." She looked down shamefully, her shoulders slumped. "I begged my parents to change it when I was ten because I didn't like how weird it sounded. I refused to go to school for a while. There weren't exactly a lot of mixed kids at the time. I would hide from the nanny before drop-off. It got so bad that my dad would take me himself and walk me in. Even then, I would sneak out. After a few weeks, they bent, and we made Saanvi my middle name."

The idea of a ten-year-old Sloan evading every adult in her life made me smile.

Defiance personified.

Henry went to boarding school in Switzerland until high school. After his experience, their parents decided Sloan wouldn't go to boarding school. She went to one of the most exclusive private schools in Manhattan. One of the most interesting things I learned while becoming so successful was just how ignorant the upper crust of society could be.

It was nauseating and made me glad I went to public school in a boring suburban town.

"That story, about the fight and everything with Julian," she began. My muscles tensed. I had tried my best to keep my promise and let things be when all I wanted to do was find him and put him in the ground.

I nodded. She leaned against me, her head on my chest. "I broke up with him because he made me feel like that girl again, the one who was ashamed of her own name. And when I go to events like these, I feel like I don't belong. Then I remember just how hard I tried to make sure I never would."

"We don't have to go if you don't want to." I dropped a kiss on the top of her head. "But from my perspective, you've always fit in. And if it's something that makes you happy, the hell with everything else."

It was a massive simplification of everything she was going through, and if she really didn't want to go, I was happy to stay home. But I wanted that to be a choice she made because of what she wanted and not what she thought was expected.

She walked a tight rope between meeting and defying expectation every day of her life. All I wanted was to give her a place to land when she eventually got tired.

She was still for a few moments longer and looked up at me nervously as if she was about to say something. She stopped herself, then smiled. "Let's go."

* * *

As expected, Sloan had an amazing time. After the part of the festival where everyone ended up covered in an array of colors, she ran to me, throwing her arms around me with an excitement that reminded me of when she finished racing the McLaren.

"Careful." I reluctantly stepped back and peeled her arms off me. "You're going to get us caught."

"And we've been so good all day." She swept the powder-filled hair out of her face. Her laugh made our attempt at concealing our relationship worth it.

My heart swelled at the smile she gave me. "I make no promises once we get home."

"I'm going to grab some jalebi, and then we can go?" She looked around and gave me a sly peck on the cheek before running off.

Once she was out of sight, I looked at myself and smiled. I attempted to dust some of the power off and failed horribly.

"Xander's brother, right?"

Jay walked up beside me the second Sloan walked away. We had briefly greeted him politely when we arrived, and he introduced us to people who ran in similar circles as we did. But largely, to my relief, Sloan and I spent the day together.

Sloan was like Xander, always making friends. While I found it tedious, I played along because it made her happy. "Sloan told me she's seeing someone, so you can stand down."

He didn't know we were together. I had no reason to dislike him . . . other than the fact he made it known that he wanted to sleep with my girlfriend. "Her request to leave her alone isn't enough? You need the threat of someone enforcing it?"

His lips thinned, and he smiled. "You're taking bodyguard duty very seriously. I wonder, how's her boyfriend feel about your . . . protectiveness?"

"I don't often concern myself with how other people feel."

"Whatever you say." He shrugged with a knowing smile. "Well, whatever secret you two have, I have no vested interest in revealing it, so as I said earlier—you can stand down."

I didn't respond. I simply turned back to look in the direction

Sloan would be coming from any second. Xander was right. It was hard to hate this guy, but practice made perfect.

He turned to walk away but left me with one comment that left my jaw on edge. "I always figured it would be Xander."

Never mind. Hating him would be easy.

It would be a while before statements like those didn't piss me off.

* * *

WE ARRIVED AT my place exhausted, covered from head to toe in an array of colors, but seeing the fire that lit Sloan's eyes filled me with a second wind. "Want to help me change?" She walked a few steps ahead. She didn't turn back for an answer.

Something came over me in that moment. I was filled with a rush of deep yearning, an ache to tell her something. I didn't follow her. Instead, I grabbed her hand and pulled her back to where I stood.

She looked up at me with surprise. Just as she opened her mouth to say something, I said it.

"I love you," I told her. Her eyes went wide. Before she could say anything, I pressed my lips to hers. The scent of sandalwood and jasmine filled the air. "Sloan"—kiss—"Saanvi"—kiss—"whoever you are."

She giggled, and I kissed her again.

I pulled back, cupped her face in my hands, and swept the tears that welled in the corners of her eyes away with my thumbs. "I love you. Drunk on Christmas, patching me up on Thanksgiving, nearly set alight by a sparkler on Diwali, covered in colors on Holi, or eating paella on a random Wednesday. In whichever of the five languages you speak. In whatever outfit you make me want to rip off. I love you, Saanvi Sloan Amari."

Before being with Sloan, I was trying to forget.

Now all I wanted to do was remember. Every laugh, every smile, every single second. She lit up my world and made each moment better than the last.

Her chin wobbled. She took my hands in hers. A few stray tears streaked down her cheek. "I love you too."

Relief washed over me, extinguishing the fear and igniting something entirely new.

Chapter 43

SLOAN

Marcus loved me. And I loved him.

There were so many times I wanted to say it, but something had held me back: the lingering feeling that I would always take a back seat to other things.

But he loved me, and for now, that was enough.

I dragged his head down to mine and pulled him into a deep, passionate kiss. My fingers laced into his hair. Not breaking the kiss, I stepped back until I was stopped by the entryway wall.

All I wanted at that moment was to feel his lips and his body against mine. To be surrounded completely by him.

His fingers found the zipper and drawstring that held my skirt in place and released both. It pooled around my feet and left me in the red lace he loved so much. He growled with anticipation as I slid the skirt aside with my foot. His statuesque body pressed mine hard against the wall. The feel of his thick arousal against my groin sent delicious chills up my spine.

"Let's go to bed," he groaned in my ear. The air was thick with love and lust swirled together. I knew what he wanted—to take me to his bed and show me just how much he loved me. Over and over again until I was nearly passing out with exhaustion.

But I couldn't wait. I wanted him here. Now.

"No," I rasped. My body trembled with emotion. "Here."

My frantic hands found the bottom of the kurta and undid it. He took a tentative step back to remove the rest before his lips met mine again, pressing me back against the wall. The powdered colors on our bodies stained the white paint.

His touch scorched my skin as he slid his hand up my back to the tassels holding my top taut. He pulled it open.

"Is there red lace under here too?" His breath along my neck threw my senses into a frenzy. He pulled it down to find there was nothing underneath, leaving me standing in just my panties for his appraisal. He stopped for a moment to pull back and take me in. "Fuck. I love you."

"I love you." I traced my finger down his chiseled chest over his abs.

His mouth collided onto mine, quickly moving to my neck and then to my breasts. He took a hard peak into his mouth and teased me roughly with his teeth. The tightness in my body wound harder and harder. It begged for release. "Marcus. Please."

His hands reached my hips and slipped off the lacy barrier between us. He hooked my legs around his waist and pressed my back hard against the wall once more. "Anything you want, Sloan." He pushed his length into me slowly with uneven breaths. The pleasure seeped into his words as he read my body like he'd already memorized it. "I'll give it to you."

His arm reached out and braced against the wall while the other remained on my hip. He thrust deeper and harder. His tempo picked up. "You." That was all I had to gasp before he was fully unbridled. The familiar sound of his hips crashing against mine filled the entryway.

My fingers clutched his already well-marred back and sank into it as I tried to hold on. The pleasure building inside me became overwhelming. Finally, the feeling of densely packed heat exploded from my core through my entire body, leaving me trembling against him at his unrelenting pace. He followed moments later. "I love you, Sloan," he whispered softly in my ear.

"I love you." I wanted to say it over and over.

We remained that way, entwined against the wall, for a bit longer. He finally lifted his forehead to lean it against mine, our breathing slowed. He wiped a few tears I didn't realize I shed. My hands moved to the back of his neck and tugged gently.

"Mine," I commanded.

He smirked. "I've been yours for years."

"I love you." I cupped his face in my hands and enjoyed the feeling of being wholly secured in his arms.

"Never stop saying that."

"You're going to have to get this wall repainted." I laughed into his shoulder as he carried me to the couch that we collapsed onto. "And the couch cleaned."

Laying a soft kiss on my lips, he glanced at the now colorful wall in the entryway. "I should have it framed."

We lay there, tangled in each other's arms. "You taste like jalebi." Marcus broke away from a lazy kiss and smiled against my mouth.

"I don't think I ate anything else today. I'm pretty sure jalebi is why I had so many cavities as a kid."

My grandmother made them for me anytime we visited, and I made sure to eat all that was available to me. Thinking about her always brought up a wave of disappointment, mostly in myself. I wished I spent more time loving the parts of myself I tried so hard to hide as a kid.

I sighed deeply.

"You okay?"

"Mmmm." My nose nuzzled into the hollow of his neck. "I wonder if I'd feel less like an imposter at these things if I had stayed Saanvi."

"A rose by any other name." He ran his fingers through my hair. They gently brushed against my scalp. I loved that he caught onto my little game of scavenger hunt.

"Maybe when I have kids, I can give them more traditional names." I was thinking out loud, not really considering how that might sound until after I said it. Having known him for so long, I often forgot that we'd only been in a relationship for a couple of months. I winced at the inevitable assumption that we were moving too fast.

"Pick whichever first names you like." Marcus laid a kiss on my forehead. "Our kids will be Suttons regardless."

Our kids.

I'd have fallen into a full-on swoon if I wasn't already lying down.

Chapter 44

SLOAN

I peeled off my coat and walked into the kitchen.

"How's Penelope?" Marcus looked up from his laptop. He stood, leaning forward against the kitchen counter, looking at the laptop in front of him.

Penelope and I had brunch that morning. She and her ex had an awkward reunion over the weekend and she needed to rant about it. I'd only met her ex once when she first started at the firm. He was handsome and charming, and Penelope had a hard time getting over him for good.

"Good . . . well, she will be." I walked behind him to get a cup of coffee and he, seemingly acting on instinct, closed what looked like a set of bylaws he was looking at on his laptop screen.

I tried to ignore it, pressed a kiss on his cheek, and walked to the fridge.

It was probably work.

Marcus was always a very private person. He only said about a tenth of what he was thinking. Anyone close to him would eventually get used to deciphering what those few words meant.

It wasn't my business, whatever he was reading. If it *was* work, it was probably highly confidential, given the nature of his company.

I knew that.

It made sense.

It still made my stomach turn. Insecurity made me mistrustful. The last few weeks had been heavenly. We were in love, and everything between us felt strong and stable, like nothing could tear us apart.

That one stroke of the trackpad brought back all the insecurity that the Zurich argument unearthed.

"Worried about corporate espionage?" I asked as mildly as I could. I walked over to the other side of the counter and put the cup down. Technically, I was the competition. I owned stake in Amari Global and would eventually have a board seat, but it all seemed distant to me now.

He stood straight up and crossed his arms. There was a look of indecision before the corner of his mouth tipped up. "If you want information, I can think of much easier ways for you to get it out of me."

I didn't say anything. Today, the flirting didn't make me delirious. It made me suspicious. I left the coffee on the counter and turned down the hallway. I didn't want to fight, and I knew if I stood there and let the frustration build, we would.

There was a certain amount of built-in trust when it came to Marcus. He wouldn't do anything to ruin his relationship with Henry. While I hated the idea that the only thing that kept him from being truly deceitful was answering to my brother, it provided some cover. I only wished I was the reason.

"Can I show you something?" his voice called from the kitchen. I stopped for a moment and turned around, taking a few steps back.

"Sure," I said half-heartedly.

I walked over and stood in front of his laptop. He put his arms along either side of me and leaned forward. His chin dropped to my shoulder.

The screen was populated with a contract, a Swiss deed written in French. It wasn't what he was looking at when I walked by, but I tried not to overthink it.

It took me a lot longer than Marcus to translate French. After a minute, I realized what I was reading.

"You bought a house?" I asked. I inhaled sharply when I scrolled down to see both of our names were on the deed. "You bought us a house? In Switzerland?"

He didn't say anything as his fingers moved along the trackpad and opened up another screen. Pictures of a ski chalet in Zermatt.

"You don't need to buy me ski chalets, Marcus." I pressed a kiss on his chin. It was sweet, but only made me feel worse. The gift seemed generic, especially from the man who bought me the most thoughtful gifts I'd ever received. "My real estate holdings are more than sufficient."

His laugh was warm and heavy, a weighted blanket that smothered my insecurities, even if temporarily. "Trust me, Counselor, I know you don't need anyone to sweep you off your feet with extravagant gifts. You don't want a Prince Charming. And you don't need a knight in shining armor."

I turned back to the screen. "Then what are you?"

"Your future." His breath skittered along my collarbone. "And this is a small part of it."

I knew our relationship was serious, but the only future I ever imagined Marcus planning was the one for Sutton Industries. Occasionally he would say something that made me believe he was thinking about one we had together, but I was always too scared to talk about it. Too scared of the possibility that I'd be an afterthought.

My knees trembled, and I leaned back into him. "What does the rest of the future look like?"

I kept my eyes on the screen. My unsteady fingers scrolled down the page as I glanced at the details of the ski chalet.

"Winters spending some time skiing in Zermatt because you love it there. And you love it there because you used to visit Henry when he went to boarding school."

Henry hated his time there. My grandmother was dead set against sending him but was overruled by the rest of the family. So, she would take me to visit him all the time. The three of us would spend time along Lake Geneva in the spring, and in the winter we'd go to Zermatt. She would bring books in Hindi along to make sure neither of us forgot how to read or write it.

I was sure it came up at some point over all the years I'd known him, but how did he remember?

"Summers in East Hampton. In that blue Cape Cod–style house next to your family's house in Lily Pond. The one you always admire whenever you're there," he said. "We can take the jet to Goa because you love Vindalho and the beaches. But you hate swimming in the actual ocean. Stop in Singapore to see Penelope because you're going to miss her whenever she decides to move back."

His arms wrapped around my waist and paused. A long, drawn-out exhale followed, warming my neck with delightful sparks.

"Then, later, the kids will go to school in Manhattan. I worry about kids who go away to boarding school because . . . well, you've met Henry."

I laughed.

"Did I miss anything?" he whispered.

My words got caught in my throat. A life, built entirely with me in mind. Us in mind. The lingering fear that I wasn't a priority was finally silenced.

"Yeah." I turned and ran my hands up his chest and sucked in a deep, shaky breath. "What do *you* want?"

"I already have what I want."

I paused. I couldn't place the worry, but it remained. "Is everything okay?"

He nodded. His hand moved from my waist to cup my cheeks. "I'm sorry for how I scheduled the Zurich trip."

"I know." I ran a hand through his hair. He had trouble with situations he couldn't control, like when we disagreed. It gave him more anxiety than he ever showed.

"I can't ever lose you, Sloan." A deep fear coated his words.

A sharp ache grabbed tight hold of my heart. I always figured that was the fear that underpinned his reluctance to get close to people. He'd finally opened up to tell me.

I placed my hand over his. "You won't."

I leaned up to kiss him. Kiss away the pain, the fear, whatever it was that was between us. He groaned, pulling me closer, kissing me until my lips tingled. He pulled me into the bedroom, my shaky legs following.

Marcus took his time peeling off my clothes, and his fingers lingered on every dip and curve of my body. He crawled on top of me in the bed and kissed me again, mapping every inch of my body with his mouth, like he was trying to memorize it. Touching me like he wanted to slow time.

His lips trailed down between my legs, his stubble leaving a trail of goose bumps along my inner thigh.

"Marcus," I whimpered. My head arched up against the mattress when he parted my legs.

"I don't deserve you," he whispered as he laid a kiss at my entrance. "But I will." His lips kissed and grazed gently over my clit. "I promise I will." His tongue finally swept over me before he drew my clit into his mouth, sucking and grazing with more pressure.

I jolted up from the heated flare it sent up my spine. "Marcus, please." My hand ran through his hair.

The breathy plea was all he needed. Marcus spread his hand along my navel and pushed me flat against the mattress while his mouth kissed, licked, and sucked me. His fingers entered me, curling and thrusting with a well-practiced precision.

The pressure built until my body writhed with ecstasy. It exploded in waves I couldn't control. The moans, the tears, the pleas burst out of me without warning. His movements didn't stop until every wave of the orgasm had calmed.

My eyes were barely open when I felt him shift in the bed. His turbulent gaze met mine. He leaned over to kiss away the tears. "I love you," he whispered before he pulled away.

I shuddered as he positioned himself at my entrance. His eyes locked on mine, and I didn't dare look away. Not when he looked at me like *that*. Like nothing else in the world existed. Just me. My heart hammered in my chest, a boat on choppy waters. "I love you," I panted weakly in anticipation.

He pushed into me slowly, enjoying every pulse around him. His jaw flexed as he tried to maintain restraint despite the overwhelming pleasure.

"Never stop saying that." Marcus's husky voice sent electricity in all directions. He started a slow and sensual rhythm, leaning in to kiss me softly. I moaned softly in agreement.

"Never." His voice drowned under the sound of our bodies moving together, erasing everything else in the world. Each slow snap of his hips and every buck of mine got me closer. His taut muscles strained with each thrust.

His fingers pressed into my hips, angling them up to hit the spot that drove me to the edge. His thumb stroking rough circles over my clit pushed me over. My body erupted in pleasure again. His hips didn't stop, and he continued to climb until he released a loud, guttural groan. He paused, deep inside me, and climaxed.

Marcus lowered and leaned his head against mine and brushed a kiss on my lips. Our gazes locked. In his eyes, I could see our future. They held every hope I had for us.

Chapter 45

MARCUS

Weeks passed like days. Sloan's London project was wrapping up, and my work at the London office had been done for a while.

I had spent the last couple of weeks making the arrangements to formally turn operations back over to the New York office. With the work of the expansion complete, I was beginning to delegate more off to my executive team.

Not working fourteen-hour days left me with some time. I spent it rediscovering parts of myself I'd long buried, like a love of reading I'd ignored because it didn't make sense to waste my time on it. That, and trying to figure out how to get Sloan to move in with me. We were practically living together already.

There was the detail of telling Henry and her family. There was still a lot hanging in the air between that and telling her about the Amari Global Board discussing an alternative CEO when their grandfather eventually stepped down. Everything I did, I did to help. I hoped she'd see it that way.

I found myself unable to sleep. I lay in bed staring at the ceiling. My mind ran in a million different directions at all the uncomfortable conversations to come.

I should have told her today. I should have told her any day since

Brussels, but the fear of losing her had stopped me and kept me silent.

I looked over to her side of the bed and smiled.

Sloan slept peacefully next to me.

After I succeeded in distracting her from the movie we had planned to watch, we ended up in bed earlier than usual. Sloan fell asleep quickly after. The lead-up to the end of her project must have been wearing on her. She'd been more stressed recently.

I was shaken from my thoughts by a buzzing.

I looked over to see Sloan's phone lighting up on her nightstand. She was so sound asleep that she didn't hear it. After the first call went to voicemail, two more followed.

It was Henry.

He called multiple times in succession.

A chill trailed up my spine.

The calls stopped for a moment before my phone lit up.

My heart rate ticked up.

I swallowed hard, quietly moved off the bed, and made my way out of the bedroom as I picked up the phone.

"Hello?" My voice was almost a whisper. Now would have been a terrible time for Sloan to wake up.

"Shit, sorry. You guys are sleeping. Time difference."

I remained silent and tried to figure out what he knew before getting too worried. He sounded out of it.

"I called Sloan, but she's not picking up," Henry went on.

"It's close to midnight here," I said.

"Right." He paused. "She's sleeping."

"Henry." A shudder passed through me. "What's wrong?"

"It's, umm, it's my grandfather." My heart dropped. I felt my legs beginning to give way and was forced to lean against the wall. "He died today."

I was silent.

My mind immediately raced at the implications. I didn't allow myself any time to process or react to the news. He was a mentor, a friend, and the reason I was able to achieve what I had. That was what I did when I lost someone close to me. I kept moving.

"Can you get Sl—"

"I'll tell her. Whenever she's ready, we can head back to New York. I'll let you know when." I knew what he would ask: find Sloan, tell her, and get her home.

A sigh of relief came through. "I can't tell you how grateful I am for you. Thanks."

"I'm sorry, Henry." I tried to ignore the guilt seeping through me at his words. At that moment, his little sister was asleep, naked, in my bed.

I loved her. I wouldn't hurt her. He was still pissed about my absence for so long, so I knew when I told him about Sloan and me, he would be angry. Eventually, he'd understand and be okay with it. I didn't want to think of the alternative.

"Yeah. Me too."

The phone clicked.

I slid down the wall until I felt the floor beneath me. My heart beat loudly in my ears. The death didn't just mean I'd lost my mentor and Sloan her grandfather. Without him as cover, it meant my hope to keep my involvement in the Amari Global board a secret was gone. It was a matter of time now.

The sound of the clocking tick taunted me as I waited with a morbid anticipation.

* * *

MOST OF SLOAN's things had made their way to my place over the past few months, so packing for her was easy. When I woke her and broke the news, she wouldn't be in the headspace to pack things for herself. I figured anything I missed could be easily replaced when we landed in New York. I didn't want to wake her until I had to. Tonight was the last peaceful sleep she'd get in a while.

I sat in the kitchen, calling to get the jet ready for the morning when I heard the floor creak.

"Marcus?" Sloan walked slowly out of the hallway, her eyes adjusting to the light. She looked at the packed bags sitting a few feet away. Dressed only in one of my old college T-shirts, she nervously twisted the fabric between her fingers. "Is everything okay?"

I sat her down at the island beside me and broke the news. She cried for a moment at the shock, but after the immediate reaction, she showered and dressed quietly.

She remained that way on the plane. Her face was devoid of emotion while her eyes were a hurricane of them. Henry and Sloan had a difficult relationship with their parents and grandfather. Their childhoods were filled with nannies to raise them and great expectations to crush them. The only person who seemed like a true parental figure was their grandmother. There was a resentment still hanging around in both of them.

It wasn't until we landed in New York, arrived at my place, and saw Xander waiting for us that she cried. As if she'd saved up all of her vulnerability for when he was around to take it, she wrapped her arms tightly around his torso and sobbed deeply, ripping a hole in my chest at the sound.

She didn't mean anything by it. She was grieving. He was her best friend.

It made perfect sense, but it didn't placate the pressure in my chest, the feeling of my heart being removed with a rusty ice pike.

* * *

AFTER SLOAN WENT to sleep, Xander spent the next hour telling me not to read anything into her reaction. It bothered me, but that wasn't what weighed on me.

Xander and I sat quietly across from each other in the living room. It was almost three in the morning. We didn't really know what to do with ourselves. I was exhausted, but sure I wouldn't sleep. He seemed a little lost.

"I need to tell you something," I said. If he found out on his own, it would be worse. I was already on thin ice with Xander and Henry, and I couldn't tell Henry. Telling Sloan felt impossible.

He looked up and sat up straighter when the seriousness registered.

He was stone-faced and silent as I told him.

The board. The vote. The secret I'd been holding on to for over year.

"I get not telling Henry, for now. But you have to tell her." Irritation laced Xander's tone, and tension lined his shoulders. "Soon."

"I know," I said, mostly to myself.

Xander stood and raked a tired hand down through his hair. He took a breath and grabbed his keys off the coffee table. "I mean it. Soon," he repeated.

I nodded, and he started toward the door.

I went upstairs to try to get some sleep, knowing full well I wouldn't.

Chapter 46

SLOAN

We got into Manhattan early in the morning. I didn't sleep much on the flight.

I was exhausted when we got to Marcus's place. I fell asleep almost immediately when my body hit his mattress. These were not the circumstances I thought would precede my first night in that bed.

When I woke, I could hear voices downstairs talking. Henry was here. At some point, I felt Marcus curl up next to me. He probably had set an alarm to ensure he was out of bed before anyone else came by. I pulled myself up and remembered I probably should have gone to the guest room for that exact reason.

Marcus had the foresight to move my bags there. He left some clothes out on the nightstand for me to change into.

Always a step ahead.

I smiled at the thought. The idea that those skills were used to care for me filled me with warmth.

"Hey," Henry's voice greeted me as I descended the stairway. "You okay?"

They were all seated on the couch around the coffee table. Marcus and Xander turned to greet me. Marcus's gaze lingered, and his expression deflated when he realized I wouldn't be cuddling up against him in my still sleepy state.

I shrugged and plopped down next to Xander. More than anything, I felt guilty that I didn't feel more upset. When my grandmother passed, I remember being devastated and sobbing for hours on the couch at my parents' house. I was in my first year of law school and took an entire week away from classes to mourn.

It was the first funeral since the Sutton parents passed.

Xander handed me a cup filled to the brim with coffee. "What happened?" I asked.

My question summoned the horror the night the Suttons were in the accident. The broken pitch in Marcus's voice when he asked me the same question was something I couldn't forget. It was too late by the time he and Henry arrived at the hospital.

Xander had played the match of his life that day, and his parents were there to see it all. They always were. I tagged along to a celebratory dinner, and we all decided to head up to the Sutton family house for the weekend. We usually went out and partied with the team, and his parents went home after dinner. But that night was different; he was set on going home. Xander and I drove a few miles behind his parents' car.

There was a rain delay. The match started later than scheduled. The roads were still slick and coated in wet fallen leaves. When we caught up to the crash scene, it was gruesome. I tried to keep Xander from seeing it. The sound of his blood-curdling sobs rang in my ears for years.

Xander was a shell of a man for months. Marcus too. My hands shook at the pain they must have been going through today, another funeral reminding them of all they had lost. Another name added to the already long list.

"Doctors say it was cardiac arrest, probably a silent arrhythmia."

Henry shrugged and pulled me from the memory. The tears welled in my eyes. "Probably didn't feel anything."

The memory made my body rattle with the sobs I tried to contain. The tears fell like raindrops into my coffee. Xander's arms wrapped around my shoulders, and his chest muffled my low sobs.

The Suttons' death affected all of us differently. For me, it made any drastic change something to fear. A morbid anticipation of the fallout made me wary.

"Are you okay?" I asked him. The fear that something would shake them from the happiness in their lives terrified me, especially for Xander. I couldn't watch him fall back into the pit he was in years ago.

Xander gently pushed me back, his hands on my shoulders. The look of deep concern softened. "You have to stop worrying so much about me."

"Marcus?" I looked over at him; his expression was pained. Not jealous. Not possessive. He wanted to be the one to comfort me. The secret seemed so minor now. I wish we had told Henry when Xander found out.

He nodded. My gaze lingered on his before it moved to Henry.

I wondered how Henry felt about all of this. To say his relationship with our grandfather was strained was an understatement. "Are you okay?" I asked him.

Henry shrugged again. "I guess."

"Is it okay that I'm sad but not all that sad?" I asked him. He was the only one who'd understand it. I didn't know how to explain it. Of course, I was upset that my grandfather was gone. It left a hole in my heart. Almost all the happy memories of my childhood were of his house with my grandmother. Losing him felt like the doorway to that idyllic past was slammed shut. But most of my emotion around today was a fear of how Xander was handling all of it.

I was always close to my grandmother, but my grandfather always had a distance. The company was the most important thing in his world; we were often an afterthought. He loved us, but we never developed any type of relationship with him that centered around anything outside of the company.

"That makes two of us." Henry smiled softly. "He was a complicated man."

After I finished getting myself together, Henry and I went to see my parents. Services would be tomorrow, so Henry and I decided to stay with them for the night.

Chapter 47

MARCUS

After the services, the family returned to their Manhattan home.

Sloan and Henry's father, Shaan, let his children know what everyone long expected. He planned to step away from duties with the company. It was an open secret and the reason why the board was so keen on monitoring Henry's behavior.

Xander and I were going to leave when Sloan brought a pile of albums out and laid them on the coffee table. "You guys, look at these pictures of Henry at his first tennis match."

She pulled the photos out of the album, and we settled back in for a while longer. The moments when the family settled together always bothered me. Xander seemed to melt right in, but I always felt slightly out of place.

"Marcus, would you help me with some of these photos?" Sloan's mother, Beatrice, asked. It surprised the entire group, but everyone was absorbed in another photo a few seconds later. It was a well-known fact that she loved Xander. The two had a standing lunch in the city for years.

"There are a ton more albums downstairs," Sloan explained, not looking up when Xander drew her attention to another embarrassing picture of Henry.

Resting behind an unassuming brick façade, the Amari residence in Manhattan was deceptively large. Its five stories unfolded around a central spiral staircase, each depositing you to a sprawling marble landing. I only stepped out of the salon a minute after Beatrice, but by the time I walked through the corridor, she was gone down the grand staircase.

The distinctive clack of her heels led me downstairs. The first floor housed an expansive gym, a playroom, and an office. A box of albums sat in front of the office. I walked to the office door, and spindles of dread wrapped around me. I never been far enough into an adult relationship to meet the parents. But I'd known the Amaris my entire adult life. That had to count.

Beatrice stood behind the large mahogany desk in front of a stack of books with an open photo album at the top. There was a stack of old albums on the desk next to the pile of books, and a few strewn about the room. It was the most disorganized I'd ever seen it.

"These?" I asked. She shook her head and motioned for me to look at the album she'd opened. Beatrice was amiable, as always. Her light brown hair was pulled back into a neat bun, a proper society mother. Her perfectly manicured finger pointed to a photograph.

"This was taken at a rugby match."

I couldn't help but smile. The picture was of Henry and me before the match began. He was injured in the scrum, and after that, he stuck to tennis or boxing. Ironically, he sustained far more serious injuries from those endeavors.

"You two were inseparable for years." She smiled warmly and took a long pause. "When are you planning on telling Henry?"

Her tone lacked any irritation, but I felt my pulse tick up again. How did she know? "About?"

She raised her eyebrows. "I may not know my daughter as well as I should, but I know her well enough to know when she's in love."

My eyes darted around the floor. Beatrice became more moth-erly after our parents died. By that point, however, Sloan and Henry weren't really interested in her support. She did try, though. There was no point in lying to her. "Soon"

"Good. He'll be happy for you."

I had trouble believing that. Probably because Henry and I got into a lot of trouble together. He knew and saw everything. She didn't say anything about how she felt about my relationship with her daughter. Beatrice played it close to the vest.

"You're okay with it?" I asked. We'd concealed our relationship for months from the entire family. Beatrice was stoic, but she had to have some opinion on the matter.

She laughed. "Do you remember Sloan's law school graduation?"

I did. Every minute of it. She wore a red dress and sky-high heels that made her nearly as tall as me. She wore them in an act of defiance, knowing everyone would tell her she was too tall to wear them. The graduation was outdoors; I still remembered the way the wind picked up the loose waves in her hair. She was excited about her job at the firm. She wore the same perfume as she did now.

"I suspected for some time before that." She closed the album, handed it to me, and continued. "But that day, I knew. The way you looked at her, like you'd stop breathing if you looked away. My daughter isn't known for her patience. I'm surprised you waited so long."

I grinned and suddenly felt lighter. The boundaries I thought I'd crossed when pursuing Sloan seemed inconsequential now.

"There was a brief period I thought maybe I was wrong." She walked to me and laid her hands on my shoulders. She shook her head in disappointment. "I was starting to think you'd run away forever."

"I won't ever leave her."

"Good." She stacked the albums and handed them to me. "I

expect you to be at Thanksgiving every year from now on. No exceptions."

* * *

THAT NIGHT, SLOAN came home with me.

She stood in the kitchen in her pajamas, the short silk ones that drove me crazy, reading some documents for work.

Enraptured by a merger document, she didn't hear me walk up behind her. She jolted back when she felt my breath on her neck. "I'm going to take a quick shower," I whispered in her ear. She let out a contented sigh when I pulled her into me. Her shoulders fell, and my face got lost in the hair that swept along her neck.

I needed to tell her about the board, the last secret between us. Her body leaned back against mine, fitting against me perfectly. The temptation of holding her tightly all night was too strong to deny today.

I would tell her in the morning.

Chapter 48

SLOAN

The will would be read to the family at my parents' house tomorrow. I was drained already. The only silver lining to this day was coming home to Marcus's place. All I wanted was to lie in bed, wrapped up in his arms. We'd tell them soon. The weight of the secret was taking a toll on him. I could feel it.

I reviewed a few merger agreements, then turned my attention to the twelve names that would soon decide Henry's fate.

The board.

With my grandfather's passing and my father taking a step back from the company, Henry would be interim CEO. It meant the board would have to vote to retain him in perpetuity. Normally, it wouldn't be a concern. Henry could handle the job. But his extra-curriculars were getting attention. I knew that meant we needed to ensure he had the votes to remain at the helm.

I tried to figure out how we could get to six votes. A tie would mean a stakeholder vote, and the family had enough stake to keep Henry in charge, but that wouldn't look great publicly.

Ideally, we would have seven, but I was stuck at three definitive yes-votes.

I was a board member now since my grandfather's passing,

which meant I would have the second largest stake in the company. My yes-vote made four.

There were four swing votes. Three that were probably no-votes. And one I didn't know anything about. Marie Therese Anderson.

The original acquisition papers stated it was the board seat added by the Ellory acquisition, but I tried to find something, anything about a woman by that name in the industry, and nothing. She presumably had a stake in the company prior to the acquisition, but all I could find was her name on papers and no evidence of her.

Something didn't fit.

It was a French name, which was odd given that Ellory was based in the United States. Thinking harder, I searched my mind for any other way that name was familiar. I was randomly reminded of the Bourbon line.

The French royal house.

Louis, Philippe, Marie Therese. All legitimate heirs of Louis the Fourteenth, the Bourbon French king who built Versailles and adorned it with the coat of arms and the fleur-de-lys.

My heart beat loudly in my ears.

My mind raced.

Xander's middle name was Phillipe.

Marcus's was Louis.

Their mother was a French history scholar, and half the reason I knew so much about it was her.

It couldn't be.

Marcus having a proxy board seat didn't make sense. My hands began to tremble as I scanned the kitchen and came upon his laptop sitting on the couch.

I stopped for a moment, frozen in fear. It couldn't be him. I was being paranoid and not thinking clearly out of grief. Why would he want a secret seat on the board?

I knew the reason but refused to believe it. Not the man who said he loved me, the one I'd practically been living with for months. He wouldn't keep something like that from me. A fog of hurt and betrayal hung over me.

My legs and arms moved of their own accord. I opened his laptop to the password screen before I realized I had done it. I stared at the screen and knew it had to be related. The Sutton brothers hardly ever talked about their parents to anyone other than Henry or me. The connection to French history was something I overlooked a million times when I reviewed the board names. It was the perfect password.

It clicked. With trembling hands, I typed "Clovis."

As the legend went, he was the King of the Franks when the fleur-de-lys symbol became an established symbol of the monarchy. It was a fact I only knew because of their mother.

Another ten-character code followed. It would be something nobody would assume. No names or places. Something he hid, but could never forget. Not his parents, that was still publicly available information. Not Xander, his only remaining family, that could be guessed.

A sharp pain pierced my chest, and I typed in *my* phone number. I was in.

Almost like it was waiting for me, the Amari Global board list was open. I scanned through a few files to confirm what I feared. Ellory was a smokescreen; it was a shell company. The entire acquisition was for the board seat. The one Marcus now had control over.

He had stake in the company, a seat on the board, a list of the members he'd need to sway.

My stomach hollowed, and something caustic filled it.

No.

What I thought couldn't possibly be true. He couldn't be trying to take over.

So dizzy at the revelation, I didn't hear the shower turn off, the footsteps down the stairs, or even him when he called my name the first time.

"Sloan?"

I was caught reading confidential material on his computer, not that I was the one who had any explaining to do.

"Marie Therese?" Waves of nausea rolled through me when I turned to him, and his expression was all the confession I needed. My voice shook, and tears welled in my eyes as I tried to control the deep, gut-wrenching betrayal. "Why is a dead French princess on our board?"

"Sloan." He approached me slowly, like he was walking toward a viper. He may as well have been with all the anger and hurt threatening to boil over. "Let me explain."

"Explain why you have a proxy seat on the board?" The searing pain from his lie fueled my anger as it sped past logic. "Why else? A board seat means control with my grandfather out of the way."

He recoiled like he'd been slapped. His body was tense, jaw tight, eyes in a fury. "Sloan, that's not—"

"It has to be the reason. It's the only real competition."

I'd been so enveloped in figuring out how to get the votes Henry needed, I didn't think about what the alternative was. In the event Henry got a vote of no confidence, the board would nominate someone else. That someone else needed a stake in the company and favor with the board.

"God, listen to yourself, Sloan." He raised his voice, hiding the pain from my accusations. "You have spent your whole life wishing for something you don't even fucking want. What makes you think I want it?"

The realization that Marcus was lying to me whipped me into a frenzy. The lie was a means to an end, but I hadn't taken a second to understand what that end was. I chose the worst option and ran with it, knowing the accusation alone would hurt him. Judging by the look on his face, it worked.

I couldn't think straight. The room felt like it was spinning, the only thing that grounded me was my anger. My enraged brain kept reminding me that Marcus was always calculated. He didn't make mistakes. He didn't slip up.

Every move was purposeful.

We'd learn our inheritance tomorrow, but I already knew I'd have the second largest stake in the company. His stake in the company, through the Ellory board seat, meant he could be nominated to take over as CEO.

My vote would be useful. And he knew that.

He's always been hiding something.

I could feel it every night we went to bed. He was always holding something back.

"Was I a part of the plan?" My voice broke, and a sob slipped through.

I'd never seen that face before. The one of complete and utter devastation. The question leveled him.

Silence passed for a moment.

He closed the space between us and cupped my face in his hands. I let him. I wanted it to go away, the anguish and betrayal. I wanted him to make it all go away. "Of course not, Sloan—"

"Then why?" Another sob slipped loose. I pulled his hands off me, but I didn't step away. The memories of all those nights we stayed up talking and making love replayed like a spiteful movie. "Why have you been lying to me?"

There was a war of indecision in his eyes. "Ellory is my company. The acquisition was purposeful. Your grandfather asked me to do it a year ago. It meant an additional seat on the board, one that would vote in favor of Henry's succession."

My hand flattened against on his chest and lay there a second, unsure. I pushed him away.

"Why?" My voice regained its steadiness, and my heart hammered in its place.

"Someone he could trust to vote in Henry's favor, if it came down to it when he retired." He took a step closer to me. "I wanted to tell you."

"Why didn't you?" I snapped, even though I knew he was probably asked to keep it a secret. "And a promise to my grandfather is a flimsy reason."

He was silent.

It didn't make sense. If it was that simple, then he could have told me. He *would* have told me. He didn't intend to contest Henry's succession; he meant to strengthen it. Then what was it that kept him from telling me? Keeping it a secret from Henry made sense, but me?

I paused.

I had a stake in the company.

I had a board seat and was more than qualified.

"Who were they planning to nominate?" Venom coated my tone. "The board. If not you, then who?"

"Sloan, I thought you didn't—"

"Who." I didn't want an explanation. I wanted an answer, even though I knew it.

His eyes darted away from my face. "You."

"The McLaren, the books, Zermatt," I listed off with a bitter laugh. The anger concentrated into spite. "All ways to distract me so I wouldn't mind when you helped ensure I didn't get the only thing I've ever wanted."

"Do you? *Actually*, want it?"

"It doesn't matter, you should have—"

Before I could answer, a new voice filled the room, then suddenly stopped. "Marcus, when were you going to tell me about having a seat on—"

Caught up in our argument, neither of us heard Henry enter. We looked at him at the same time. His mouth was agape, his face etched in disbelief.

He stood stunned into silence at the sight of us. I was in my silk pajamas. Tight silk tank top and short bottoms that ended just below my butt were never something I wanted to wear in front of my brother.

The room was stuck in silence, and his eyes darted between us. It only took a few seconds to put it all together. I was supposed to be at home. Clearly, he'd just showered, and we were both dressed for bed.

"Henry." Marcus's voice was stern but with his trademark control, trying to head off the inevitable implication. "Listen—"

"My *little* sister?" Henry took a couple of determined strides toward Marcus. Fury poured off him in waves. I grabbed Henry's arm and yanked him back with surprising force. The logical part of my brain finally cleared the fog. I knew the argument would escalate out of control if I let it. "I'm going to fucking kill you."

Whatever civil conversation Henry planned to have wasn't going to happen now.

"Yes, Henry, because that's what you need right now, an assault charge." I stood in front of Henry, but he was entirely focused on Marcus. Marcus would never escalate a fight, but the accusation that he might would hurt him, and that's all I wanted in that moment.

Henry finally took a step back, and I shoved him further. I stood between the two of them.

"Lying to me about Ellory, abandoning us for years, that isn't enough?" Henry shook off my hand and took a step closer, his face flushed with anger. "You screwed Sloan? What the fuck is wrong with you?"

"Listen—" Marcus's voice rose over Henry's.

"No," I interrupted calmly. My heart raced, but I wasn't going to let Marcus have any more of my anger. He'd taken enough from me. I looked directly at Henry. "Outside, now."

"Sloan—" Henry protested.

"Now," I barked. He recoiled in surprise. Henry wanted to fight. Hell, so did I. But we needed to leave, before I said something I couldn't take back. Not for Marcus's sake, but for Xander's. "I mean it. I want to leave."

Henry looked at me, and his features immediately softened. His pinched expression changed to concern for me. For the first time in years, it didn't make me angry. My protective older brother was always there, behind the man that bickered with me.

"Do not call her," Henry warned Marcus, stepping backward as I pushed him to the door.

I threw a jacket over the little clothing I was wearing. Too angry to think, I grabbed my bag, laptop, and Henry's arm. I pulled him out the door. I stopped in the threshold and met his gaze one last time.

"Sloan, please let me explain."

The pleading sound in his voice almost made me stop.

"Despite what my grandfather thought, I could lead just as well as Henry. But it's nice to know you agreed with him."

I walked out knowing exactly how much it would hurt him.

* * *

WE WERE SILENT for a few minutes in the town car on the way back to Henry's place on the Upper East Side.

"The board seat is to ensure the vote," I said into the silence, staring at the floor of the town car. That was why Henry was there;

he figured out the same thing I did. "With my vote and his, all you need is one of the swing-votes."

He sighed. "Yeah. I figured." He gently shook the rolled-up papers in his hand. "Grandfather was always a few steps ahead."

"At least now, it's probably one less thing to worry about." I knew the vote weighed on Henry more than he had let on the last few months.

"You know, you'd probably get the votes you'd need if you wanted to unseat me," he suggested. The corners of his mouth tipped up. "Do you?"

I grinned at his levity; I was sure he was joking. "You were meant for it, not me."

He was always the future of the company. For a long time, I thought I wanted it. What I actually wanted was acknowledgment that I could do it. Approval. If I was completely honest with myself, I had stopped caring about the approval too. I held on to to the resentment because letting it go felt like agreement. My anger was largely out of spite. It was way past time I let it go.

"Doesn't answer my question." His tone became serious.

I exhaled a deep breath. "No. Honestly, I don't."

He looked out the window, and the car got quiet again. "Stay with me tonight. You shouldn't be alone," he offered, his eyes fixed on the passing traffic. We were entering the part of the conversation that made him uncomfortable.

"I'm fine."

"Sloan." His lips thinned. "For once, let me help."

My shoulders slumped. "Fine."

"Are you okay?" His eyes met mine.

I nodded.

He opened his mouth a few times, but said no more. We were silent the rest of the car ride.

"Sloan?" Henry stopped me after we arrived and stood in the

foyer. He laid his hands on my shoulders. "I'll kick his ass if it makes you feel better."

I laughed. I missed Henry. Competing had turned us against each other. I couldn't let that happen again. "I'm okay, Hen." I shrugged. "At least now you know."

Chapter 49

MARCUS

I swirled the whiskey in my glass and took another sip. It was close to midnight, and I couldn't sleep.

I tried to go to bed, but the pillows smelled like her from the other night.

It was a fight, a big one, but couples did that. It would be fine. It had to be.

For the record, I wanted to stay out of it. But I owed it to their grandfather. I owed it to Henry too. He went through a lot in the last few years, and the only person he ever leaned on wasn't around.

Henry and Sloan's grandfather, Rishi, called me a little over a year ago and told me his plans to step down and pass the company directly to Henry, circumventing Henry's father. I thought it was a great idea. Henry was more than capable.

The only problem was the terrible press Henry seemed to get. He was dangerously close to being voted down as the next CEO when Rishi eventually stepped aside. The last year was spent trying to avert some of the bad press, to avoid a vote of no confidence. When that didn't work, we tried to ensure the vote—adding a seat to the board, swaying members as we could.

Nobody associated with the company could have set up a shell corporation to be acquired by Amari Global, so I was the perfect choice. I had the capital to do it, and Rishi could trust me to eventually vote in Henry's favor when the time came. The circumstances also meant keeping all of it quiet was essential. Henry couldn't be involved in any of it.

At the time, the impact on Sloan was an afterthought. I always assumed she was past it. By the time Sloan and I were on the jet on our way to London after the new year, the wheels were well in motion. By the time I realized how much it weighed on her, I couldn't tell her. I was too scared to. I hoped it was something she'd never need to know. If Rishi hadn't passed, he would have retired in a couple years and Henry would have succeeded him, as planned.

Over the last couple of months, I wanted to show her that it would be different with me. Instead, I lied to her and proved that it was more of the same. Everyone else's wishes ahead of hers.

I was roused from my thoughts when I heard a knock at the door.

My pulse picked up with hope. All I wanted was to go to bed with her in my arms. We could figure everything out tomorrow.

It was Henry and Xander.

"I told him why you have the board seat, and everything else," Xander explained flatly at my surprise. "And before you ask, she's at Henry's place. You can fill Henry in on *those* details."

Xander walked past into the entryway, leaving Henry looking down at the steps with indecision.

I opened the door wider and stepped out of the way. Henry silently passed over the threshold and followed Xander. He and Xander took seats at the dining table. I poured the three of us glasses of whiskey and joined them.

We sat in silence.

Years of friendship with Henry, countless arguments, occasional physical altercations, we'd endured it all.

"Do we have anything we'd like to say to one another?" After another few silent minutes, Xander's patronizing tone filled the room. He folded his hands on the table neatly, looking at me and then at Henry, like a disappointed parent.

Silence.

"Really? Nothing?" he pressed on. "I got pulled out of bed for this?"

"Thanks for locking the door this time. I didn't want to walk in on whoever you were *entertaining* next." Henry's fingers gripped the glass tightly.

Xander wiped his hand down his face.

The accusation was fair. He had no reason to believe I would treat Sloan differently than the other women I'd dated. He ignored the fact that he was my best friend and I'd never risk that on something fleeting. Although, how could he believe anything I said, given what just happened?

"I would never do that to her," I assured him.

"Because you're a changed man?" he scoffed with a mocking laugh. "Does Sloan know that you've done all the same shit the tabloids publish about me?"

She did. I never explicitly told her about those days, but we'd circled the subject before. She had her wild streak, and I had mine. His concern for her was expected. The secrecy was the problem. And the fact that Xander knew while he was in the dark didn't help.

"Fuck," Henry continued. "She's my little sister. What the fuck were you thinking?"

"It's not something fleeting. It's a relationship, a real one," I snapped. "We should have told you sooner."

"Yeah, you should have." His tone lost some of its sharpness. "I guess it was better I walked in on an argument than . . ." Henry stopped himself when he realized where he was going, and shivered in disgust.

"Look," I said when the room quieted again. "I'm in love with her."

Henry's brows furrowed. "What?"

"I have been for a while."

"So . . ." He leaned his head on his hand. "What does all this mean? You want to date her? You *are* dating her?" Henry looked to Xander. "Xander didn't tell me anything about the Sloan stuff."

"I want everything with her. Date her, marry her, have a life and kids with her." Despite the confession, my chest felt heavier. "I don't know how long it'll take for her to forgive me for this mess, but I'm not going to stop trying until she does."

Henry went silent again, longer this time.

"She'll forgive you." He finally broke the tension. "She doesn't want the company. She was angry." Henry shifted uncomfortably. "Just don't fuck it up." His warning sounded more like a question. "What do we do if you guys fall out?"

"We won't." I didn't have an actual plan for that scenario. Whatever happened with Sloan, I'd fix it. There wasn't a single thing I wouldn't do to make her happy. Not a single line I wouldn't cross to keep her that way. "Anything I mess up, I'll fix."

He nodded and raked a hand through his hair. "About everything else . . ."

"I should have told you."

"Yeah," Henry snapped. "I didn't need to figure it out on my own, and then have Xander and Sloan fill in the missing pieces. It's something my best friend should have told me himself."

"I know."

After a long pause, he downed the last of the whiskey in his glass. "Why didn't you tell me?"

"Plausible deniability. Rishi asked me not to. Did you think you'd take it well?" I groaned and ran a hand through my hair. He knew why. But in the past, I'd have told him. "I'm sorry."

I never wanted to get involved. But I needed to help Henry because I knew if the roles were reversed, he'd help me. I had years of evidence of that.

"Look," Henry began. "I know you and my grandfather were close, but you didn't know him like Sloan and I did. You saw the captain of industry, the one whose instincts were always right. The one who asked for forgiveness and never permission. As your friend, I am warning you, don't be like him. Because Sloan and I saw the man who put us in competition with each other from the time we were kids. The man who loved us but put his own ambition ahead of everything. He saddled us with his impossible expectations. He was a good man, a great one, but you don't owe him anything."

His words hung in the air.

I knew my success was mine, logically, but I'd felt indebted to their grandfather. And a little guilty for how Henry and Sloan often shrank under his expectations. In the end, I put his wishes ahead of telling Sloan the truth.

I had made that mistake twice now, putting other interests ahead of Sloan. I couldn't make it again.

"And thank you," Henry said, turning his empty glass on the table. "You've always had my back. I'm sorry all of *that* got out of hand."

"It's fine. We okay?" I asked.

He nodded, pushed his seat back, and got up from the table. "I think having to see my little sister in lingerie makes us even for your help with the board."

"Those were pajamas, not her lingerie." Low blow, but it was the last one. Besides, I had spent the last year helping him, even if it meant being a pretty shitty friend. He and Xander winced. "Now we're even."

He stuck up his middle finger and made his way to the door. "See you tomorrow, asshole."

* * *

THAT LEFT XANDER and me at the table. I dumped my face in my hands. It had been a long few days.

"You can say it." My hands muffled my voice.

"Say what?" Xander asked.

"That you were right."

"You look like you've been through enough." Xander sighed.

"I'm sorry."

"You've been saying that a lot lately."

"I mean it. I shut you out—not just now, but for years," I began. "I thought I was protecting you, doing what was best. I didn't want you to have to deal with certain things, so I kept them from you. I shouldn't have done that."

Xander sighed again and looked down at the table. "I know. I didn't make it easy for you to believe I could handle it."

He didn't keep a lot of serious secrets; most were silly and a part of his infuriating I-owe-you game with Sloan. The few he did have surrounded his spiral after our parents' death. There was another one I knew almost nothing about. He and Sloan sealed that off in one of their covenants.

"You ever gonna tell me about all of that?" I asked, referring to the times he spun out.

"Maybe." He gave me a crooked smile and shrugged. "I'm guessing she got a little scary-angry today?"

"Yeah." The only other time I saw a glimpse of that anger was the night of their surprise visit in London.

"I did warn you. Full-tilt Sloan is terrifying." Xander looked up at me sympathetically. "When she gets that upset, it's a blind rage. She only says and does the things she knows will hurt."

Like walking out.

I hoped it was out of spite or to hurt me because she knew it would. Not that she actually wanted an out.

"What do I do?" I hated that I had to ask.

His chest shook with a silent laugh. "You've been secretly sending her first editions of all of her favorite books, and you bought her a chalet in the place she loved because she spent time there with her favorite family member . . . and Henry." He grinned. "I think you know how to show her she's your priority."

"But she doesn't believe it," I confessed. The knife lodged in my chest twisted. She thought it was all a plot or scheme to make the truth more palatable. It wasn't. I wanted her to see it was different with me. I couldn't change what was already in motion. But from then on, her needs were the most important.

"Well, you did lie to her for months."

"I know where I fucked up," I snapped.

I was terrified to lose her. So terrified, I made an amateur miscalculation. If I'd been thinking clearly, I would've played the odds and told her. Odds were that she'd be angry, but she'd understand—she didn't want to be CEO. But with Sloan, even a chance that the odds wouldn't be in my favor was too much to risk.

"Good." He walked over to me, slapped a supportive hand on my shoulder, and yawned. "You two will figure it out."

I nodded, and Xander left for the night.

Chapter 50

SLOAN

I left immediately after the will was read. I avoided my mother's flurry of questions when she noticed I was avoiding the Sutton brothers. Needing to seek refuge and figure my shit out, I went to work.

Not that it helped. I spent the morning looking at the same names over and over again. Marcus knew better than anyone how to approach the board situation. The sensible thing to do would be to see him and figure it all out. The only benefit to coming in to work while I was on bereavement leave was getting a straight conversation out of Reese about my promotion to senior partner.

The London offer was legit. It was everything I thought I wanted. And I wouldn't need to wait. My promotion to senior partner still hadn't been officially announced, so I considered it.

Now that I was finally home, I couldn't figure out how I could make it work. Or, if I wanted to try to make it work. And then there was Marcus.

"I was half expecting bangs." Xander's voice yanked me out of the engulfing hurt. The weight of the sadness immediately lifted at the sight of his comforting green eyes and that charming smile.

"Laney took my scissors." I tapped my pen against my desk and flicked my gaze to my assistant's desk. It was too soon to be considering trauma bangs.

"I must have missed your call." He rolled his eyes. Hurt was scribbled all over his face.

I winced. We told each other everything, or we used to. "Xan . . ."

My shoulders fell in a deep sigh. He crossed the office and hugged me. Based on the level of camaraderie this morning, I gathered that Marcus and Henry had worked things out and Xander knew what had happened.

I stood so I could lean into him and he wouldn't see the lone tear that streaked down my face. I had missed my best friend. "I swear," he said, "if you've been crying to Penelope, I will—"

"She doesn't get back till next week." I hiccupped a laugh. A few silent seconds passed. "Did you know?"

He was here and relatively calm. That meant he wasn't surprised. Whenever someone hurt me, Xander became a different version of himself. A glimpse of it came out in London, but instead of playing the protector, he was mediating. If I didn't already believe Xander was onboard with the relationship, that was proof.

Xander held my shoulders and pushed me back to look me squarely in the eye. "Yes. It wasn't my secret to tell. I'm sorry."

I nodded. He was already in the middle, and now even more so. Oddly, knowing that Xander already knew made it feel less painful.

"Why not go and talk to him?" he asked.

"He lied to me." It sounded almost benign when I said it out loud.

Marcus knew everything about me. I had spent the last six months opening up to him more than anyone I'd ever dated, and he had held on to something monumental the entire time. He knew how I felt about the company, and he still kept it a secret. I didn't care that Henry would take over. I cared that he was so comfortable keeping me in the dark.

That was the crux of it. I trusted him with everything, and he still kept me at arm's length. There were moments when I felt like I was being let in, but others when I felt like I was on the outside looking in.

"And then you walked out instead of talking through it."

"Whose side are you on?" I asked. It was meant to be light, but Xander's expression grew serious.

"Grow up, Sloan. I'm on the side of what's best for you. I'm not always going to agree with you to make you feel better. Sometimes, *you* need to be pushed in the right direction." He didn't wait for me to object. "He fucked up, big. But you're in an adult relationship. You can't just walk out whenever you're angry."

"I know." I knew walking out would hurt him, that's why I did it. When I felt cornered or hurt, I lashed out and went straight for the jugular.

That's when I realized how much he'd opened to me. I couldn't hurt him so deeply without knowing him as well as I did now. I always attributed his unrelenting commitment to his career and company to self-importance. It wasn't that at all. He wanted to be needed because you couldn't be abandoned when you were useful.

"You two are exhausting," Xander groaned. "Do you want this to work?"

"Yes."

"Then you two need to fix this before you can't."

"It was just a fight." The angry fog from the argument lifted last night. I knew what I wanted, and it was always him. "Right?"

"It better be." His almost lighthearted laugh eased my nerves. "If not, we're in the origin story of Marcus's supervillain era."

"Xan." I sighed, more deeply this time. I didn't want to face it all today.

"Let's go." He took a step back and gestured to the door, knowing what I was going to ask. I wanted to sit on the couch, cry a little, and drink some wine. I needed my best friend for that.

* * *

"I TALKED TO Reese today. He didn't know about Van Der Baun's offer." I leaned against the countertop in Xander's kitchen.

Luckily, after Van der Baun's initial offer, I was able to sit down with Jay Sachi and work in some terms in the Burton merger. Those terms included my ongoing counsel . . . in the New York office. Jay was easy to convince. Even though there wasn't anything in it for him, he'd remain in London and have very little contact with the firm moving forward.

That little addition meant the firm would lose one of its biggest clients if they didn't make good on the promises made to me at the outset. Nobody double-crossed an Amari.

"Are they fighting over you now?" Xander grinned and pulled out a bottle of wine. "If so, I would like a dedicated office space in the negotiations. I don't like Penelope being around you so damn much these days."

"It's hardly a fight. Reese is drawing up the paperwork. I'll be partner here in the New York office, as planned." I took the glass he poured for me and walked over to couch. I was beginning to question if I wanted what I'd been chasing for so long. The vicious need to be perfect bled into every aspect of my life and often kept me from happiness. "And this best friend competition you have going on, Pen isn't even playing."

"So, I'm playing with myself?"

I laughed and glanced over my shoulder. "Happens to the best of us, Xan."

It had been months since we'd had a movie night, and since I wasn't in the mood to face my problems just yet, Xander caved and agreed to watching a couple of murder mysteries. I sat down on the couch and reached into my bag for my phone when I saw something.

It was the brown leather-bound journal I got for Marcus years ago.

In my anger, I must have grabbed it with my things. I put my glass down on the coffee table and opened the front cover. It was empty except for a few random notes in the first few pages. Curiosity got the best of me, and I flipped through the blank pages until I noticed the lip in the back cover. A picture fell out and onto the floor.

I leaned down and picked it up. It was the picture of the four of us at my law school graduation. On the back of the photo was my handwriting:

Don't lose this.

Emotion swelled in my chest.

Every so often, something like *that* would happen. A small reminder that I'd never left his heart all this time. I gave copies of the photo to Henry, Xander, and Marcus. Each had a different note from me; that one was his.

It went with him everywhere. He kept it like a vow. To me.

I could faintly hear the sound of Xander's voice. "You sure you don't want to talk to him?"

I nodded. "I'll call him tomorrow."

He rolled his eyes. "Call him now."

"Xan, please," I begged. Something about reconciling scared me. He owned every part of my heart; I wouldn't be able to pick up the pieces if he ever broke it.

"Fine," he groaned. "But I'm telling him you're here."

I gave him a hard look.

"Like I said." He shrugged. "Sometimes you need a push."

Chapter 51

MARCUS

Sloan ignored all my calls all day.

She was in attendance this morning, but left before anyone could talk to her. She was still angry. I tried to work, but I spent the entire day staring at my phone. The only distraction I had was that I couldn't find my journal anywhere, the one she gave me years ago. I always had it on me. That was driving me crazy.

Sloan did text me once to tell me that she was fine, but that did nothing to ease the anxiety. I left the office early, hoping by some miracle she'd be at my place waiting for me. That hope shattered when I came home to an empty house.

A lot had happened in the last week. Sloan needed time. Every reflex told me to push the pain of the argument down until I didn't think about it. Until it stopped hurting.

I couldn't do it. If there was one thing the last few years had taught me, it was that I couldn't escape what I felt for her. And I didn't want to.

Xander: She's here, she's fine.

I was going to lose my mind. She should've been here, with me.

Me: I'm coming to get her.

I couldn't spend another night without her, and I wasn't going to put anything ahead of Sloan ever again. I told her I wasn't ever letting her go, and I meant it. Thirty minutes later, I was at Xander's door.

He opened it and stepped aside to let me in. My eyes were pulled to hers immediately.

"I'm going out." Xander grabbed his keys and brushed past me. Before he left, he turned in the doorway and looked at both of us sternly. "Do not have sex on my couch."

The door shut. Sloan stood silently in front of the couch.

* * *

SLOAN

Before I could blink, he swept me into his arms. I tensed for half a second before I melted into him. It was so easy to let myself be pulled back. Staying there like that, wrapped in his embrace, was tempting.

His chest shuddered. "Don't ever walk out on me again." His tone was commanding, but it sounded like a plea. That was the part he probably kept replaying in his head. My chest clenched at the thought.

I pushed him back, shifted away, and sat down. He followed and sat beside me. "I want every detail. What happened?"

He told me everything. From the start. His involvement with the board, the Ellory acquisition, the scenario he and my grandfather were trying to avoid. The one where I became CEO.

"It was never meant to take something from you. It was meant to follow the succession plan." Marcus took my hand in his and I let him. "At first you were—"

"I was an afterthought," I spat. What used to feel like a slicing pain from rejection didn't hurt so much anymore. What hurt was the lie.

"I didn't think of how it would affect you or if it would." He didn't look away when he said it, allowing me to see the deep remorse in his eyes. His confession made the pain worse. "When I realized how much it still weighed on you, I wanted to tell you so many times."

"Why didn't you?"

"I was scared," he said, as his chest caved with a soft, regretful exhale. "That I would lose you."

A raw vulnerability painted his entire face, pulling at my heart. Every stone in the wall he put up was gone. Every defense was lowered. He was laid bare in front of me. The knowledge that he'd open himself up to devastation, again, wore at my resolve. The fact that he'd done it to repair our relationship nearly diminished it completely.

"Marcus. We can't keep doing this."

"Sloan—" His eyes searched mine as panic bled into his voice.

"Going back and forth wondering what you're telling me and what you're not. Wondering what your motive is or what the calculus on any given situation is." I looked down at the floor, tears welling. "I'm so tired."

He cupped my face in his hands. "I should have told you. I'm not good at this, but I promise you, I will be. I'm going to mess up, but I *will* figure it out. I won't hurt you again." His voice was soft but firm. "The calculus is simple, Sloan. Whatever I need to do to make you happy is what I'm going to do."

"I want to believe you," I rasped.

"Let me prove it." His thumbs stroked my cheeks, sweeping away some of the tears. "That life, the one I told you about in London? I meant every word. The only time I've ever seen a *real* future for myself was when I pictured one that I shared with you." There was a tremble in his voice.

I tried to hold in the tears, but they poured out of me with a small sob.

"I want to make that future a reality, not as a way to make it up to you, but because there is nothing more important to me than making you happy. I'll do anything for it. I'll find every book you love. Hell, I'll dig up Cervantes and make him write you a new one. Because you make me whole again, you keep me together, you make me want to feel *everything*. You are my entire future, the only thing that matters. Let me prove it to you."

He leaned in and pressed a short kiss against my lips, seeking nothing more than a chance.

"Okay, prove it me," I said softly. What I wanted, more than anything, was to spend my life stumbling upon all the ways he loved me.

He ran his fingers through my hair, I couldn't help myself, and I leaned my head against his chest. "*Main karoonga,*" he said. *I will.*

I jerked back, and my heart stopped for a second.

No way. He learned Hindi?

The words got caught in my throat until finally I gasped out a "What?"

Marcus took my hands in his again; mine weren't the only ones trembling. "I've been learning it for the past few months. After that dinner you made, the one I invited myself to, I realized how many parts of you I didn't fully know. From there, it became my mission to start learning them. Hindi was first. I will never be fluent, and the prospect of ever being able to read it is questionable. My best is somewhere around an illiterate first grader."

I laughed through the quiet, overwhelmed sob.

"I want you to feel seen. Completely. I never want you to feel like you have to hide any part of yourself. I'm going to memorize every single piece of you. The parts that I don't understand, I'll figure out. And now, if you can't describe it in English or French, we have Hindi too."

My heart swelled. My chest rose and fell with a deep, slow breath. I couldn't think of anything to say, so I leaned in and kissed him. He groaned and pulled me into him when I deepened it. Completely enveloped in his kiss, I let him pull me into his lap, and I straddled him.

He gently wiped my tears. "I have your journal. The one I got you," I told him as my lips tingled with a familiar buzz. "You kept it all this time but never wrote in it?"

"As long as there were empty pages, I had a reason to carry it around." His nostrils flared as he took a shuddery exhale. His confession felt like a love note. "It's always been you, Sloan."

The words filled me with static. "All these surprises." I wiped a few tears. "You'll spoil me."

"I'm going to keep surprising you." Marcus ran his arms around my waist and held me tightly. "I won't ever hide anything else, just the surprises."

"I do love games." I sniffled and tried to regain some level of composure. "Can I have a hint for the next one?"

"No," he drawled, his body relaxing around me.

"Please?" I asked and leaned in to drop a trail of kisses along his jaw.

"Fine, but you have to agree to my next question."

"Okay."

"Move in with me."

I could feel the tremble in his hand on the small of my back. "That wasn't a question. Are you asking me or telling me?"

"Fuck, Counselor." His tone was playful. "Main bheekh maang raha hoon." *I'm begging.*

"Now you're just showing off." I swatted his chest.

He gave a laugh, a rich and deep one. There was nothing that squeezed my heart more than *that* look. That shift, when a deeply buried joy made its way out of him. His entire face lit up in a way I hardly ever used to see. It warmed me to my bones.

"So?" He looked nervous. It was the most endearing thing I'd ever seen.

"Yes, I'll move in with you." I leaned in, pressed another short kiss on his lips, and immediately pulled away. "What's my hint?"

"You helped make it." The wolfish grin that spread across his face made me sure I needed to know more.

Before I could interrogate him for more clues, his hand gripped the back of my neck and pulled me back to his lips. Our tongues slid against each other's in a familiar tango. A shiver of warmth swept through me. I pulled away after a minute, my pleading eyes searching his.

"Take me home," I whispered.

Chapter 52

SLOAN

Henry and Marcus were certain that Henry had five yes-votes to retain him as CEO. Three were no-votes. That left four votes in play.

We needed three things. A way to secure one more yes-vote (ideally two), a way to prevent one or more of the no-votes, and a backup plan.

Preventing a no-vote was the path of least resistance. I sat on the bed and scanned the company bylaws on my laptop.

A cloud of steam distracted me when it puffed into the room as Marcus walked out of the bathroom, a towel wrapped around his waist. I looked up from my work to take a moment to admire him. Watching the remaining water droplets slide slowly down the rigid muscles felt forbidden. Knowing I was the only one privy to what was below the towel made my own sense of possessiveness surge. A part of me still squealed internally at the knowledge that I was fucking that body regularly.

We had spent the last few days working from home because we couldn't pull ourselves out of bed. I wasn't looking forward to the arguments we would have in the future, but I wouldn't mind the process of making up.

Marcus almost never worked from his home office. He never took time off. But that was slowly changing.

"I already know what you look like naked," he chuckled when he noticed me staring and pulling the sheets up around me. It was a bizarre habit, a lingering self-consciousness from a lifetime of hiding.

Instead of going to the closet, he came to the bed. He leaned in and moved my laptop back to the nightstand. He kissed my lips gently. Then, he nudged me until my back was flat against the mattress. "And what you feel like." He laid a kiss on my jaw. "And taste like." He moved down to my neck, his warm breath skating across my collarbone.

"I could say the same for you."

The smug smirk he gave when I pulled at his towel made me feel faint. He moved back to my lips as the weight of his body pushed me into the mattress. The soft playful kiss became heated in an instant. His hand tossed the towel to the floor and pulled the sheets out from between us.

"They're going to be here soon," I reminded him to no avail.

His hands ran down my sides to my hips, and he hooked my legs around his waist. As much as I wanted to get distracted again, I knew we shouldn't right now. I swallowed hard when I felt my resolve wear.

"If we're not downstairs when Henry gets here, he'll assume why," I said.

The mention of his name made Marcus jerk back. "We're finishing this later." He reluctantly pulled away and got dressed. Following his lead, I quickly showered and got dressed as well. Henry and Xander were coming over in an hour.

Once I was dressed, I sat at the kitchen table and waited for them while I looked over the bylaws. Specifically, I was looking into voting requirements for board members. Marcus thought that maybe we could change the requirements to prevent a no-vote from being able to attend the vote.

Apparently, manipulating the method by which board members voted was how the Waldorfs retained control of their family's company.

Marcus was looking into Julian. I wasn't surprised.

When Xander and I put Julian's family in the FBI's crosshairs, they were also faced with an unfriendly board of directors. Their family came from old steel money and still held managing control of the company. Allister, Julian's father, called to hold a vote just a day after changing the bylaws to require all voting members to be physically present.

The global nature of the company made it nearly impossible for key members to vote. That, and I assumed blackmail, ensured his continued control.

I spent most of the morning looking into our bylaws to see if the same method could be used. It could, with one notable exception. Proxy voters weren't permitted. It meant Marcus would need to vote in the Ellory seat, and that would raise a lot of flags, given he was a sitting CEO of the competition.

"You can't vote by proxy. The owner of Ellory must vote in person if Henry changes the voting requirements."

"Good thing I changed ownership over to Xander last week." He grinned nervously. Secrets were still a sore subject. "Honestly, I forgot about it with everything that happened."

I smiled. "It's okay." I leaned in and pressed a kiss on his lips. His heart was in the right place, and change took time.

We looked up when we heard the door open and close. Xander and Henry were being let in. After Henry's impromptu interruption a week ago, I was convinced a small staff wasn't a bad idea. My assistant found Madeline, who served as a house manager of sorts and would handle filling out the rest of the staff.

"How are things in paradise?" Xander sat down next to me and looked at the computer screen.

"Stop." Henry grimaced and took a silent seat across from us.

He shifted uncomfortably. The animosity between him and Marcus was mostly gone, but there was still some getting used to what would be the new normal. To say he wasn't entirely comfortable with Marcus dating me was generous.

"We're moving in together," I blurted. They'd find out eventually, and I didn't want to keep another secret. I looked at Marcus, who looked like he was bracing for an argument. Xander didn't look surprised, and Henry looked exactly as I expected. Visibly ill.

"Hen . . . ?" I asked. "You okay?"

"Yeah." Henry ran his hand through his hair and stared at the papers in front of him. "This is normal, boring even. Doesn't make me uncomfortable at all."

I sighed and grabbed a croissant from the large tray in the middle of the table. I had hoped this morning's get-together would be a move in the right direction with my brother. He and Marcus were seemingly okay when they were on their own, but when it was all of us, it was awkward.

"Ground rules." Henry exhaled loudly. "Can you keep the kissing and general PDA to a minimum? And lock doors—"

"Good luck with that." Xander laughed.

"A problem easily remedied by knocking," I reminded him.

"Can we focus?" Marcus asked. He was quiet during the exchange, feeling equally uncomfortable.

"Yeah," Henry said. "I'll change the by-laws to require board members be present for votes. Then, I'll call one."

"Good. We confirmed all five of the friendly board members are available and in the city. We know two-no votes may not make it," I added.

"And the swing-votes?" Xander asked.

"I've been meeting with all of them for the past month," Henry assured him. "We should have at least one."

I sighed. "We don't have a backup plan."

"We do," Henry said, the corner of his mouth tipping up. "Technically, we have a spare."

I smiled. "I don't want any part of being CEO. So, this better work."

We were quiet, uncomfortably quiet, over that possibility.

Marcus and I hadn't talked about what that would mean for us. I couldn't be a partner at the firm and CEO at the same time. The firm might be open to a sabbatical of sorts, but that was a longshot. Then there were the personal implications. If I headed the largest pharmaceutical company globally and Marcus was at the helm of the largest biotech, there would be scrutiny. While not illegal or unethical, the optics weren't great. The last thing I wanted was having to keep our relationship a secret any longer.

"It will work." Marcus slid the folder that laid beneath my laptop to Xander. "Do not, under any circumstance, let Sloan or Henry read any of that."

"Blackmail on the board?" I grinned. Why was that so hot?

"Yeah, on all twelve board members. Using it was an absolute worst-case scenario." Marcus eyes narrowed on Xander. "It would turn an otherwise amenable board member into an enemy, and no CEO needs that. If it needs to be used, Xander, you have to do it."

"Corporate espionage is fun." Xander paged through the documents. He closed the folder quickly and pressed his hands on top of it. "Holy shit." His eyes were wide.

Marcus's hand found mine. "I couldn't tell you be—"

"Plausible deniability." My thumb stroked the back of his hand. "I get it."

Our life together was always going to be a little complicated, but easy was never something that interested me. I wanted the messy, overwhelming, all-consuming love I had with him over something simple any day. Everyday.

Chapter 53

SLOAN

The day of the board vote, I had to run to the firm to get a few things since my promotion meant a new office. Henry and I got everything settled at the Amari Global board room before I made a quick trip to the firm and came right back.

When I got back, thirty minutes ahead of the meeting, Henry was talking to the board members who had already pledged allegiance to him. Watching him made me recognize just how much I didn't want his job.

Xander, the newest member of the board, sauntered over to me. His eyes darted up and down my blouse for a second, and a wide grin erupted along his mouth. He leaned in and stifled a laugh. "Your blouse is inside out."

I let out a small gasp when I realized he was right. I grabbed my suit jacket laid on the chair behind him and threw it back on.

"Seriously? You were gone for like forty-five minutes." He chuckled.

"What?" My smile confessed for me. Ever since we made our relationship public, there had been an ease about Marcus. There was also an insatiable need to have me everywhere. Over the past few weeks, he'd pulled me into coat closets, empty offices, and town cars.

This morning, he intercepted me at my new office. I was his, and he was making it known.

"Please," Xander said with a roll of his eyes. "Don't think I don't know why it took both of you so long to get to dinner last week."

I felt the blood rush into my face. We were terrible at covering our tracks. "I don't know what you're talking about."

"If you get pregnant, I call godfather."

"Not really something you can call dibs on."

The prospect of children excited me more than I expected it to. We were moving a little fast, but sometimes it didn't feel fast enough. There were no plans to do anything past living together, for now, but the idea of what the future held made my heart swell.

The room fell quiet as Henry called everyone to attention a few minutes before 9 a.m. We took our seats and watched the clock. The bylaws required a ten-minute grace period for all voting members to arrive.

The board meeting was tense.

As counsel, I regularly sat in on board meetings, but I'd never had my entire career riding on one. The first order of business was to address the immediate changes in the wake of our grandfather's death. Henry looked like he was going to be sick before the meeting, but during it, he was a pro. I was proud of him.

The vote to retain Henry was the first item in the meeting. Things went a little sideways.

We had the votes to retain Henry, but the board voted on a stipulation. Henry would continue as interim CEO for the next year, but he was saddled with a morality clause. The board would re-evaluate his tenure in a year and had the power to remove him if his behavior didn't meet the specific stipulations of the clause.

We were powerless to oppose it.

Once the day was done, we waited for him at our townhouse to celebrate. It was still a victory.

"To Henry." We clinked our champagne glasses together.

"To you three," Henry corrected. His ego had taken a back seat over the past few weeks. Likely humbled by the board. "We'd be pulling poor Sloan up off the floor if it wasn't for your efforts."

"You know what's wild?" Xander took a large gulp from his glass. He pointed to Marcus and me. "They've fucked all over this city, and the tabloids continue to follow Henry around."

Met with no laughter, he backtracked. "Okay, well, maybe not 'ha-ha' funny."

"We should celebrate," I said. The last few months had been rough for a variety of reasons. This was the final cloud looming over us. I felt Marcus move behind me and wrap his arms around my waist. He yanked me back against him, caring less and less about Henry's protest about PDA. "Low key. Nothing to write about. But properly."

A few moments of silence passed. "Got it. Everyone, get packed for the weekend." Xander snapped his fingers. "Hamptons."

Chapter 54

MARCUS

I t was bright and humid the day I decided to visit the cemetery. It was early on a Saturday morning when I told Sloan, who was still in bed. It was a few weeks after the board meeting, and Sloan was now fully moved in.

I had never come here. Not once since their funeral. I was overwhelmed then, and later I told myself it was better avoid it all. My eyes scanned the granite headstones. The guilt crashed over me in one large wave. I didn't realize how much I'd buried until my feelings for Sloan shook it all loose.

But it wasn't as hard as I thought it would be.

I leaned down and picked up old flowers sitting beside both of their headstones.

Someone was here recently?

"Sloan and Henry take turns changing them out every few weeks," Xander's voice called from behind me. I turned to see him walking up the path with fresh flowers in his hands.

"Sloan told you I was here?" I asked, even though I was sure she called him to tell him where I was going. "I guess I should get used to that."

He grinned. "Yeah, she called me this morning and told me to bring peonies."

Xander handed me the flowers, and I replaced the old ones. I stood back up and sighed, eyes fixed on the names in front of me. "They've been doing that all this time?"

Henry was still a little distant with me, and it wasn't just because I was dating Sloan. We had each other's backs for our entire adult lives. He was still angry that I left for so long. He felt abandoned at a time he probably could have used his best friend. I couldn't blame him, especially when I was reminded of all the ways he'd been there for me.

Xander nodded. "That's something like"—his eyes looked up in thought—"two hundred and eighty-six flower exchanges over the years."

We got lost in our own thoughts for a few minutes.

"You finally made it here." Xander stuck his hands in his pockets.

"Yeah . . ." I sighed. "As it turns out, I may have a problem with ignoring the things I don't want to deal with."

He barked a laugh. "Maybe just a little one."

"What do you guys do when you come here?"

Xander's eyes floated around the expanse. "Henry updates them on you and the company. Sloan usually has a checklist of things she tells them about. I don't really do anything. I don't come up as much as they do."

I nodded. We four looked out for each other in different ways.

"Want to go run some agility drills?" I asked after a few more minutes of silence. Xander hadn't played soccer since their death. I wasn't the only one who might benefit from some aversion therapy. "The club has fields on the lower roofs."

He tensed for a moment and shook his head. "No, but I'll help you with Sloan's birthday."

I didn't push. I'd try again another time.

"Thanks." I'd missed the last two and sent gifts instead. She called to thank me for both; I had the voicemails saved. Sloan forgave my absence more quickly than Xander and Henry, but I needed to make it up to her too. Not that throwing a giant party for her would do that, but she'd get to dance the entire night away. She'd love that.

We stayed awhile longer before heading back.

* * *

"How was it?" Sloan asked. She was sitting on the couch reading when I got back to our place.

"Good." I pressed a kiss against her lips and sat beside her.

"Henry's coming over for brunch tomorrow." She leaned into my shoulder and looked at the text message from her brother. She sighed and placed her phone on the page she'd stopped at in the book. "So that's good news."

"See? He'll come around."

She nodded.

I looked at the last box of her things in the corner. "Does it feel like home yet?" I asked.

"Mmmm." She smiled, then jolted forward in excitement. She got up and walked down the hallway, only to return a few moments later. This time with a wrapped gift in her hand. It looked like a picture; I had a feeling I knew which one. "I got you something." She handed it to me and sat back down.

"Now we have two." I pulled away the wrapping paper. She'd enlarged the photo of her graduation from my journal. Her photo was already hung in the upstairs hallway. "Is your note still on the back?"

"Yup, I added it this morning. Don't lose that."

I released a contented sigh.

Over the last few years, that picture and the journal were my connection to her.

A tether.

Now, it could hang on the wall forever. I didn't need it anymore; I had her. That simple fact would keep me grounded and incandescently happy for the rest of my life.

Epilogue

SLOAN

Two Months Later . . .

Getting settled into my new office was odd. It would remain the same if I ever became managing partner. That goal had lost some luster, now that I didn't feel the need to prove myself to anyone.

I had been a senior partner for a couple of months now, and it was everything I expected. Thinking back on it now, I realize all of the accolades were confetti. They were nice to have and made things brighter, but from now on, I'd enjoy my accomplishments and only pursue what I genuinely wanted.

I sat down at my desk and took a second to take it all in. A gleeful squeal escaped me when I pulled my legs up onto the chair and twirled myself around in it.

"I saw that," Xander said as the chair swung back around. I shook off the quick dizziness and stood to greet him. He handed me a paper. "You see this?"

**AMARI PRINCESS ON THE ARM
OF THE COMPETITION**

"Yes." I rolled my eyes and threw the gossip rag on my desk. It was a photograph from a benefit all the partners attended. Marcus and I waited until everything with the board was settled before attending public events together for that exact reason. It was the first event we attended together. Henry was there too, but he went alone.

"Now that Henry's on his best behavior, it looks like they're interested in you again."

"Fabulous." I was getting used to it, but I knew it made Marcus uncomfortable. He had always managed to stay out of the public eye, and so had I. After deciding on law school, the papers didn't have any interest in what I was doing. It would seem Henry's compliance with his new PR consultant made him boring, and our relationship sparked some interest.

For now, it seemed they were interested in us because we were new. A shiny headline to capture attention for a few weeks. Henry's head of public relations, Selena, told us to lean into it. The papers loved drama, so if we continued to be nauseatingly in love, they'd quickly tire of us.

That wouldn't be too hard.

"Ready to go?" Xander picked the paper off my desk and threw it into the trash bin. Now that I was back from my short stint in London, Xander and I could grab lunch like we used to.

"Sloan?" Marcus walked through the door, typing quickly on his phone. He looked up, and his smile fell when he saw Xander. He wouldn't be bending me over my desk today.

"Are you third-wheeling our lunch?" Xander asked.

Ignoring his brother, Marcus looked at me. "I got you something." He pointed to two movers bringing what looked like a large painting into my office. I couldn't exactly tell what it was. "Which wall?" His sly smile had me interested.

Xander and I looked at each other with confusion, and I pointed to the one directly to my left. The other side of the room was a bookshelf that spanned the entire wall. Behind me was a wall of windows.

We turned to face the movers as they began to mount the piece. Marcus walked into the office to stand beside Xander and me as it was hung. The brown protective paper still concealed the painting.

"You buy her a Rembrandt?" Xander asked.

"No, the artists are relatively unknown." Marcus's tone was almost bored, but his eyes told a different story. He had that look in them. "Well, in the art world, anyway."

Finally, the covering was removed, and I gasped when I realized what I was looking at. An array of colors smudged across a white canvas. Except the canvas was actually drywall with a clear sealant painted over it. I was staring at the piece of wall he pressed me against after we said I love you for the first time.

Framed beautifully. Hung in my office.

His arms wrapped around my waist from behind me.

"You helped make it," he whispered in my ear. It was the hint he gave me a couple months ago about my next surprise.

I turned to Marcus and looped my arms around his neck. "I love it."

He leaned in and pulled me into a soft kiss. My body arched into him instinctively. And today, that was what turned something sweet into something wicked. A low groan vibrated out of his throat, and my hands began to get lost in his hair.

"I don't get it." Xander's voice rang through the lust-filled cloud. It was his way of reminding us he was still in the room. His head tilted, and he looked at the artwork with confusion.

"You better not." Marcus's tone lacked any sharpness.

"Whatever." He shrugged and made his way to the door. "Ready for lunch?"

"Tumhari." *Yours*, I whispered in Marcus's ear before I turned to join Xander.

"I know." He followed us out of the office.

* * *

MARCUS

Four Months Later . . .

Henry was hosting a New Year's Charity Gala. To be more accurate, the entire family was hosting it. I asked Henry and Xander to come by beforehand while Sloan was out taking care of a few last-minute details. And I asked specifically that they came alone.

I paced back and forth while I waited for them. I'd poured a glass of whiskey for myself and left a couple of glasses and the bottle on the coffee table for when they arrived. The glass I'd had already didn't ease the nerves.

"What is so important that you need to drag me away from absolutely nothing?" Xander walked into the main living area. His carefree expression changed to concern when he looked at me. "Jeez, what's wrong?"

If it was this hard to ask for their blessing, how the hell was I going to ask Sloan? *What if she says no?* My mind began to reel at the possibility. She would say yes, right? It was fast. Maybe it was too fast.

"What the hell is wrong with him?" Henry arrived, and I stopped pacing. Xander took a seat on the couch, and Henry joined him.

"Sloan's pregnant?" Henry and Xander looked at me as if Xander's question had any merit.

It probably had some merit. We didn't have much in the way of restraint when it came to sex.

"What?" I shook my head and sat on the couch across from them. "No."

The room was silent for a few minutes. Henry and Xander awkwardly drank their whiskey before I finally spoke up.

"I asked you both here because I wanted to ask you something." They exchanged confused looks before the realization began to dawn. No other part of my life made me nervous, but anything that had to do with Sloan would give me a reaction I wasn't expecting. I felt like I was going to be sick, and clearly, I wasn't hiding it well. "I'd like your blessing to propose to Sloan."

We were moving quickly, but I didn't want to wait. I wanted her to be my wife. I wanted to have children with her. I wanted things with her that I never thought I could have. She found the parts of me that I thought were lost for good.

"Of course you have my blessing." Henry smiled warmly, refilling my empty glass and lifting his for a toast.

"Xander?" I asked. He looked at his glass, making me pause.

"Duh." A smile stretched along his face. He lifted his glass.

"To the acquisition that finally put Marcus Sutton through his paces." Henry proposed a toast. Our glasses *clinked*. "And please never tell Sloan I referred to her as an acquisition," he added with a laugh. "In classic Rishi Amari fashion, our grandfather wanted the family ring passed to whoever got married first. I think he left it to my mom."

"Yeah, that's also what I needed to talk to you about." I pulled three rings out of my pocket. All three sat in the same velvet box. The Amari family ring, the one I picked out, and my mother's ring.

"We get it. You love her." Xander laughed and picked up the rings before stopping at the familiar one. Our mother's ring. "She doesn't need three."

He stared at it for a moment.

"Mom left me her ring," I told him.

Xander's expression was unreadable. He never actually read the will or anything that had to do with our parents' estate. I took care of all of that. Lost in thought, he chewed on his lip, emotion threatening to overcome his carefree demeanor.

"If she likes it, she should wear it." Xander smiled and looked at the ring. "But, honestly, I think she'd probably prefer the one you picked for her." Xander sniffled and took a step back.

"Wait," he said, handing the rings back to me. "Who's going to be your best man?"

"She has to accept first."

"She will," they said in unison.

I hadn't given much thought to my best man, having the ring and actual proposal to think about. I just assumed it would be Henry. Besides, no way in hell Sloan would let me have Xander.

"Who would be Sloan's maid of honor? Or should I say man of honor?" Henry's motive was transparent. "Because, if it's not Xander, it would be Pene—"

"I don't know, Henry. Who would Marcus prefer to plan her bachelorette party?"

My face fell into my open hands. Xander bounced between remarkably sincere and chaotic faster than most people blinked.

"When are you going to do it?" Henry mercifully changed the subject.

That part I already planned.

"Do what?" Sloan's voice came through the hallways. I shoved the ring box back into my pocket, and the three of us tried to look casual. Why, all of a sudden, it became impossible—I'll never know. Her eyes narrowed when she looked at us, knowing Henry and Xander weren't expected here for a few hours. Neither of them was dressed for the event.

She walked a few more slow steps toward the couch. Her hair was up in an elegant bun, like it had been the night of the gala last year. "What?"

"Nothing." Henry stood and looked at Xander. "We should go."

"Did you do something with your hair?" Xander was notoriously bad at lying to Sloan, and he knew it. "Looks great."

A few seconds later we heard the door close.

That left me to explain the bizarre exchange. "What did I walk in on?" she asked.

"Nothing. They just stopped by for a drink."

She didn't buy it. "I'll get it out of you later." She sighed, placed her purse on the end table, walked over to me, and threw her arms around my neck. "You know what I was thinking about earlier? Remember a year ago?"

The Hightower New Year's Ball was an event I'd never forget. It was the night things shifted. "Do you?"

She laughed. I ran my hands around her waist and pulled her close. "You never told me what happened." Her eyes shimmered, and she brushed her lips against mine. "I know I wasn't a perfect lady."

No truer words were ever spoken. I thought about that night a lot, especially before Sloan and I got together. She didn't drink excessively, but she hardly ate anything. By the time we got to the town car, she was clearly intoxicated.

When we got back here, she was a little difficult to steer in the direction of the guest room. She insisted she wasn't tired. Then, she complained that the dress was too tight, and instead of going to the guest room to take it off, she unzipped it and let it fall as she ascended the steps. That left only the lace thong and strapless bra she had worn underneath.

I watched for a moment, frozen in delighted disbelief. If there was any confirmation needed that Sloan felt the same as I did, at least physically, that night provided it.

Being a gentleman, I looked away. Being a living man, I only did so after a second of registering what I was looking at. I'd seen everything I needed to plague my dreams for months.

"Your dress." I leaned my head against hers. "You took it off while you walked up the steps."

Rose tinged her cheeks, and she smiled. I thought she remembered at least a part of that night. "What a gentleman."

"You damn near killed me that night, Sloan," I said with a chuckle. "It took every bit of restraint not to stare, let alone keep my hands off you."

"Let me make it up to you?" Her hands moved down my chest to my waist. Her fingertips ran across the top of my belt. "When we get home tonight." A disappointed groan rumbled up my throat. We had plenty of time before the party. "We can't mess up my hair. It took two hours."

"I'll be gentle."

"No, you won't." She giggled and pulled away from me. She grabbed the purse off the kitchen counter. "Besides, we can't be late for Henry's big night."

"Tonight, you're mine."

She looked seductively over her shoulder to me. "I'm always yours."

And I'm yours. My fingers rhythmically tapped the box in my pocket.

Bonus Epilogue: The Proposal

The press was becoming increasingly bothersome in Manhattan. It was a near constant barrage these days, aimed mostly at Henry, but Sloan was catching their eye more frequently too. She'd been staying inside more than usual. So, I suggested a short reprieve in Paris.

"Let's cross to the other side." Sloan smiled at me from over her shoulder, a few steps ahead. The chill from the cool February air rattled through the sweeping windows in the hall of mirrors as she began her way through. Her reflection glinted across the antique glass, the soft light of the chandeliers, and the early evening sunset casted her in a warm glow.

I'd rented Versailles for the day, so Sloan and I could visit without running into other tourists. The freedom to roam without being recognized was already improving her mood; the weight on her shoulders had lifted and she'd been grinning all day. Versailles was one of Sloan's favorite places on earth, and the chance to visit the château alone was the perfect alibi for bringing her here.

"Right behind you," I told her, reaching into my pocket and nervously checking for the ring. Again.

Planning a surprise proposal for anyone was difficult, but planning one for Sloan was near impossible. She read me too easily and remembered all the small details. If I'd taken her on an impromptu trip to London or Brussels, she could have pieced together the city's significance to our relationship and known something was amiss.

Versailles, however, was a place we'd never been to together before, so I hoped she wouldn't guess my intentions.

Whenever I actually managed to take Sloan off guard, she was overjoyed. Those were the games she loved to lose. I just hoped today would go the way I'd imagined.

First, I'd ask her about the room. "I feel like we look different in every mirror," I said, glancing at her as she looked up at the gilded ceiling.

Then she'd say: "Did you know that these giant mirrors are actually composed of hundreds of smaller ones?" She leaned toward one, pointing to a hairline space in the glass. "So, technically, we're looking at hundreds of reflections."

I smiled.

I did know that. And I was so sure she knew it too, that I'd bet the entire proposal on it.

"Really?" I said, watching her finger trace the line where the glass met and became one. "So, a different Sloan in each." I stepped forward and took hold of her hand. She looked over her shoulder at me, brows raised. "And I love every single one."

Her lips drew up at the corners as I pulled her in. She looped her arms around my neck, looking at me with an intrigued glint in her eye that warned I didn't have much time until she figured it out. "Marcus?"

"Sloan . . ." I whispered, resting my hands on her waist. "Saanvi Amari."

Her bright smile dissolved into something more serious, registering my nerves. Her lips parted but she didn't say anything. My heart hammered in my chest.

"I don't know exactly when it was that I fell in love with you, but once I did, I was done for. I was yours." I let go of her and began to kneel, pulling the box from my pocket. Her chest rose with a deep inhale, eyes wide. I'd managed to surprise her after all. "I'll spend the rest of my life trying to make you feel even a piece of the happiness you've given me, if you let me."

Tiny tears began to prickle at the sides of her eyes, glittering like the crystal chandeliers above our heads. Her throat shifted with a hard swallow.

I pulled her hand into mine. "Marry me, Sloan."

Her fingers trembled and she nodded. "Yes."

Relief flooded through me. I lifted myself from the floor and I swept her into my arms, pressing my lips against hers.

She pulled me closer, deepening the kiss. A small moan escaped her lips as I swept her hair back. Then I pulled away, cupping her face in my hands. "I love you."

My thumb wiped the tears from her cheek. She looked at the box I was still holding. I'd entirely forgotten to put the ring on her finger.

"Why do you have three rings?" She hiccupped a laugh.

I took her hand again, turned her around, and wrapped my arms around her, dropping my chin to her shoulder. I held the open ring box in front of her and she ran her fingers over the three bands.

My mother's ring.

Her family's ring.

And the one that had stopped me dead in my tracks.

Months ago, I went to Harry Winston to buy her a gift. I hadn't intended to look at the rings, but one caught my eye. The rays of light that shot through the diamond were brilliant and warm; it reminded me of Sloan's eyes when she smiled.

But it wasn't for sale. It was on display, on loan from a private collector. But I knew, that eleven-carat, oval cut, internally flawless ring was perfect for Sloan. Rare. Luminous. Almost unattainable. I could imagine it on her finger, glinting as she went about her day, as she came home to me at night.

And right then and there, I knew I needed to propose to Sloan.

I pulled the sales associate over and pointed it out. Thirty minutes later, the original owner had been contacted and convinced to part ways with the gem. It was set in platinum and put in a box for me.

A week later, I asked her parents, Henry, and Xander for their blessings.

Originally, I planned to just use this ring—something new, a symbol of a fresh life we'd build together. Henry could give the Amari ring to his bride one day, and my mother's ring could be passed to Xander. But our pasts were part of us too, and I wanted to let her choose. So today, she could pick one or two or all three for all I cared. As long as she was mine.

"I wanted to let you pick," I told her.

Her index finger traced the diamond on the Amari family ring.

"Henry will need this soon," she said resolutely. I raised an eyebrow, wondering if she knew something I didn't. She winked at me. "Trust me on that one."

I nodded.

She turned back to the box. Her fingers brushed over my mother's ring. She took a deep, long inhale and let it out slowly. "One day, Xan will be okay. And when he is, the person that finally gets though will deserve your mom's ring."

"Sloan," I whispered gently. If given a choice, she would always make sure Henry, Xander, and I were happy before herself. "Pick the one *you want.*"

"I am. I want this one." She pulled out the ring I'd picked out. She shut the box, turned, and handed it to me. "I want to spend the rest of my life looking at it, knowing you picked this just for me."

She held her hand out and I slipped it onto her finger.

A warm realization spread through my chest. We were living the future I'd imagined for us. Together.

"The rest of our lives sounds pretty good," I said, and lifted her chin to pull her into another kiss.

Extended Epilogue

SLOAN

Two years after that . . .

Before we were married, I hardly ever visited Marcus at his office. The occasional romp on his desk was the only real exception. Something about an Amari on Sutton territory felt forbidden. It did make the desk sex extremely gratifying, though.

But now that we'd been married a while, I found myself here more often. It probably had less to do with the name change and more to do with the fact that pregnancy made my patience even thinner. I needed to take breathers from work more often these days. And Marcus's office was closer than home.

"He free?" I approached his office, and his assistant nodded.

Engulfed in whatever he was reading on his screen, he didn't notice when I walked in. That, or he was allowing me to live in the illusion that my eight-month pregnant belly was still "barely showing." Marcus looked up from his screen and gave me that smile. After all the time that had passed, it still made my knees wobble. He immediately got up and ushered me into a seat.

"Please tell me you didn't walk." There was concern etched all over his face. He took another chair and pulled my feet up onto it.

"I needed to get some air."

He sighed and brought me a glass of water. Marcus went from protective to downright overbearing when I told him I was pregnant. And he wasn't the only one. Henry treated me like I was made of glass. Xander, who held out the longest, started to become almost as bad as Marcus when I entered my last trimester.

Their well-meaning protectiveness didn't bother me like it used to. It came from a place of love.

"What happened?" he asked as he leaned against his desk.

"One of the associates made me angry."

"How?"

"I don't really know." I laughed when I thought back on it. One of the associates asked me something about a litigation case. It wasn't my area of expertise, so I sent him to see Maya Malhotra, one of our senior associates. She was fantastic and happened to be Rohan's little sister. I didn't know why I was so annoyed by the encounter, but he seemed annoyed at my refusal to help him. He was audacious, and I didn't love it. I did feel a little bad that he became Maya's problem. "Your daughter is making me crazy."

He laughed and knelt beside me. He rubbed my belly, and our little girl kicked beneath his hand. "Maybe she's reminding you to slow down."

He spent most nights trying to convince me to start my maternity leave early. I was due in three weeks, and I probably should, but I hated the idea of someone else doing my work. Besides, I felt great.

"The doctor said I'm fine."

He sighed again. We went round and round with this exact conversation most nights. "Why don't we take the rest of the day off?"

That was something new, too. After we moved in together, we continued our ritual of making dinner together some nights. Regardless of what we were doing, we both made it home around seven. Since announcing the pregnancy, he was a lot more willing to delegate his work and would come by my office almost daily to pick me up.

Whenever he wanted me to slow down, he would slow down with me.

"The senior partners met." I didn't leave the office only because of an inane question from one of the associates. "When managing partner comes up next year, I'm on the shortlist."

He beamed for a moment. I ran my hand through his hair and sighed. His smile morphed into a knowing grin. "You don't want to be CEO of the firm?"

That's basically what a managing partner was. It was a step back from any of the actual legal work. I would be in charge. I would make some of the most important decisions regarding the firm's direction. My impact would be global.

It sounded terrible. I loved my work; I didn't want to give it up to run the firm. Watching Henry and Marcus made me more thankful every day that I had dodged that bullet. Turns out, I already had everything I wanted. And I was happy with myself. "No offense. But your job sucks."

He laughed. It was deep and joyful. Our little girl kicked in my belly at the sound. "Then say no."

I nodded. I was planning on it. "Come on, let's go home."

Marcus pulled the chair out from under my legs and helped me up. I ran my hands up his chest and gave a contented sigh. He pressed a short kiss on my lips.

He said a few things to his assistant and joined me at the elevator.

"Another short day, Sutton?" I teased him. He threw his arm around me and kissed the top of my head.

He laughed again. The baby's kicking didn't cease. "I don't mind giving Henry some time to catch up."

* * *

MARCUS

Then, two years after that . . .

N o! Dis one." Meera's brown eyes darted to the books on the higher shelves. She ignored the rows of age-appropriate books we filled on the shelf and pointed to one of Sloan's books. The one I got her while we were in London.

Over the last few visits, we had reorganized the expansive bookshelf in my parents' old study. We moved my mother's journals and her favorite books to the higher shelves. Sloan filled the shelves Meera could reach with books appropriate for her, but they never interested Meera. She was an unrelenting contrarian, just like her mother.

She jumped and reached for the book she'd been eyeing, turning back to me with an expectant grin when she couldn't reach it. "Daddy! Up."

The power a two-year-old had over me was remarkable. I followed my orders and picked her up to reach for the book she wanted.

"Sweetheart." I sat down on a chair beside the window. Meera ran her hand over the cover, then looked up at me and smiled. She looked like a little clone of her mother. "That's a little long. Your uncle Xander is going to be here soon."

Her face lit up. Xander spoiled her rotten. She was the first baby in the family, so Henry and Xander competed to be her favorite uncle. Henry bought her anything she wanted. Xander let her live a life without any rules.

"Snow?" Meera asked as she turned to the window. It usually didn't snow this early in the winter, but Xander loved to be the one who could change the weather for her. Last year, he hired a ski resort's staff to ensure the snow covered the house.

I nodded.

The year Sloan and I got engaged, we decided to have Christmas at my parents' house. It was supposed to be something nice for the holiday that year, but it became a tradition after that.

Meera giggled, jumped off my lap, and ran ahead of me out of the study to find Sloan, who was sitting with her feet up on the couch in the living area. Meera placed the book at her side.

"Meera, did you pick this?" Sloan had a faraway look in her eye for a moment as she ran her hand over the soft leather.

"We're still negotiating terms." I picked Meera up and sat her beside me. Meera gently leaned forward and rubbed Sloan's belly.

"She's going to be a lawyer." Sloan smiled. She was due in a couple of weeks. We had planned to stay in the city this close to her due date, but Meera convinced us otherwise. She loved this house, and I had trouble saying no to her. I had a feeling this next one would be the same.

"Well, it's a good thing Sutton Industries has a spare." I leaned down and pressed a kiss against her belly. Thankfully, this pregnancy was just as uneventful as the last.

"And what if he's a lawyer, too?"

"To be safe, we should make more," I whispered, not that Meera would have any idea what I meant. She chose that moment to burrow between us and push us apart, lifting the book with an annoyed look scrawled across her angelic face.

Being with Sloan and Meera filled me with a serenity I'd never known. Even with all the worry that came along with being a parent. Regardless of what I was doing, my mind went to them. The anxiety was a blissful agony.

Just as Sloan opened the book, the sound of the door opening interrupted us. "Meera," Henry's voice called from the foyer. "Your favorite uncle is here."

"And I brought snow," Xander interjected.

Meera jumped off the couch and left behind the book she convinced me she needed to read.

"Your best friend is out of control." I turned to Sloan. Xander would let her go skydiving, if she asked.

"Says the man whose best friend bought her a stable full of horses." She laughed. *That* laugh. I kissed her before getting up to chase after Meera.

The Spare PLAYLIST

Style – Taylor Swift
Back to You – Selena Gomez
In My Head – Jason Derulo
Into You – Ariana Grande
Some Say – Nea
Alibi (Under the Starlight) – Eli Rose
No One Compares to You – Jack & Jack
Find You – Nick Jonas
Lost – Maroon 5
Just Friends – Virginia to Vegas
Me Because Of You – HRVY
Come & Get It – Selena Gomez
Heart to Break – Kim Petras
Slow Hands – Niall Horan
Wave of You – Surfaces
Maan Meri Jaan – King, Nick Jonas
Nights Like This – St. Lundi
Million Ways – HRVY

Acknowledgments

To the readers – whether that means five, fifteen, fifty, or five hundred. I cannot tell you how much it means to me that you've spent your precious time getting lost in this world. When I wrote this book, it was a labor of love—one I hope you enjoyed.

To R.S. – Thank you for the time and space to pursue a dream deferred. Taking over to make sure I had time to write was a monumental task and you handled it like the man all my male main characters strive to be. Thank you for being all the goals. And finally, thank you for reminding me of my life's new motto: *I write sins not tragedies* (thank you Panic! At the Disco for the actual inspiration).

To Dimple – May our letters never be intercepted. But, let's continue to cipher them, just in case. Thank you for giving me courage by living your life on your terms. You inspire me more than you know.

To Jessica Rita Rampersad – You have to be one of the sweetest people I've met during this process. Your thoughts and suggestions for the story were amazing, but *you* are the star. I cannot wait to see what you do with your many talents. You are truly one of a kind.

To Gabby – Your feedback was incredibly helpful. I now know what a colonoscopy must feel like. Thank you for your brutal honesty when I needed it.

To Sam – You were the first set of eyes on this book, your feedback helped me grow. Not to mention, how much you helped shape this story. Thank you for finding my blind spots!

To Salma – Your voice memos were some of the most fun I had in this process. Sloan and Marcus (and the entire motley crew) would not be who they are without your honesty and willingness to share.

To Joanna & Jaime – Thank you for your amazing edits and for tapering my fascination with em dashes and semi colons.

To my ARC readers: You took a chance on this book, and on me, when not many others would. You hold a special place in my heart.

To the only person who will understand this – marshmallows are good, but . . .

Sloan, Marcus, Henry, and Xander will return in . . .

THE HEIR

He needed a perfect year. She needed a way out.

Henry sits at the helm of one of the most powerful companies
in the world. But the board is saddling him with a morality
clause before he can permanently take the post. That's where
Selena comes in. Hired in secret by his sister, Sloan,
Selena knows how to rehabilitate tarnished reputations.
At first her no-nonsense ways are an annoyance, but soon
enough, Henry has to admit that he's developing feelings for
her. But Henry will discover that Selena is harboring a dirty
secret of her own, one she can't clean up alone. They'll each
have to decide if love is worth their reputations getting messy.

NOW AVAILABLE IN E-BOOK

COMING IN PAPERBACK AND AUDIO WINTER 2025

ABOUT THE AUTHOR

AVA RANI is a contemporary romance writer who writes stories with equal parts spice and swoon. Expect big cities, diverse backgrounds, strong female leads, and plot twists.

She fell in love with reading and writing again after a decade of working in another field. In a burst of creative energy, she wrote this series.

When she's not writing, she loves to travel (fifty-two countries so far), perfect her pecan pie recipe, and introduce her toddler to every ice cream flavor imaginable (for purely academic reasons, of course).